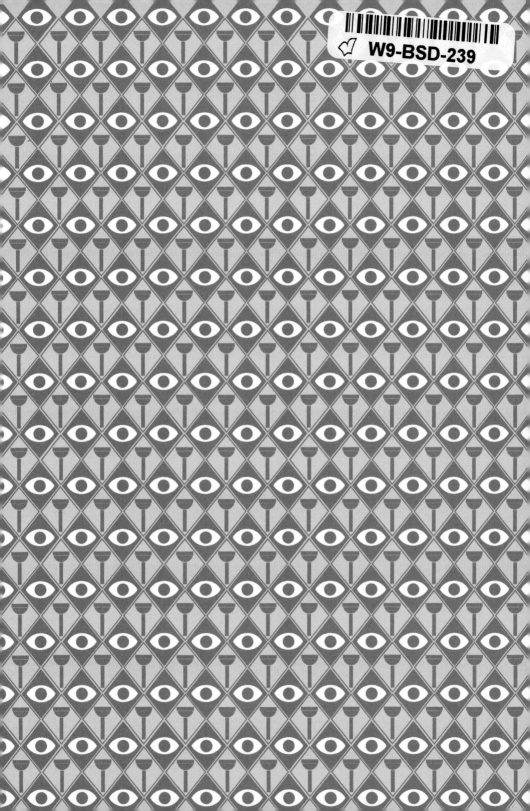

EDISON BEAKER CREATURE SEEKER

THE LOST CITY

BY FRANK CAMMUSO

VIKING

For AiVy, Khai, and Van,
the original Creature Seekers
— F.C.

VIKING
An imprint of Penguin Random House LLC, New York

First published in the United States of America by Viking,
an imprint of Penguin Random House LLC, 2019

Copyright © 2019 by Frank Cammuso
Color assist by Peter Sieburg

Visit us online at penguinrandomhouse.com

LIBRARY OF CONGRESS CATALOGING-IN-PUBLICATION DATA IS AVAILABLE.
ISBN 9780425291955 (hardcover); ISBN 9780425291962 (paperback)

Manufactured in China

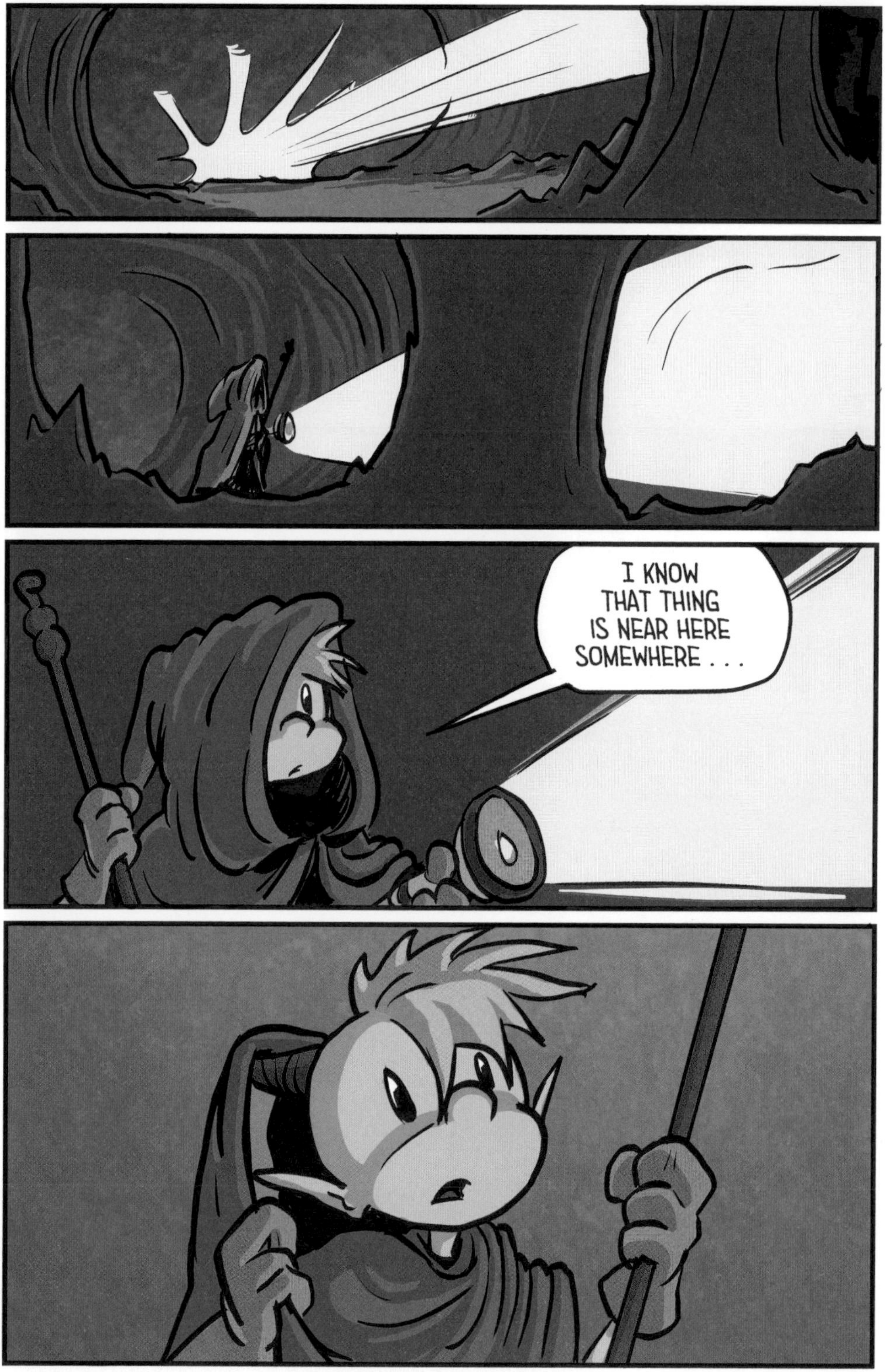
I KNOW THAT THING IS NEAR HERE SOMEWHERE . . .

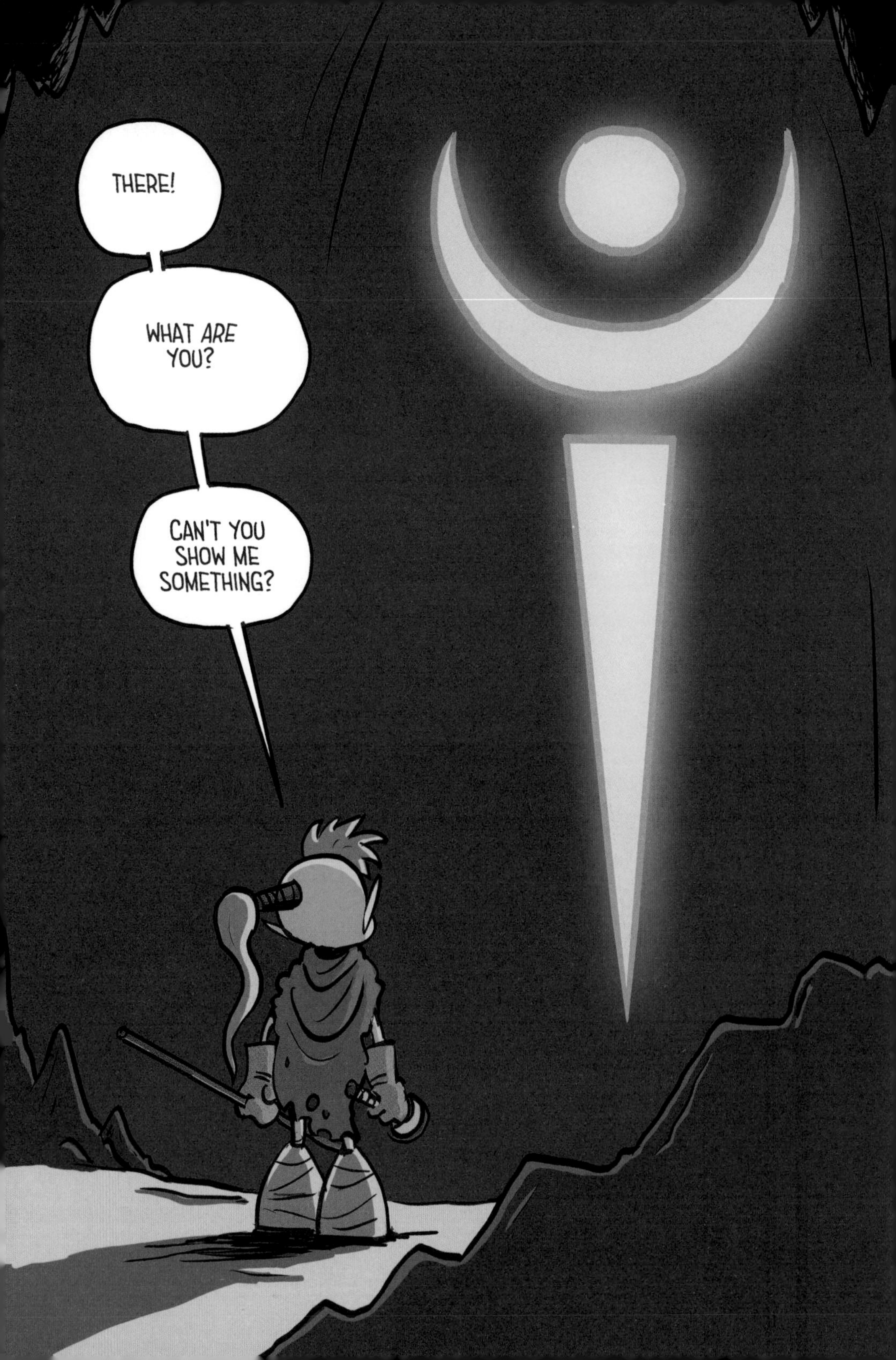
THERE!
WHAT *ARE* YOU?
CAN'T YOU SHOW ME SOMETHING?

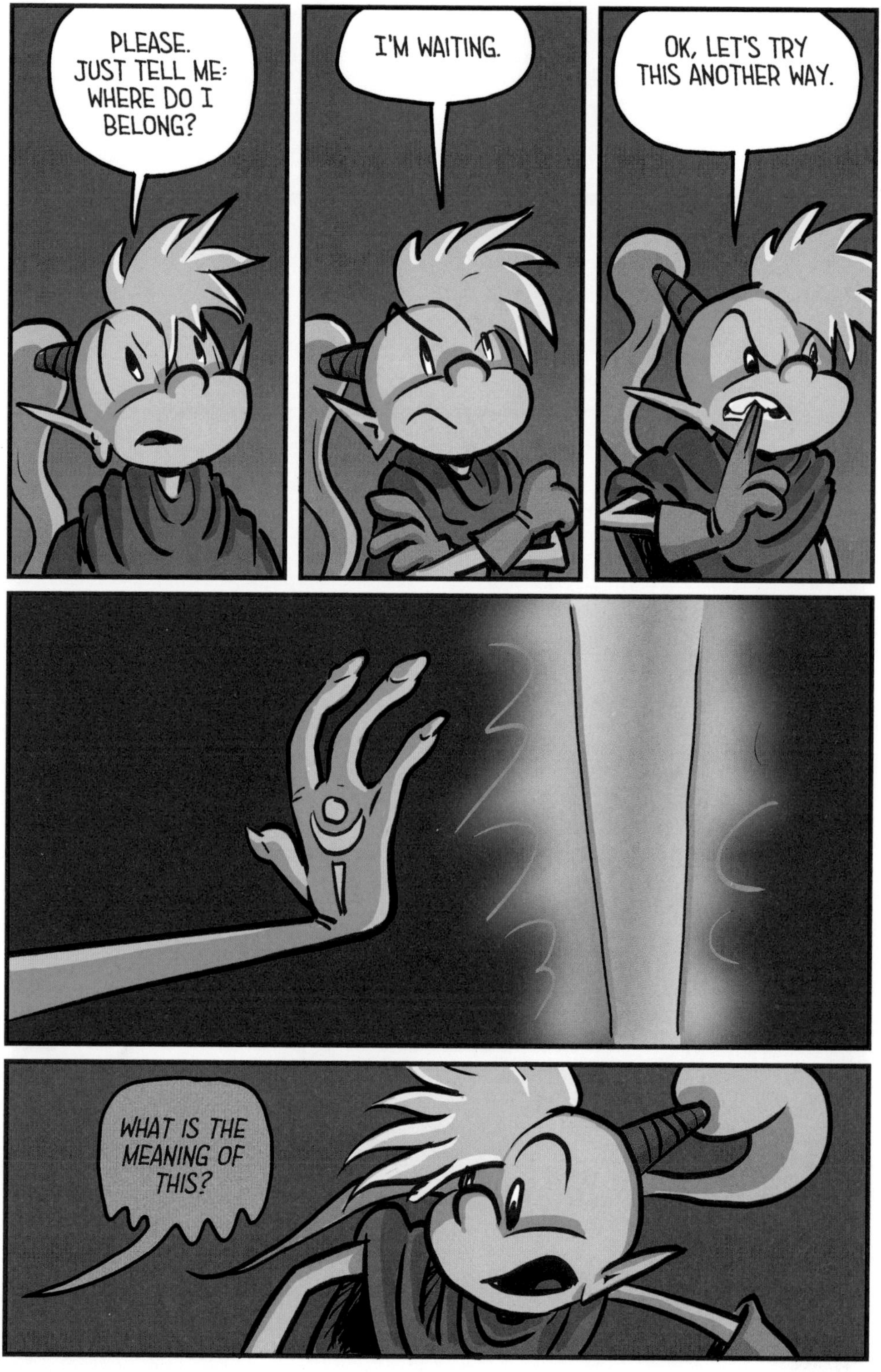
PLEASE. JUST TELL ME: WHERE DO I BELONG?
I'M WAITING.
OK, LET'S TRY THIS ANOTHER WAY.
WHAT IS THE MEANING OF THIS?

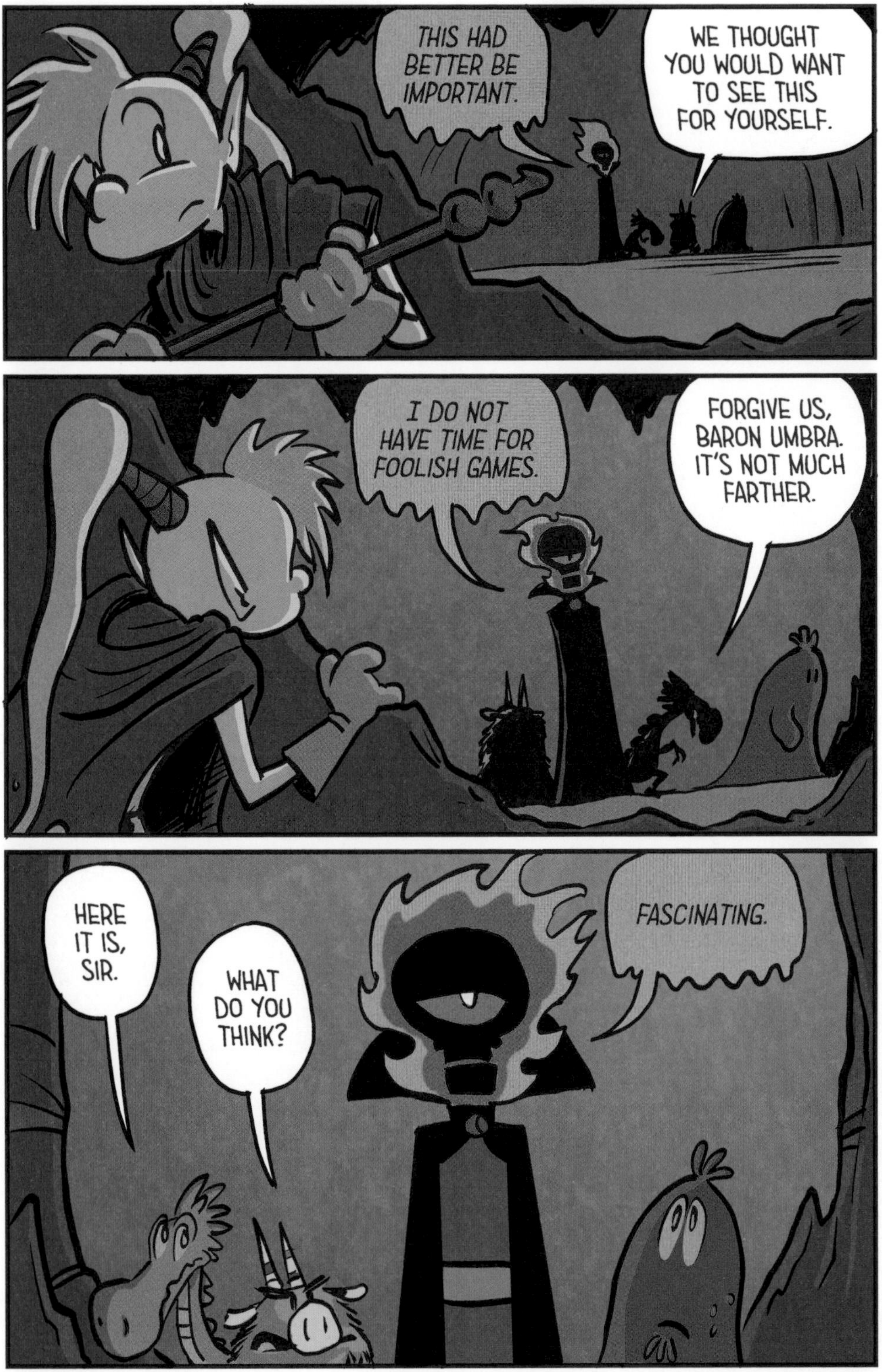
THIS HAD BETTER BE IMPORTANT.
WE THOUGHT YOU WOULD WANT TO SEE THIS FOR YOURSELF.
I DO NOT HAVE TIME FOR FOOLISH GAMES.
FORGIVE US, BARON UMBRA. IT'S NOT MUCH FARTHER.
HERE IT IS, SIR.
WHAT DO YOU THINK?
FASCINATING.

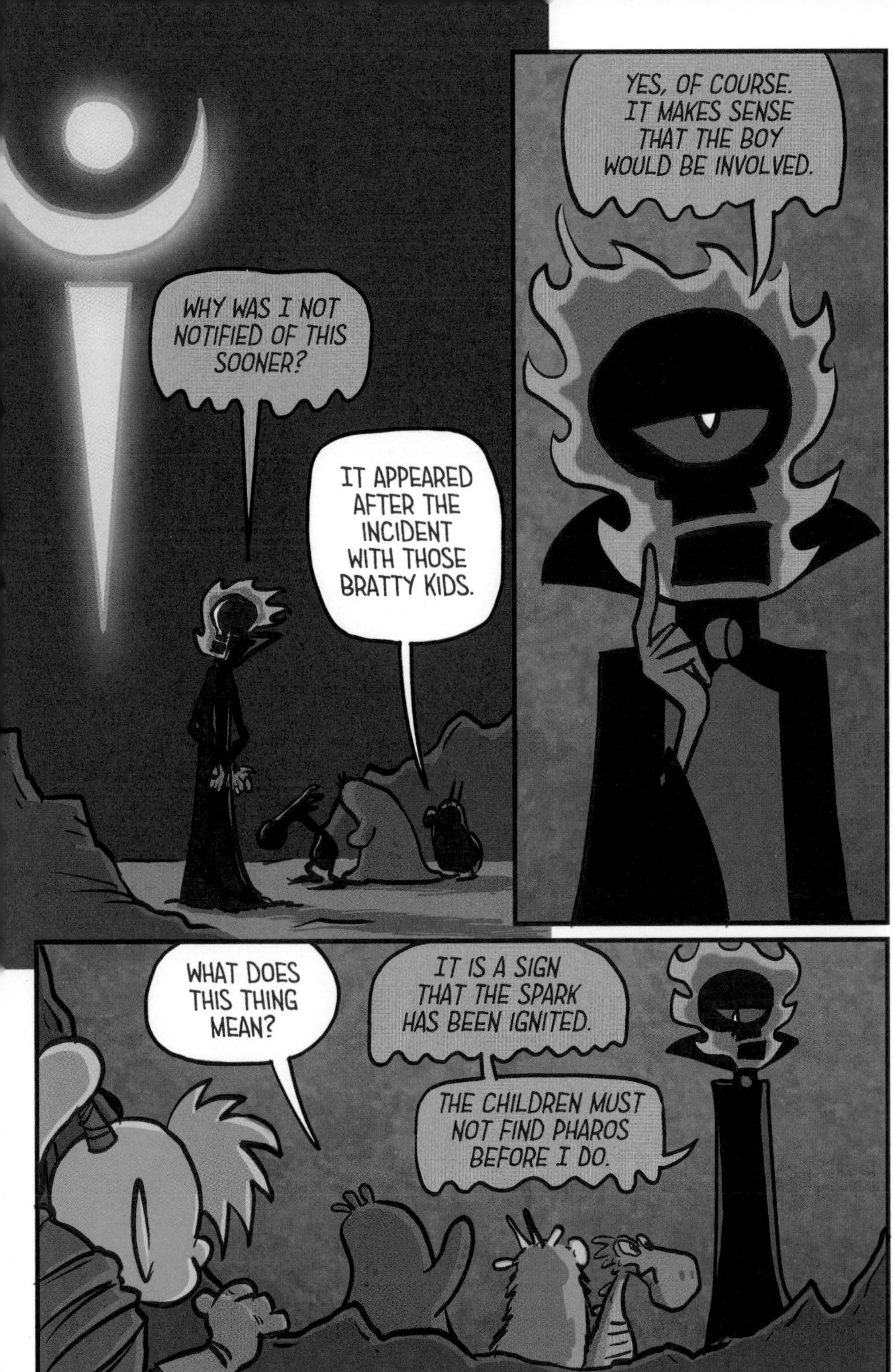
WHY WAS I NOT NOTIFIED OF THIS SOONER?
IT APPEARED AFTER THE INCIDENT WITH THOSE BRATTY KIDS.
YES, OF COURSE. IT MAKES SENSE THAT THE BOY WOULD BE INVOLVED.
WHAT DOES THIS THING MEAN?
IT IS A SIGN THAT THE SPARK HAS BEEN IGNITED.
THE CHILDREN MUST NOT FIND PHAROS BEFORE I DO.

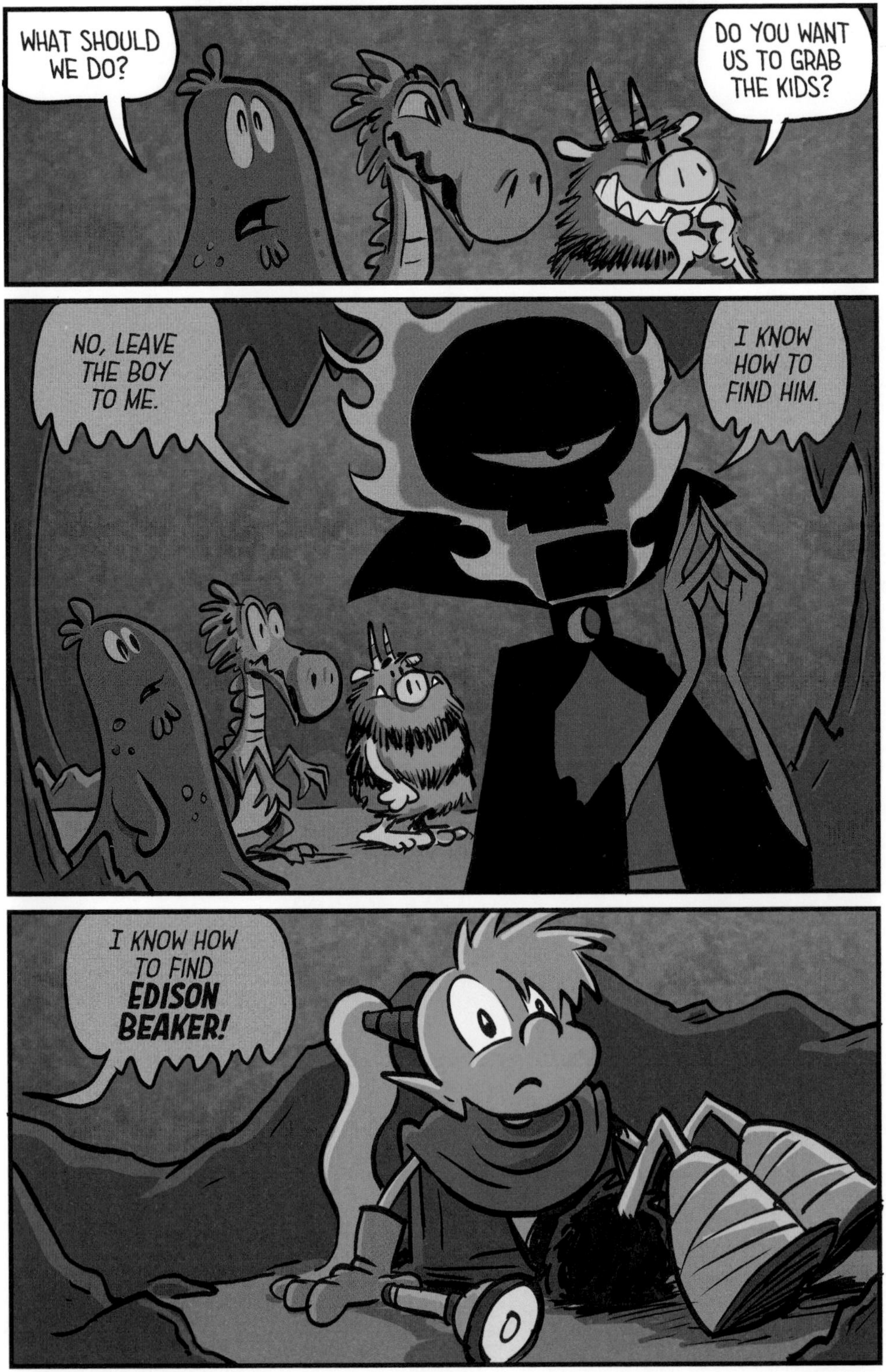
WHAT SHOULD WE DO?
DO YOU WANT US TO GRAB THE KIDS?
NO, LEAVE THE BOY TO ME.
I KNOW HOW TO FIND HIM.
I KNOW HOW TO FIND **EDISON BEAKER!**

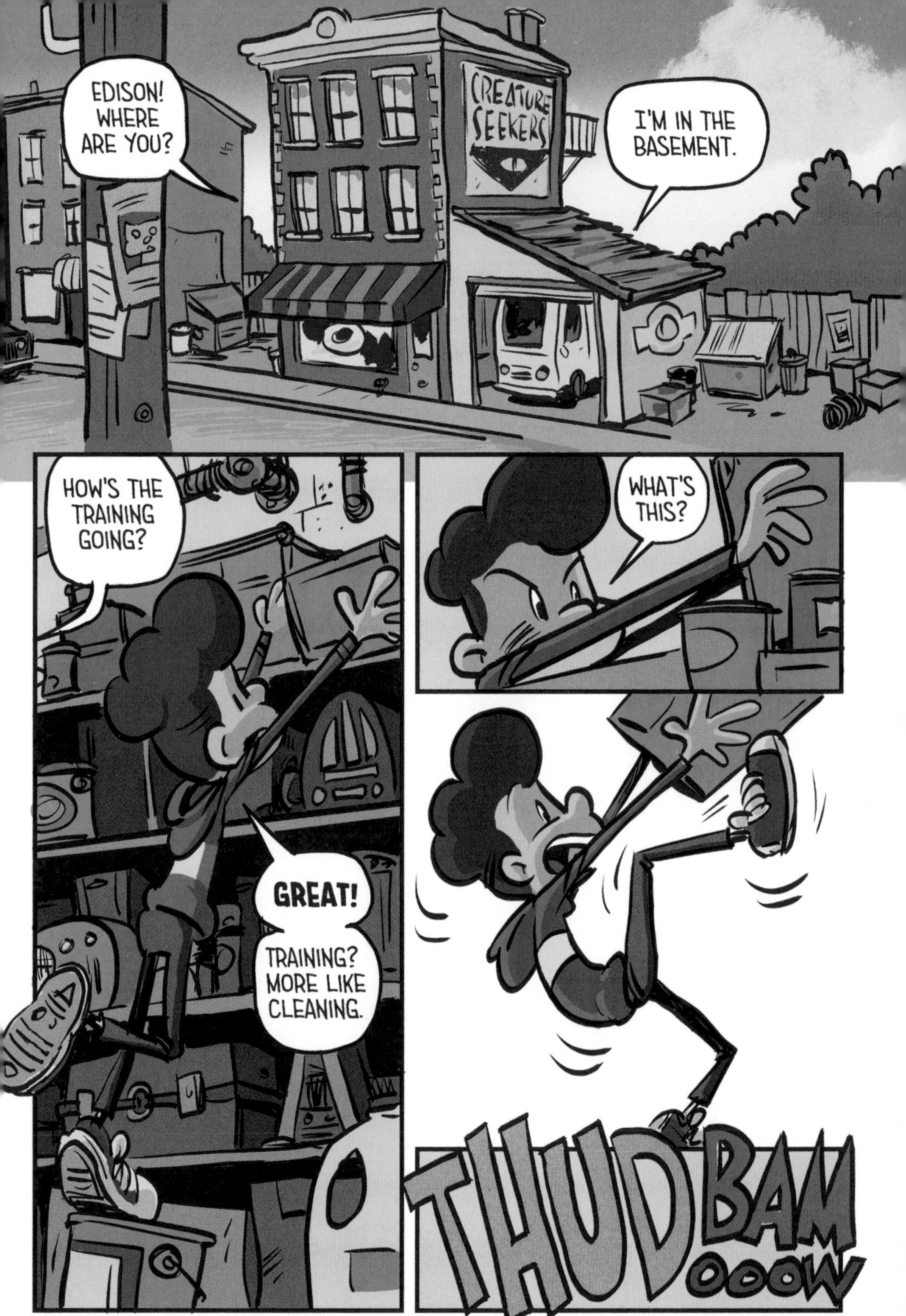
CREATURE SEEKERS
EDISON! WHERE ARE YOU?
I'M IN THE BASEMENT.
HOW'S THE TRAINING GOING?
GREAT!
TRAINING? MORE LIKE CLEANING.
WHAT'S THIS?
THUD
BAM
OOOW

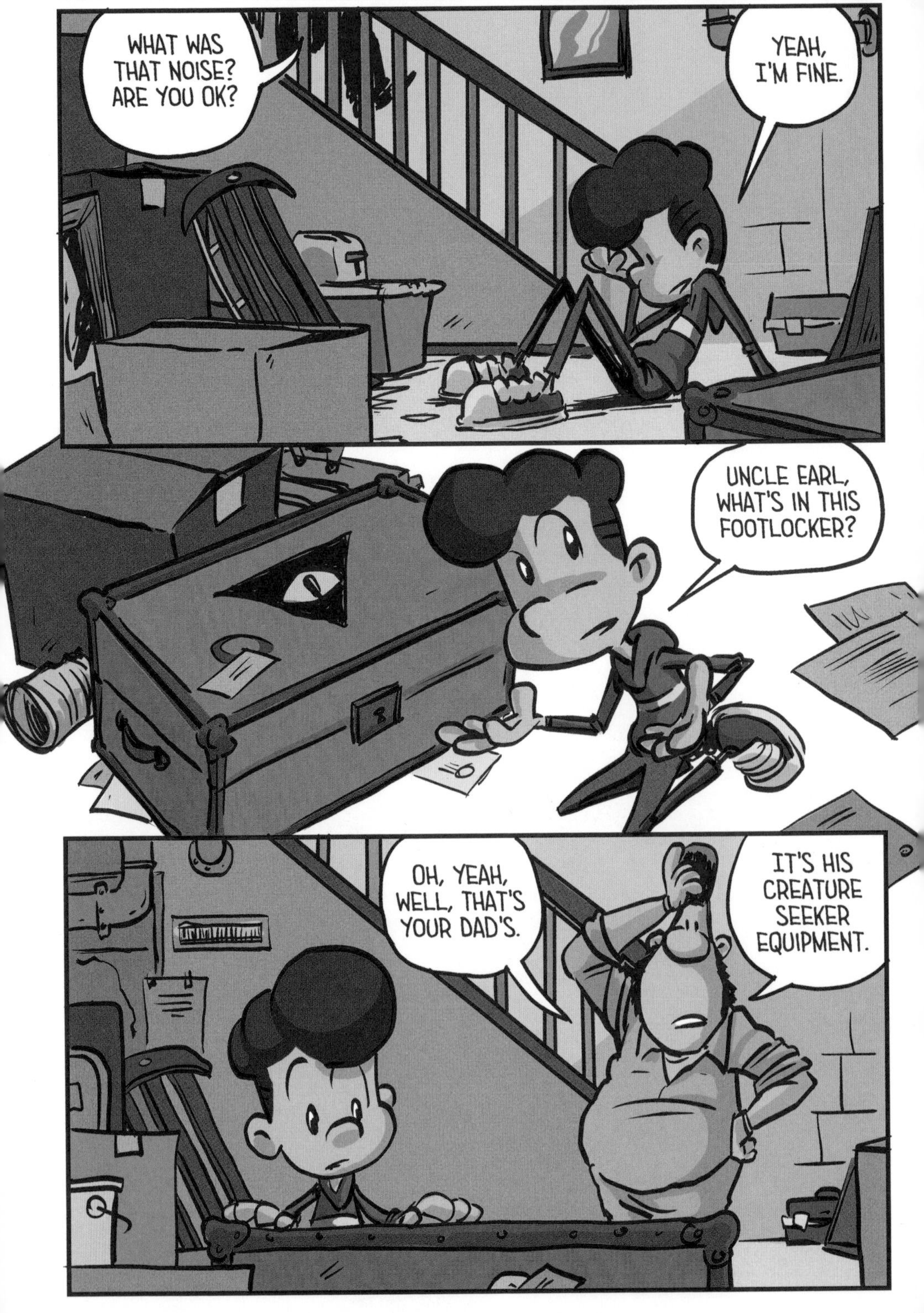
WHAT WAS THAT NOISE? ARE YOU OK?
YEAH, I'M FINE.
UNCLE EARL, WHAT'S IN THIS FOOTLOCKER?
OH, YEAH, WELL, THAT'S YOUR DAD'S.
IT'S HIS CREATURE SEEKER EQUIPMENT.

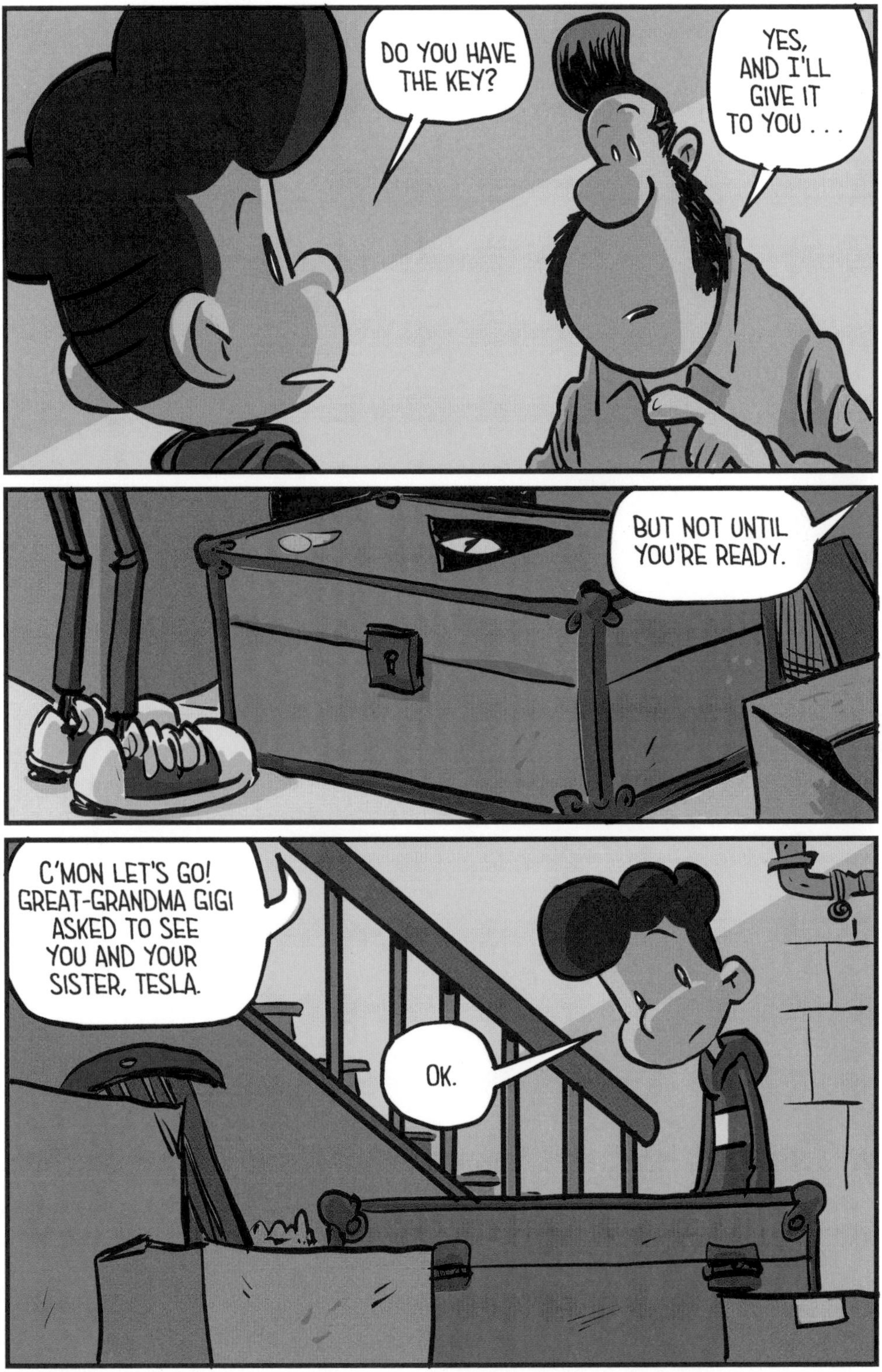
DO YOU HAVE THE KEY?
YES, AND I'LL GIVE IT TO YOU . . .
BUT NOT UNTIL YOU'RE READY.
C'MON LET'S GO! GREAT-GRANDMA GIGI ASKED TO SEE YOU AND YOUR SISTER, TESLA.
OK.

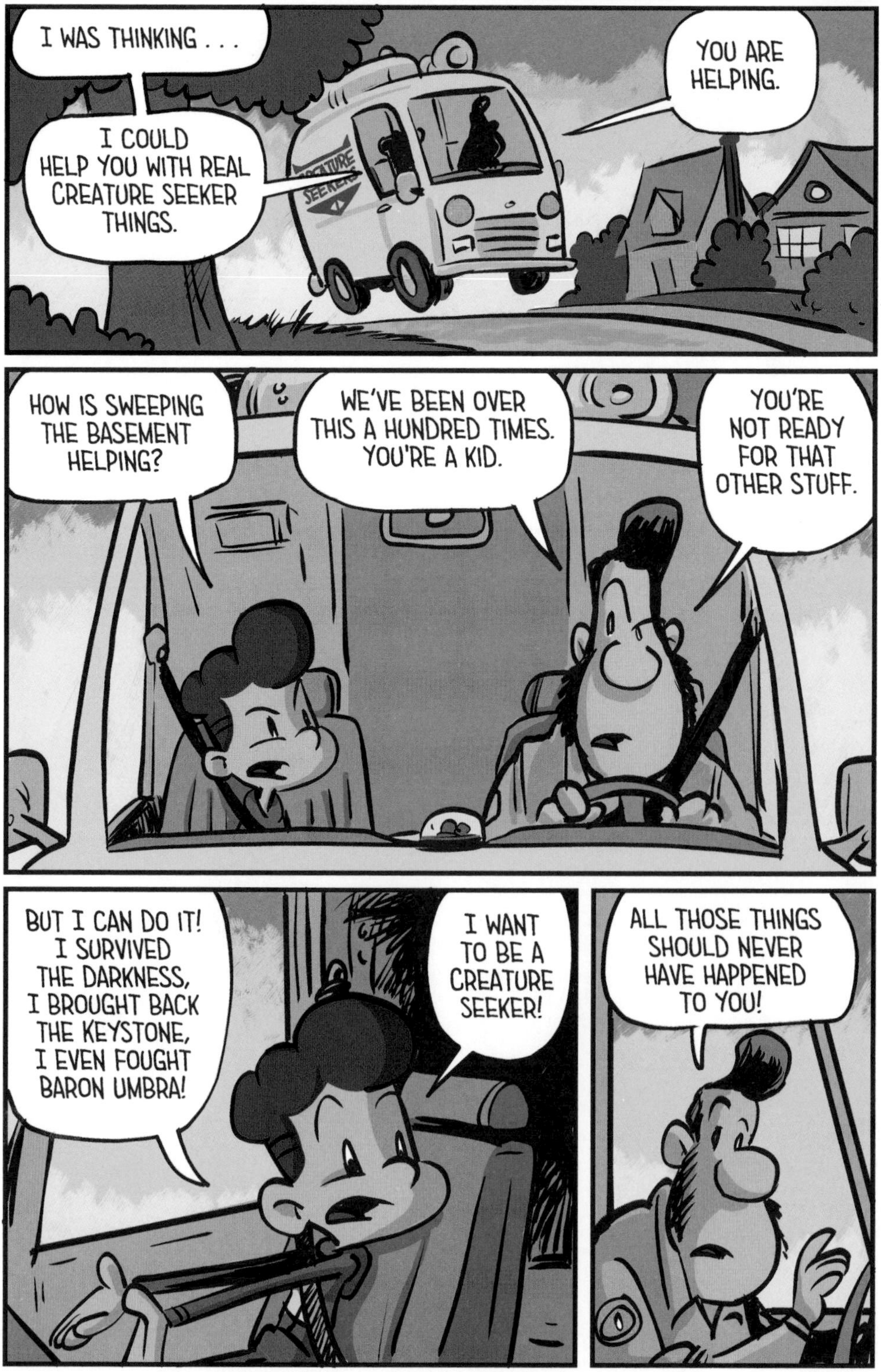
I WAS THINKING . . .
I COULD HELP YOU WITH REAL CREATURE SEEKER THINGS.
YOU ARE HELPING.
CREATURE SEEKERS
HOW IS SWEEPING THE BASEMENT HELPING?
WE'VE BEEN OVER THIS A HUNDRED TIMES. YOU'RE A KID.
YOU'RE NOT READY FOR THAT OTHER STUFF.
BUT I CAN DO IT! I SURVIVED THE DARKNESS, I BROUGHT BACK THE KEYSTONE, I EVEN FOUGHT BARON UMBRA!
I WANT TO BE A CREATURE SEEKER!
ALL THOSE THINGS SHOULD NEVER HAVE HAPPENED TO YOU!

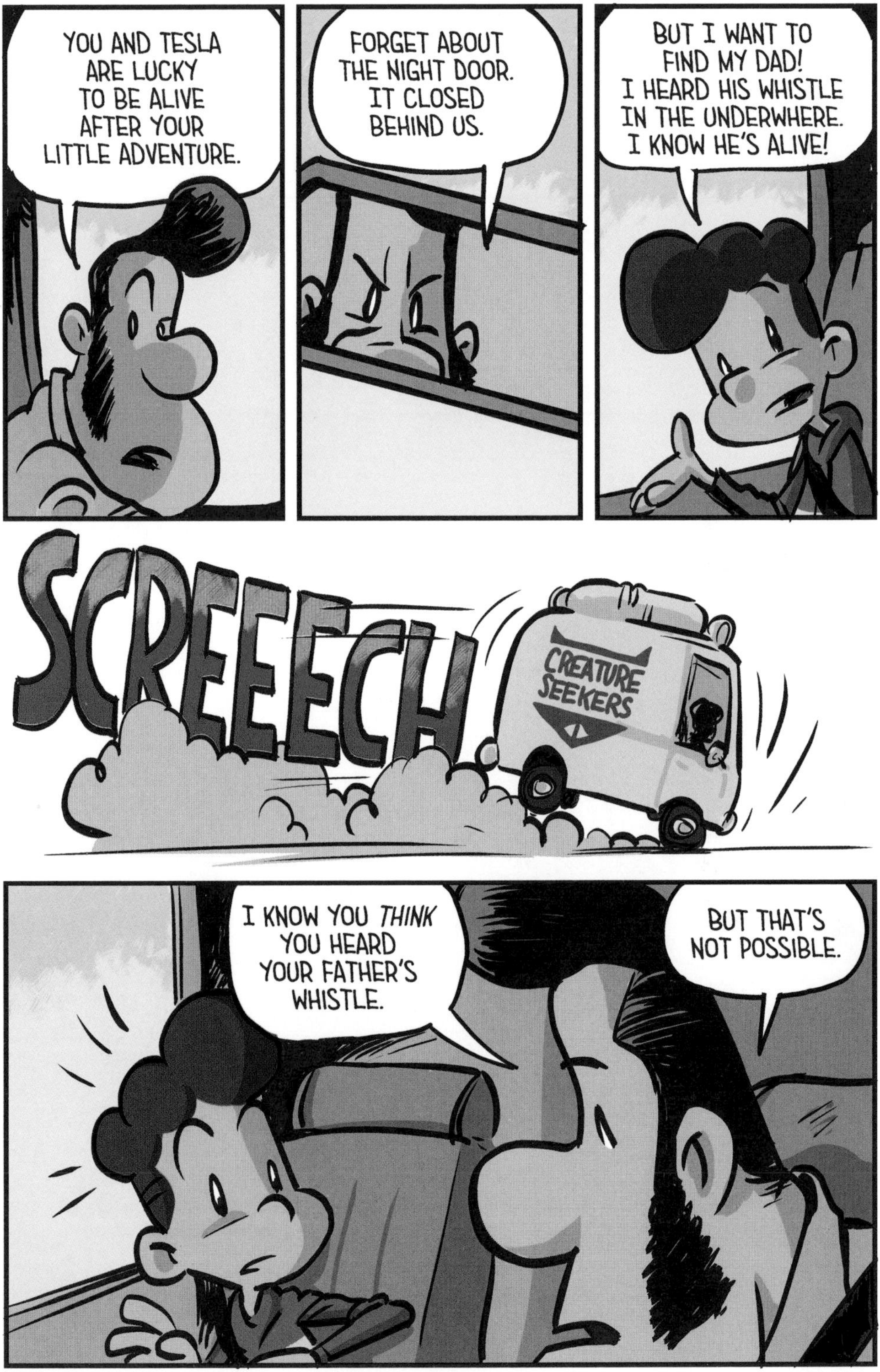
YOU AND TESLA ARE LUCKY TO BE ALIVE AFTER YOUR LITTLE ADVENTURE.
FORGET ABOUT THE NIGHT DOOR. IT CLOSED BEHIND US.
BUT I WANT TO FIND MY DAD! I HEARD HIS WHISTLE IN THE UNDERWHERE. I KNOW HE'S ALIVE!
SCREEECH
CREATURE SEEKERS
I KNOW YOU *THINK* YOU HEARD YOUR FATHER'S WHISTLE.
BUT THAT'S NOT POSSIBLE.

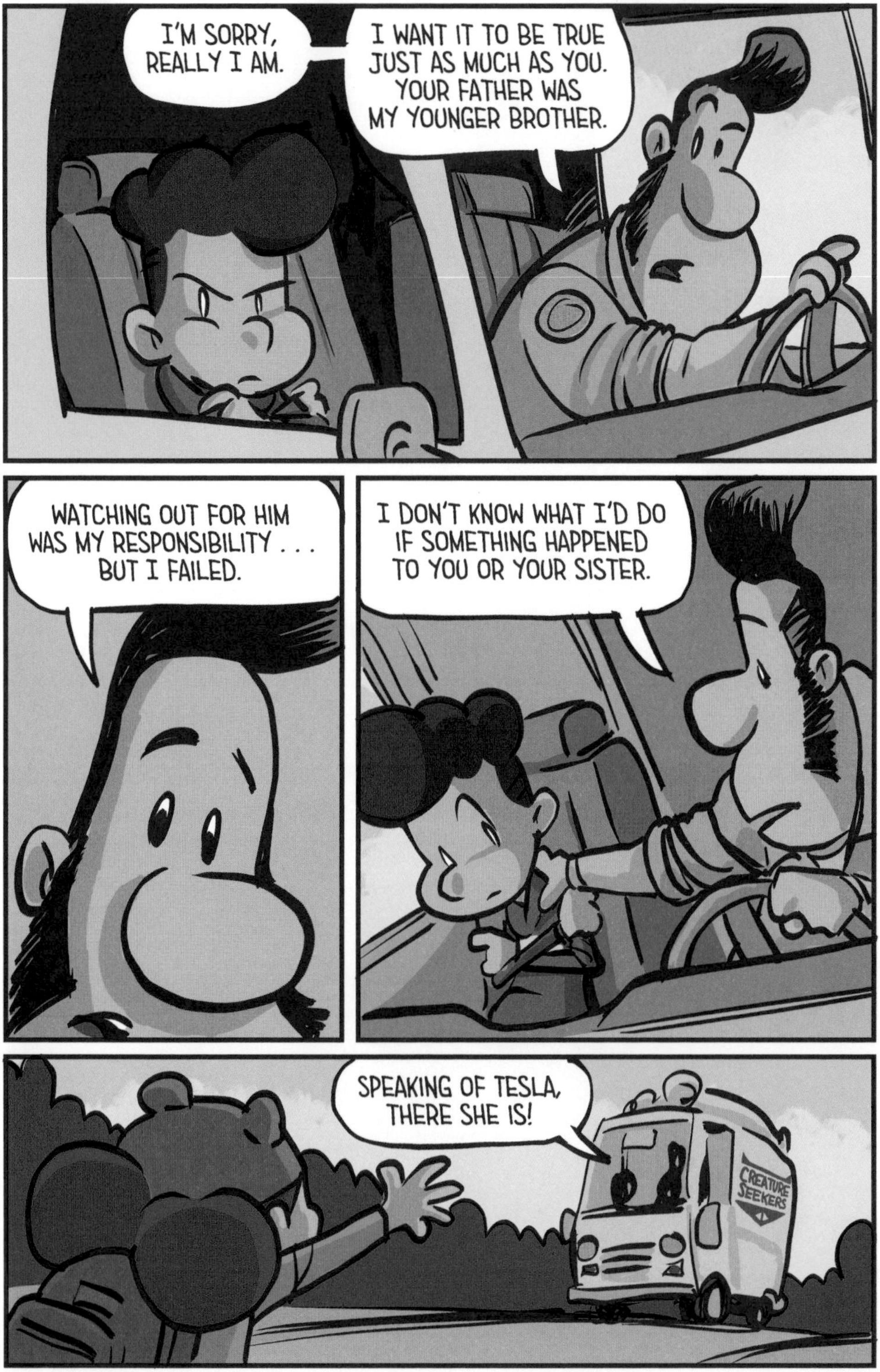
I'M SORRY, REALLY I AM.
I WANT IT TO BE TRUE JUST AS MUCH AS YOU. YOUR FATHER WAS MY YOUNGER BROTHER.
WATCHING OUT FOR HIM WAS MY RESPONSIBILITY . . . BUT I FAILED.
I DON'T KNOW WHAT I'D DO IF SOMETHING HAPPENED TO YOU OR YOUR SISTER.
SPEAKING OF TESLA, THERE SHE IS!
CREATURE SEEKERS

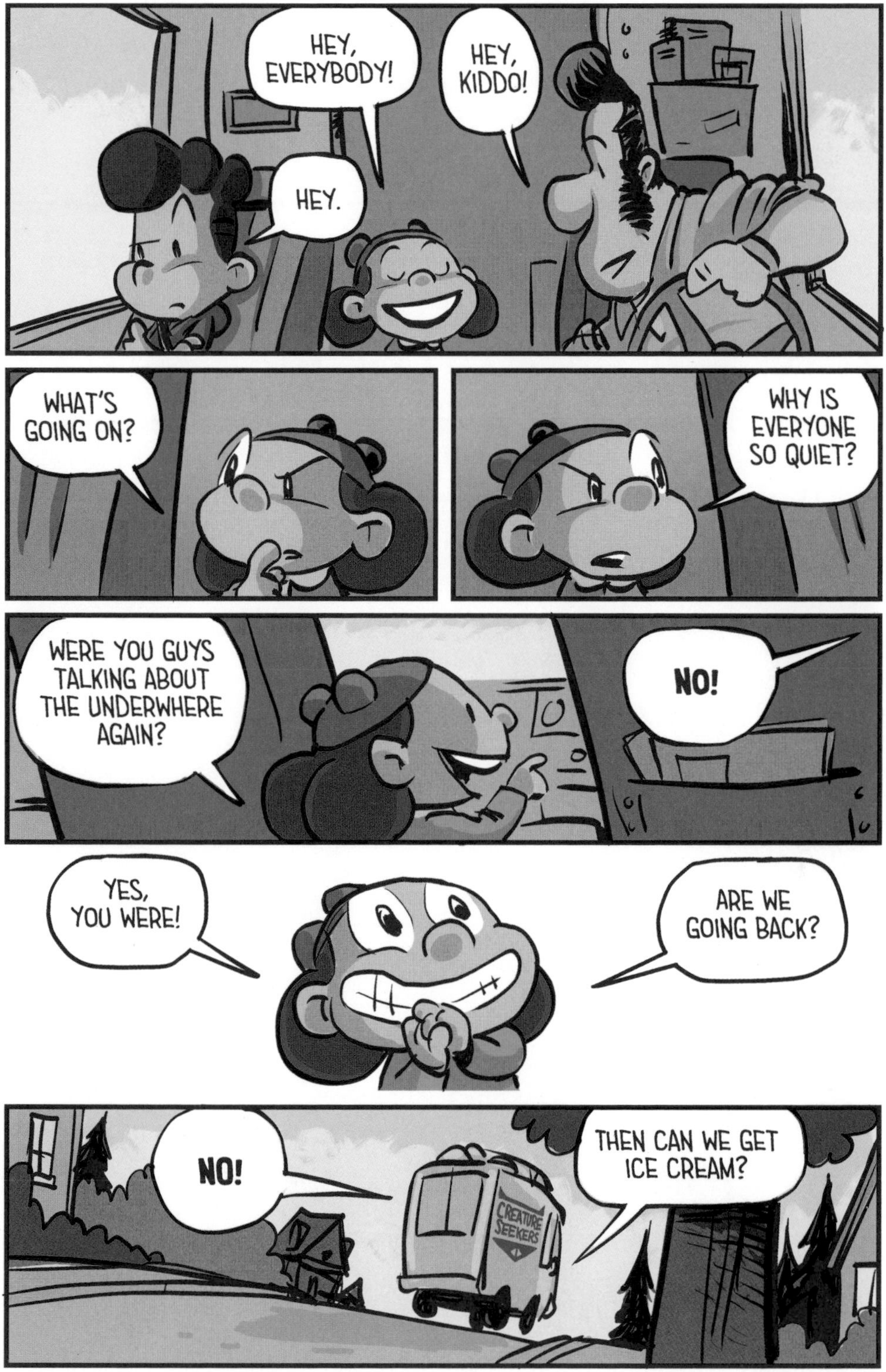
HEY, EVERYBODY!
HEY, KIDDO!
HEY.
WHAT'S GOING ON?
WHY IS EVERYONE SO QUIET?
WERE YOU GUYS TALKING ABOUT THE UNDERWHERE AGAIN?
NO!
YES, YOU WERE!
ARE WE GOING BACK?
NO!
THEN CAN WE GET ICE CREAM?
CREATURE SEEKERS

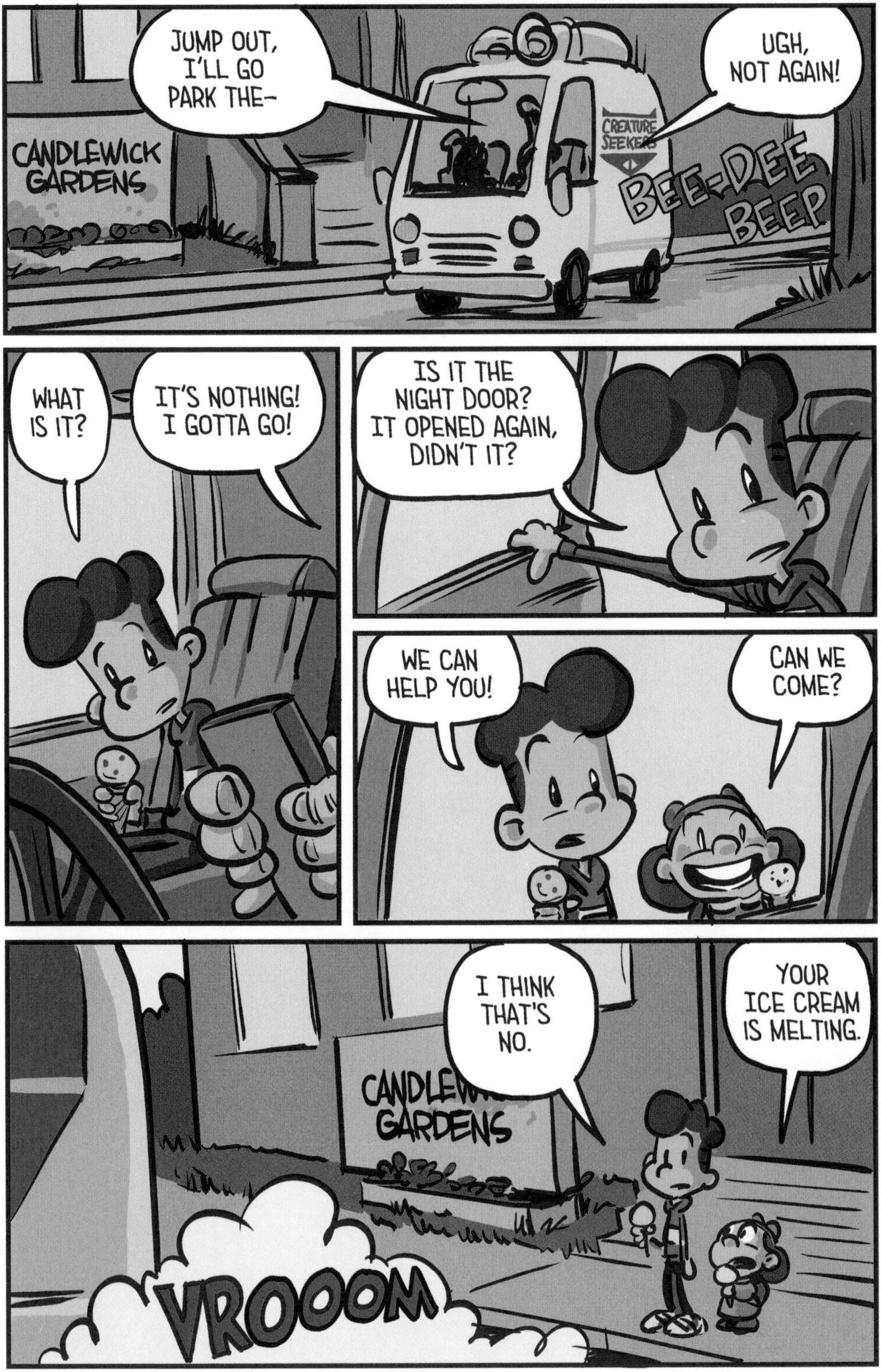
JUMP OUT, I'LL GO PARK THE–
UGH, NOT AGAIN!
CANDLEWICK GARDENS
CREATURE SEEKERS
BEE-DEE BEEP
WHAT IS IT?
IT'S NOTHING! I GOTTA GO!
IS IT THE NIGHT DOOR? IT OPENED AGAIN, DIDN'T IT?
WE CAN HELP YOU!
CAN WE COME?
I THINK THAT'S NO.
YOUR ICE CREAM IS MELTING.
GARDENS
VROOOM

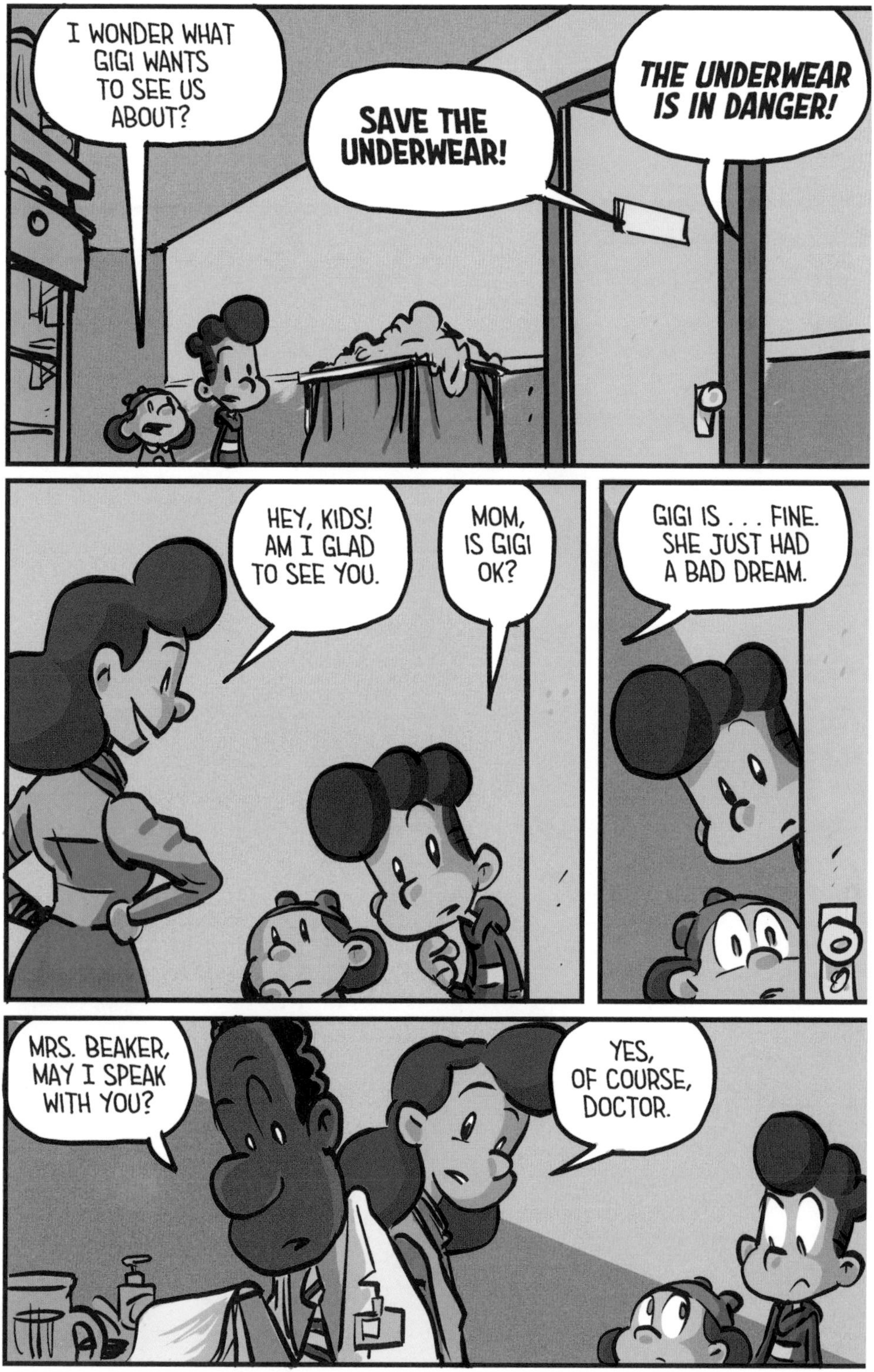
I WONDER WHAT GIGI WANTS TO SEE US ABOUT?
SAVE THE UNDERWEAR!
THE UNDERWEAR IS IN DANGER!
HEY, KIDS! AM I GLAD TO SEE YOU.
MOM, IS GIGI OK?
GIGI IS . . . FINE. SHE JUST HAD A BAD DREAM.
MRS. BEAKER, MAY I SPEAK WITH YOU?
YES, OF COURSE, DOCTOR.

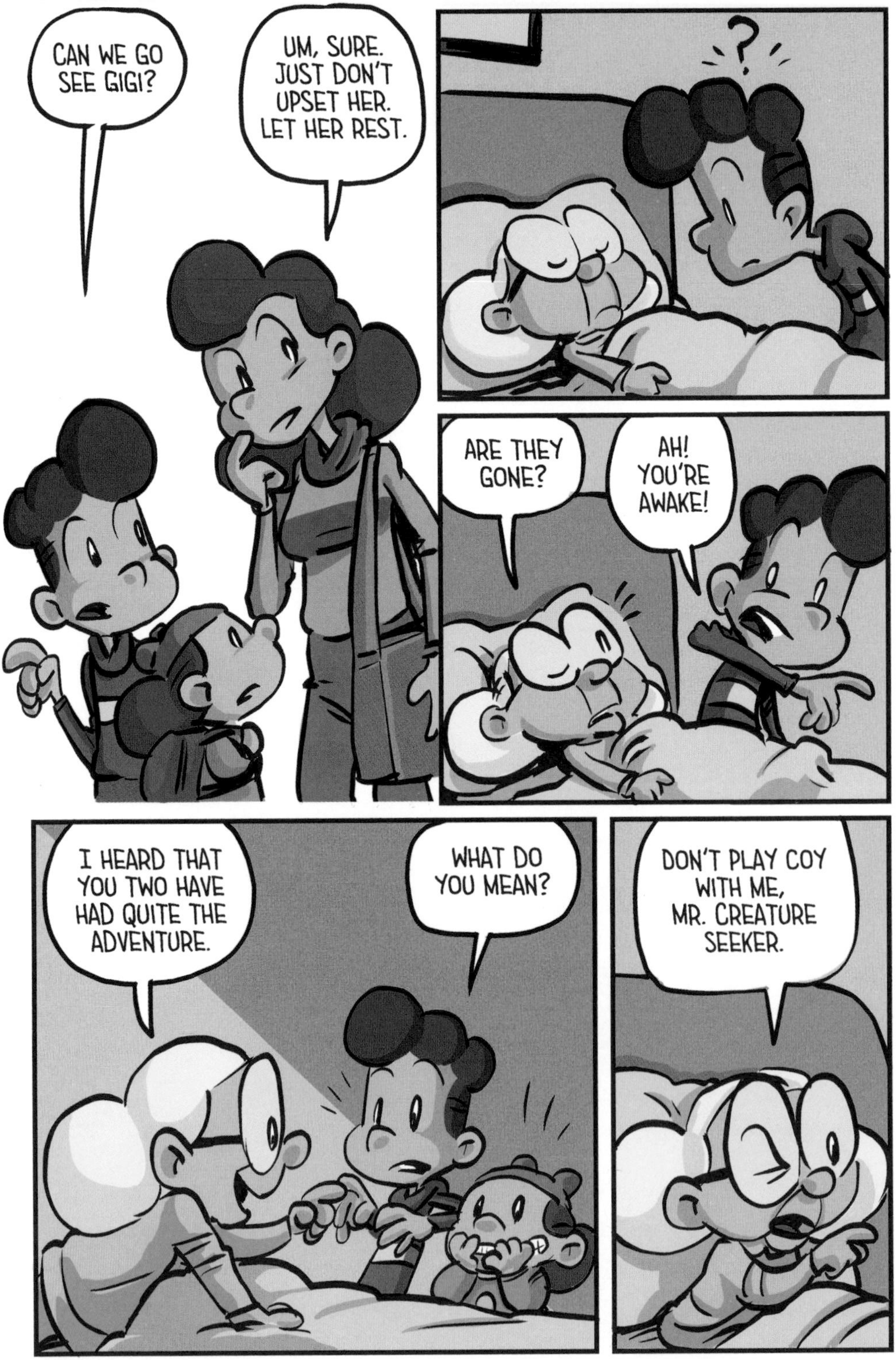
CAN WE GO SEE GIGI?
UM, SURE. JUST DON'T UPSET HER. LET HER REST.
?
ARE THEY GONE?
AH! YOU'RE AWAKE!
I HEARD THAT YOU TWO HAVE HAD QUITE THE ADVENTURE.
WHAT DO YOU MEAN?
DON'T PLAY COY WITH ME, MR. CREATURE SEEKER.

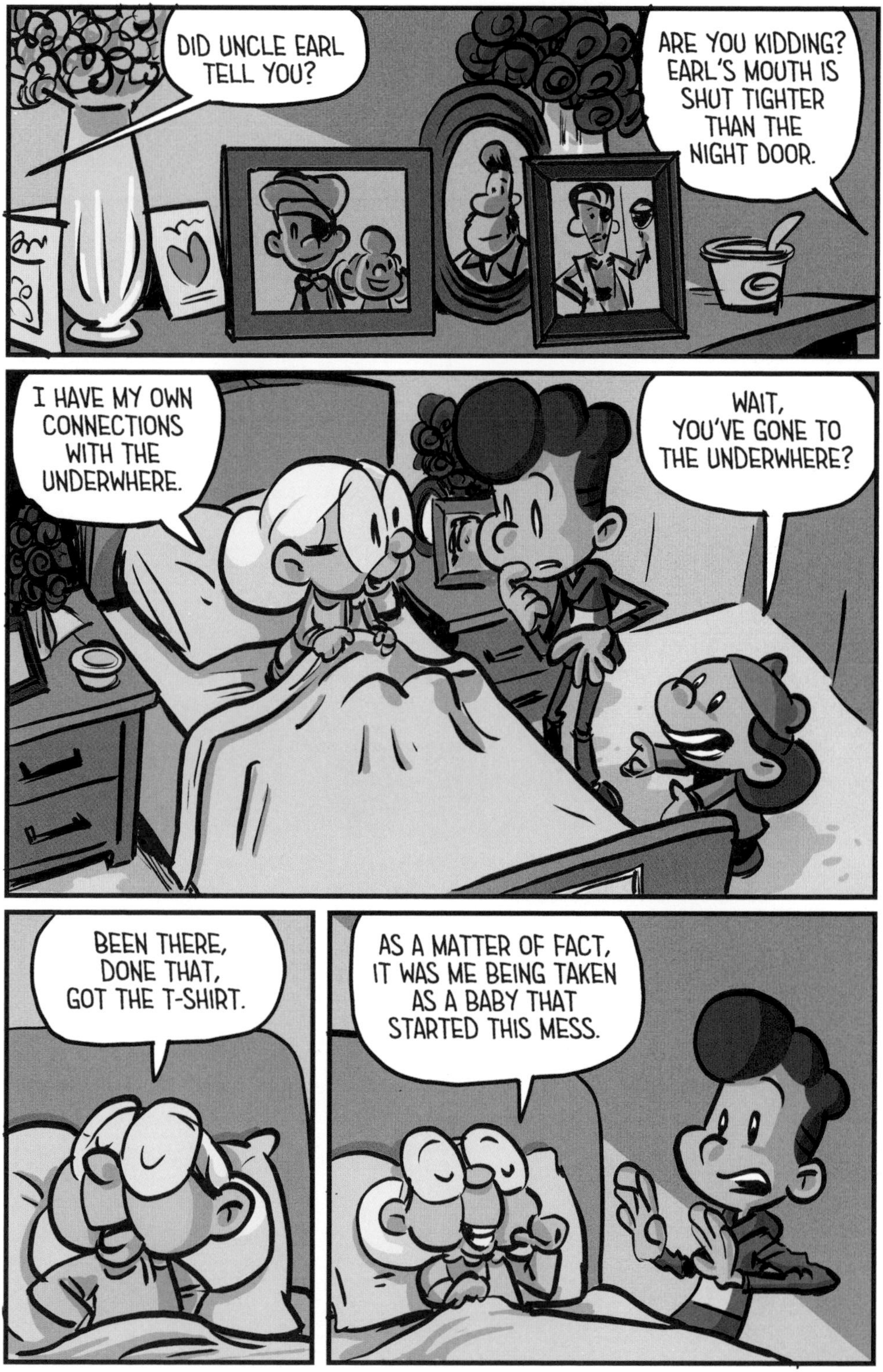
DID UNCLE EARL TELL YOU?
ARE YOU KIDDING? EARL'S MOUTH IS SHUT TIGHTER THAN THE NIGHT DOOR.
I HAVE MY OWN CONNECTIONS WITH THE UNDERWHERE.
WAIT, YOU'VE GONE TO THE UNDERWHERE?
BEEN THERE, DONE THAT, GOT THE T-SHIRT.
AS A MATTER OF FACT, IT WAS ME BEING TAKEN AS A BABY THAT STARTED THIS MESS.

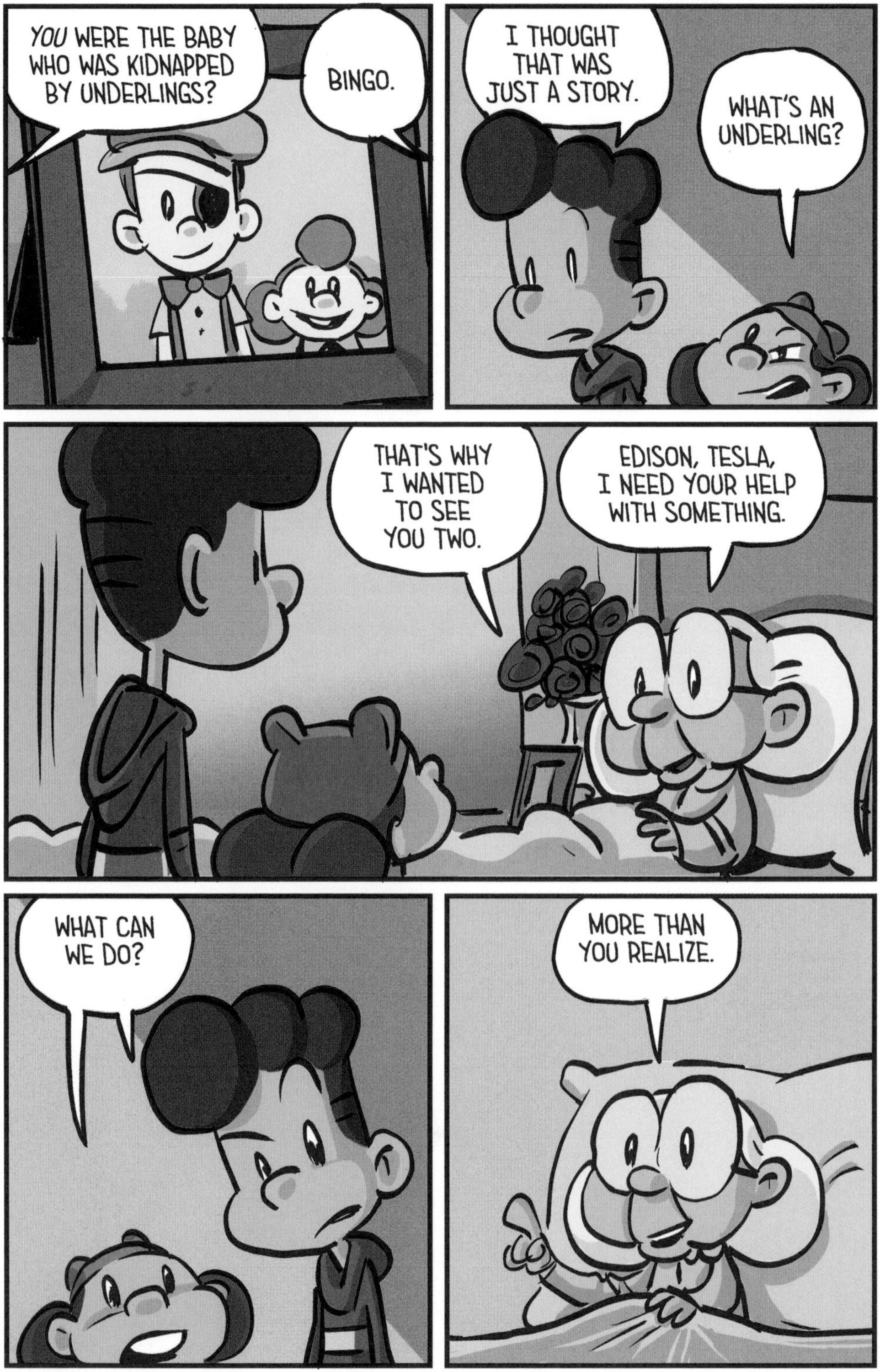

YOU WERE THE BABY WHO WAS KIDNAPPED BY UNDERLINGS?
BINGO.
I THOUGHT THAT WAS JUST A STORY.
WHAT'S AN UNDERLING?
THAT'S WHY I WANTED TO SEE YOU TWO.
EDISON, TESLA, I NEED YOUR HELP WITH SOMETHING.
WHAT CAN WE DO?
MORE THAN YOU REALIZE.

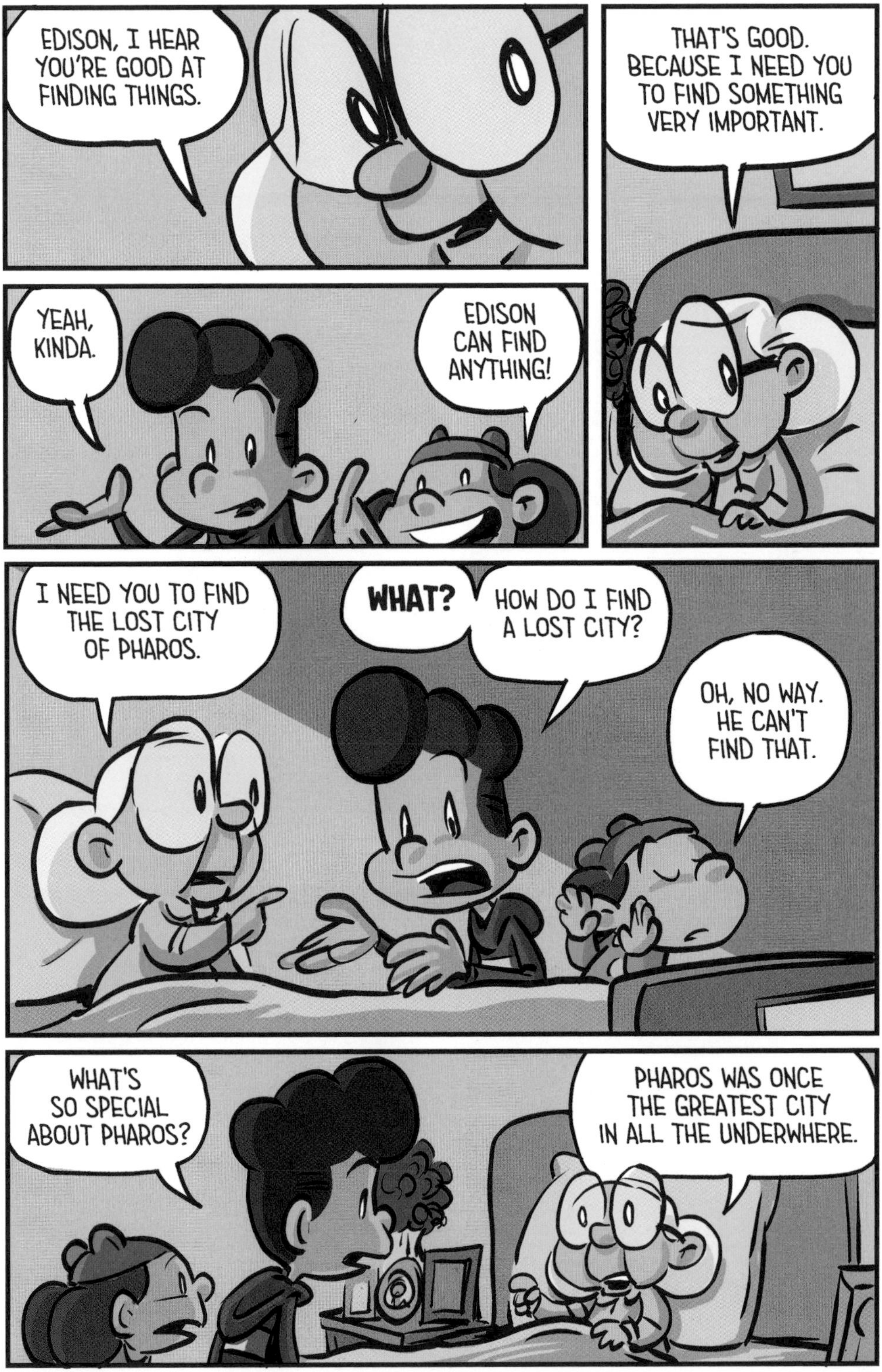
EDISON, I HEAR YOU'RE GOOD AT FINDING THINGS.
THAT'S GOOD. BECAUSE I NEED YOU TO FIND SOMETHING VERY IMPORTANT.
YEAH, KINDA.
EDISON CAN FIND ANYTHING!
I NEED YOU TO FIND THE LOST CITY OF PHAROS.
WHAT?
HOW DO I FIND A LOST CITY?
OH, NO WAY. HE CAN'T FIND THAT.
WHAT'S SO SPECIAL ABOUT PHAROS?
PHAROS WAS ONCE THE GREATEST CITY IN ALL THE UNDERWHERE.

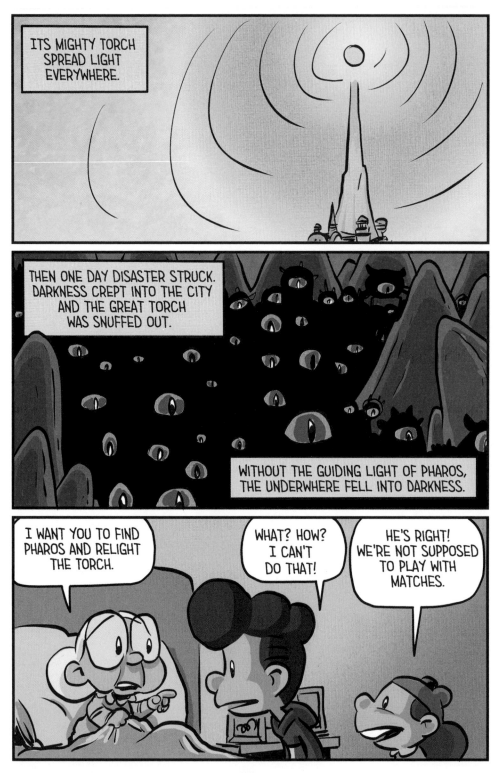

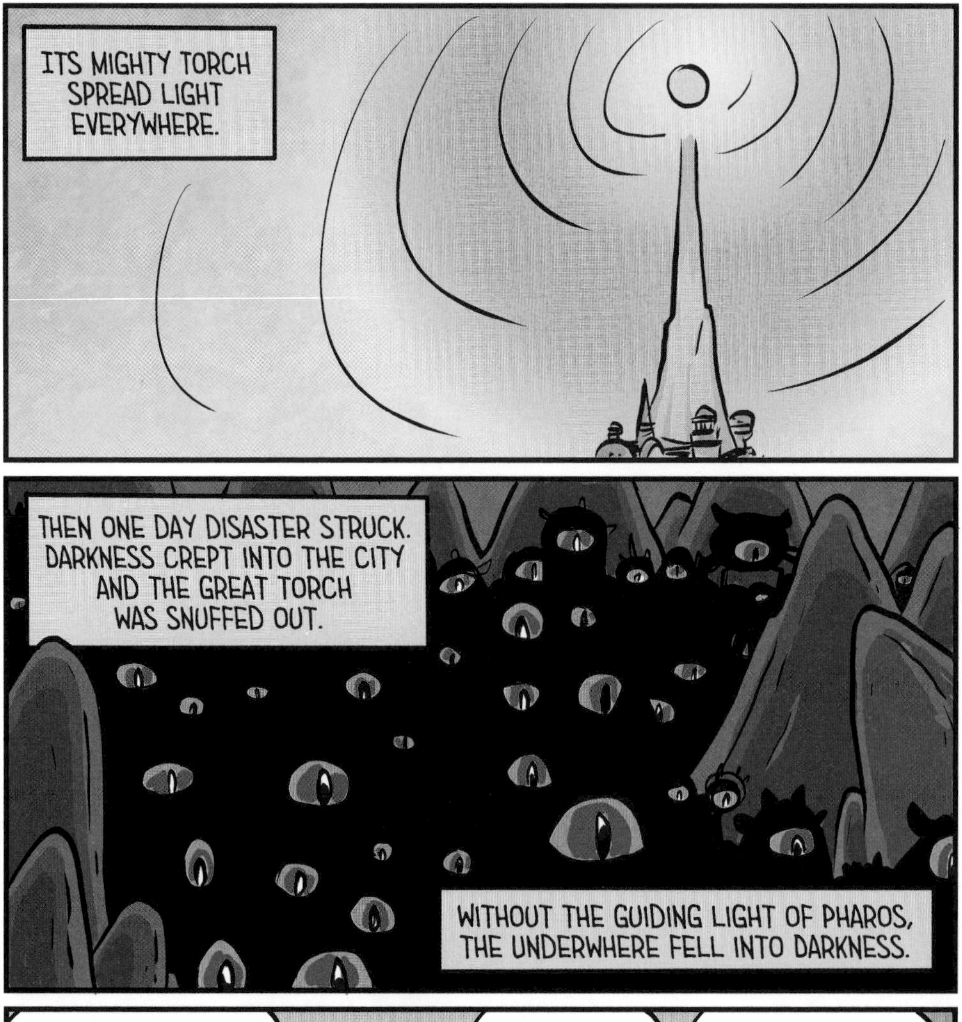
ITS MIGHTY TORCH SPREAD LIGHT EVERYWHERE.
THEN ONE DAY DISASTER STRUCK. DARKNESS CREPT INTO THE CITY AND THE GREAT TORCH WAS SNUFFED OUT.
WITHOUT THE GUIDING LIGHT OF PHAROS, THE UNDERWHERE FELL INTO DARKNESS.
I WANT YOU TO FIND PHAROS AND RELIGHT THE TORCH.
WHAT? HOW? I CAN'T DO THAT!
HE'S RIGHT! WE'RE NOT SUPPOSED TO PLAY WITH MATCHES.

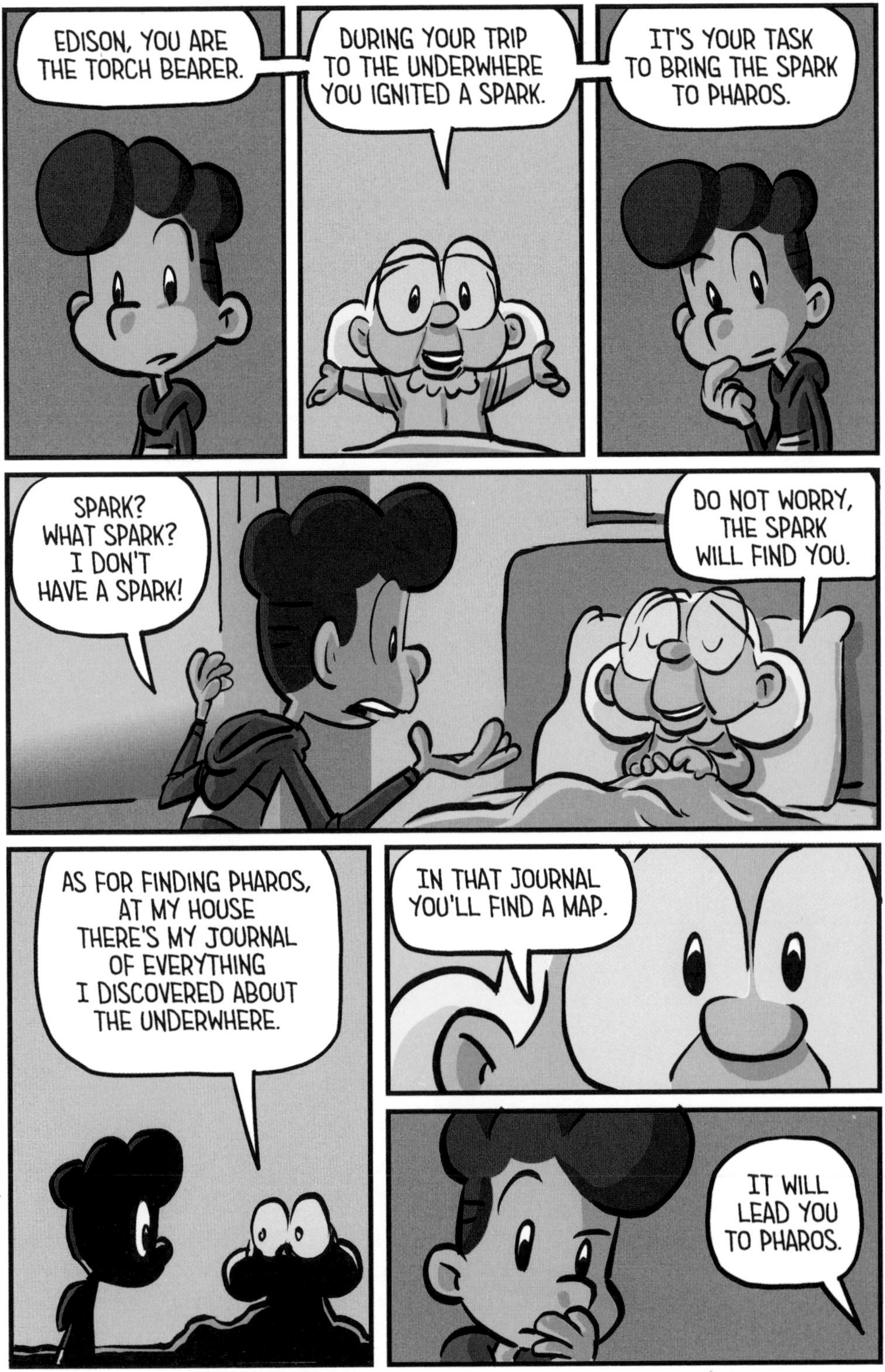
EDISON, YOU ARE THE TORCH BEARER.
DURING YOUR TRIP TO THE UNDERWHERE YOU IGNITED A SPARK.
IT'S YOUR TASK TO BRING THE SPARK TO PHAROS.
SPARK? WHAT SPARK? I DON'T HAVE A SPARK!
DO NOT WORRY, THE SPARK WILL FIND YOU.
AS FOR FINDING PHAROS, AT MY HOUSE THERE'S MY JOURNAL OF EVERYTHING I DISCOVERED ABOUT THE UNDERWHERE.
IN THAT JOURNAL YOU'LL FIND A MAP.
IT WILL LEAD YOU TO PHAROS.

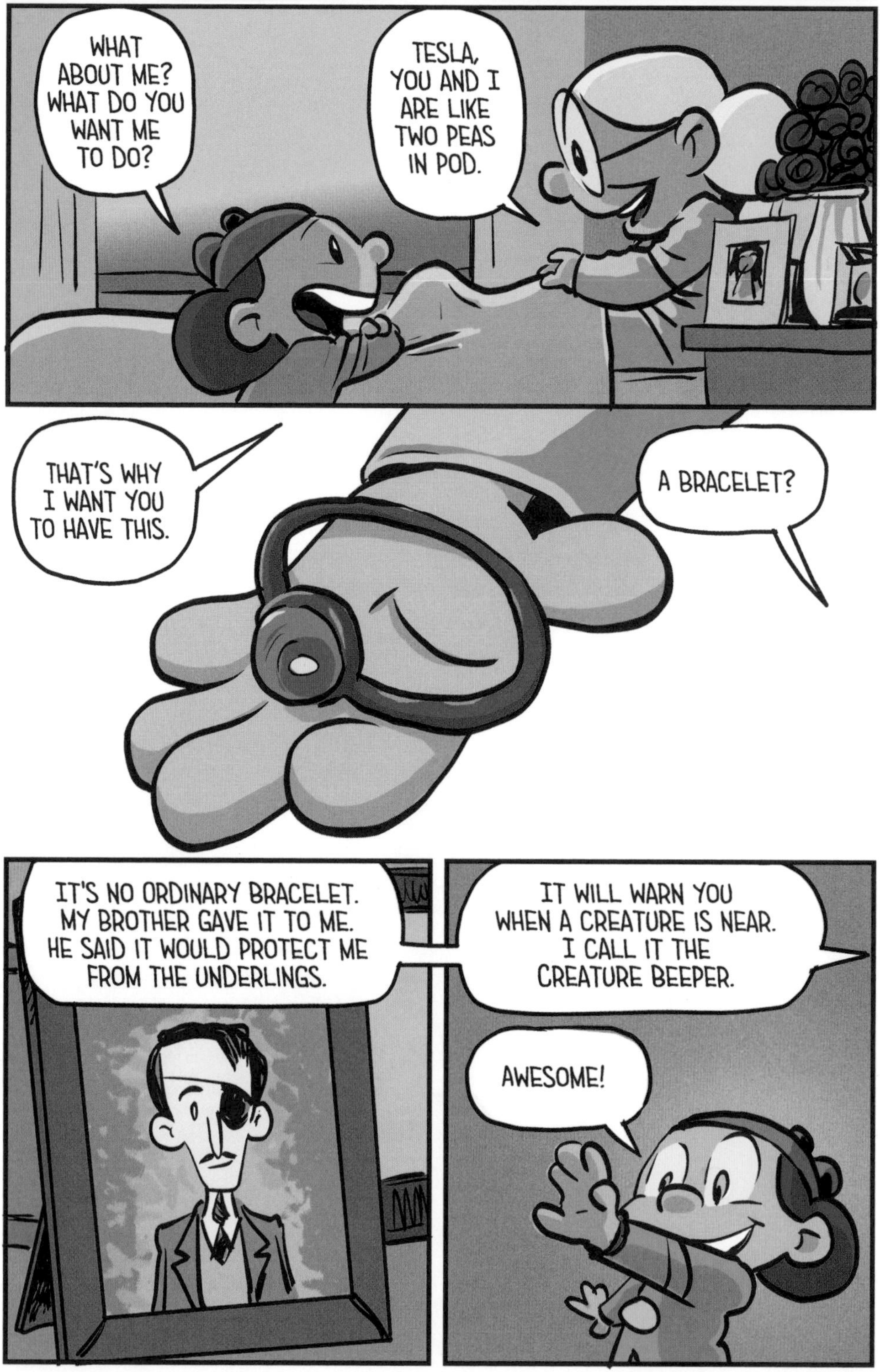
WHAT ABOUT ME? WHAT DO YOU WANT ME TO DO?
TESLA, YOU AND I ARE LIKE TWO PEAS IN POD.
THAT'S WHY I WANT YOU TO HAVE THIS.
A BRACELET?
IT'S NO ORDINARY BRACELET. MY BROTHER GAVE IT TO ME. HE SAID IT WOULD PROTECT ME FROM THE UNDERLINGS.
IT WILL WARN YOU WHEN A CREATURE IS NEAR. I CALL IT THE CREATURE BEEPER.
AWESOME!

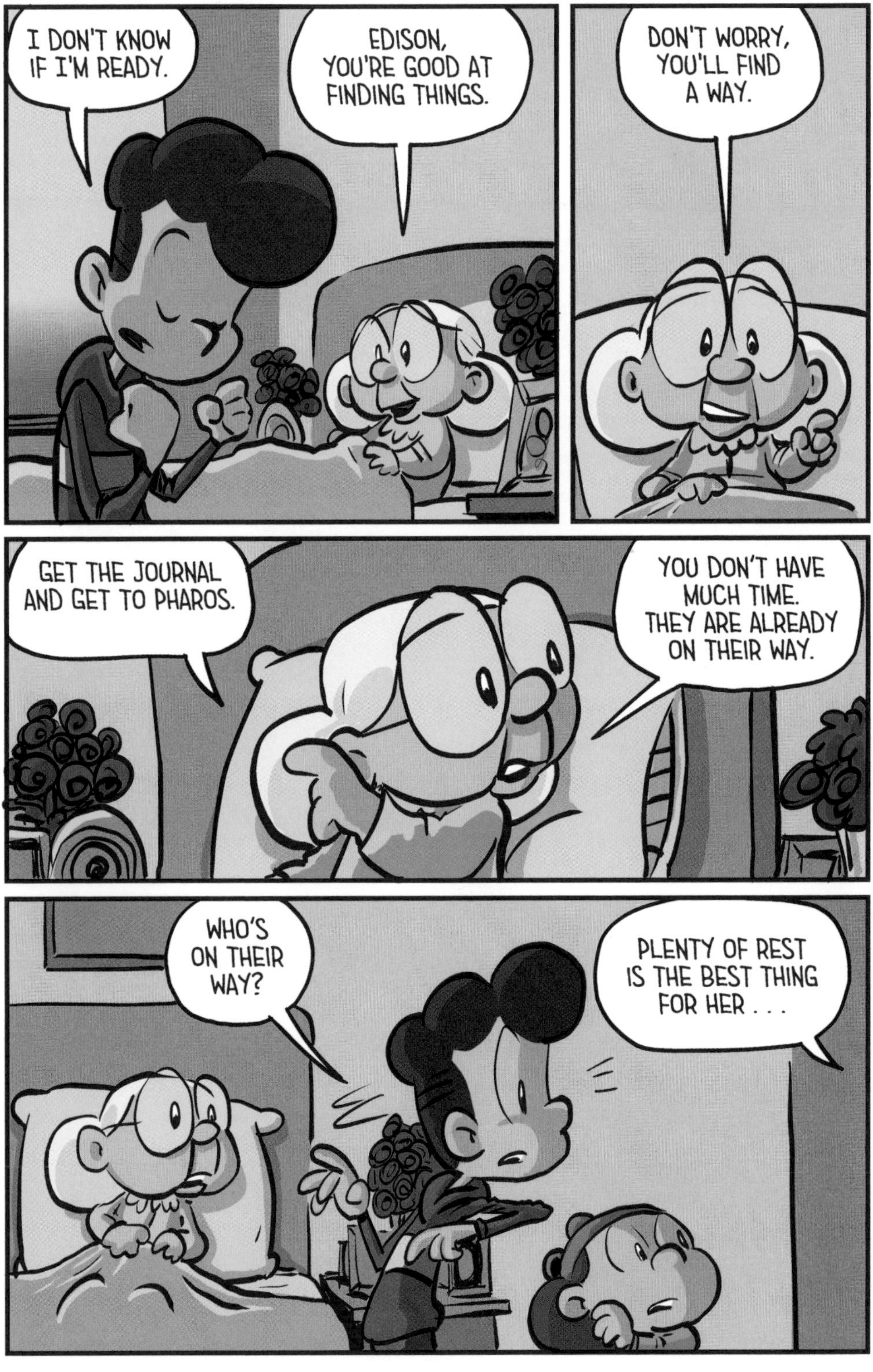
I DON'T KNOW IF I'M READY.
EDISON, YOU'RE GOOD AT FINDING THINGS.
DON'T WORRY, YOU'LL FIND A WAY.
GET THE JOURNAL AND GET TO PHAROS.
YOU DON'T HAVE MUCH TIME. THEY ARE ALREADY ON THEIR WAY.
WHO'S ON THEIR WAY?
PLENTY OF REST IS THE BEST THING FOR HER . . .

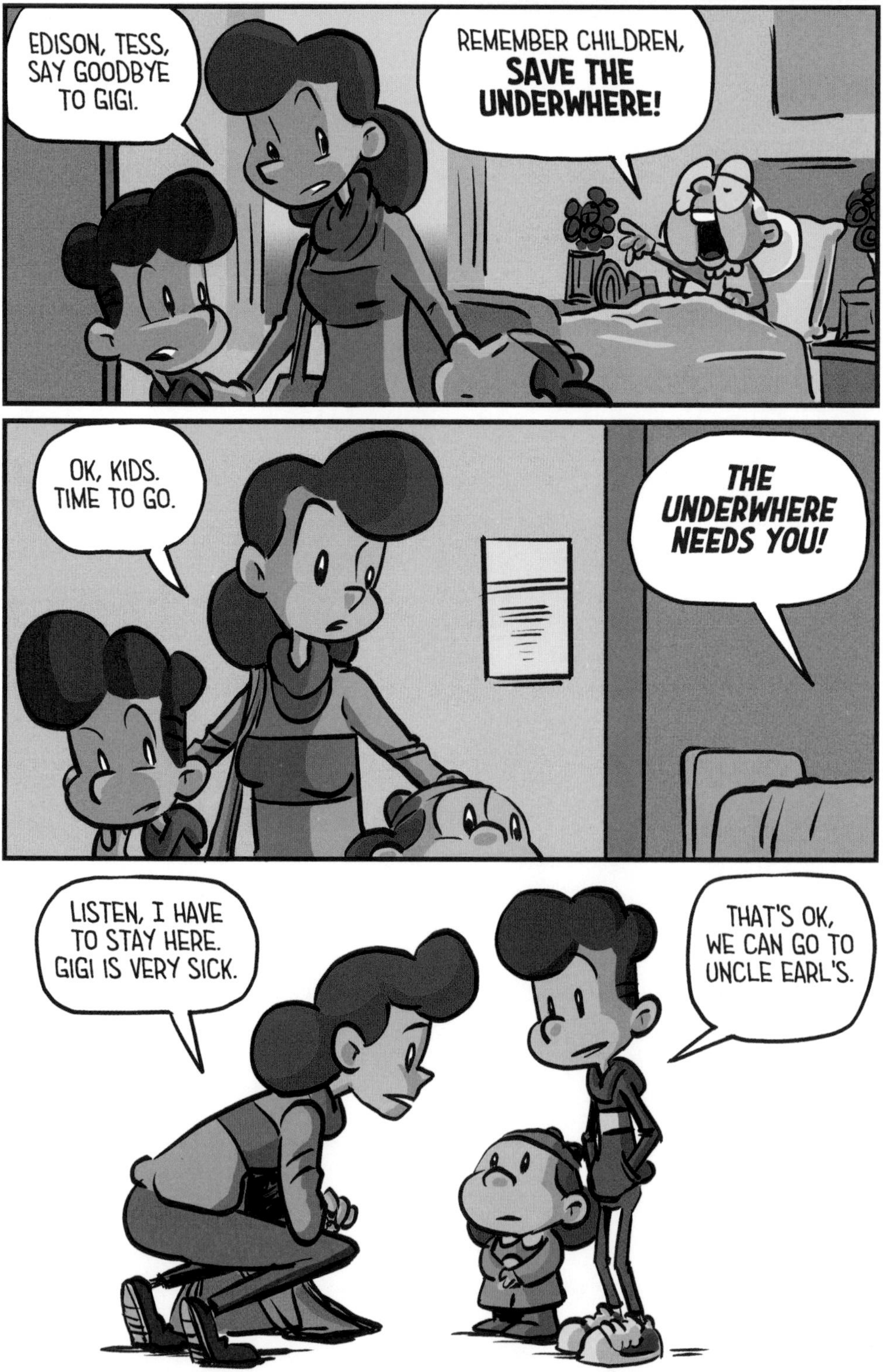
EDISON, TESS, SAY GOODBYE TO GIGI.
REMEMBER CHILDREN, **SAVE THE UNDERWHERE!**
OK, KIDS. TIME TO GO.
THE UNDERWHERE NEEDS YOU!
LISTEN, I HAVE TO STAY HERE. GIGI IS VERY SICK.
THAT'S OK, WE CAN GO TO UNCLE EARL'S.

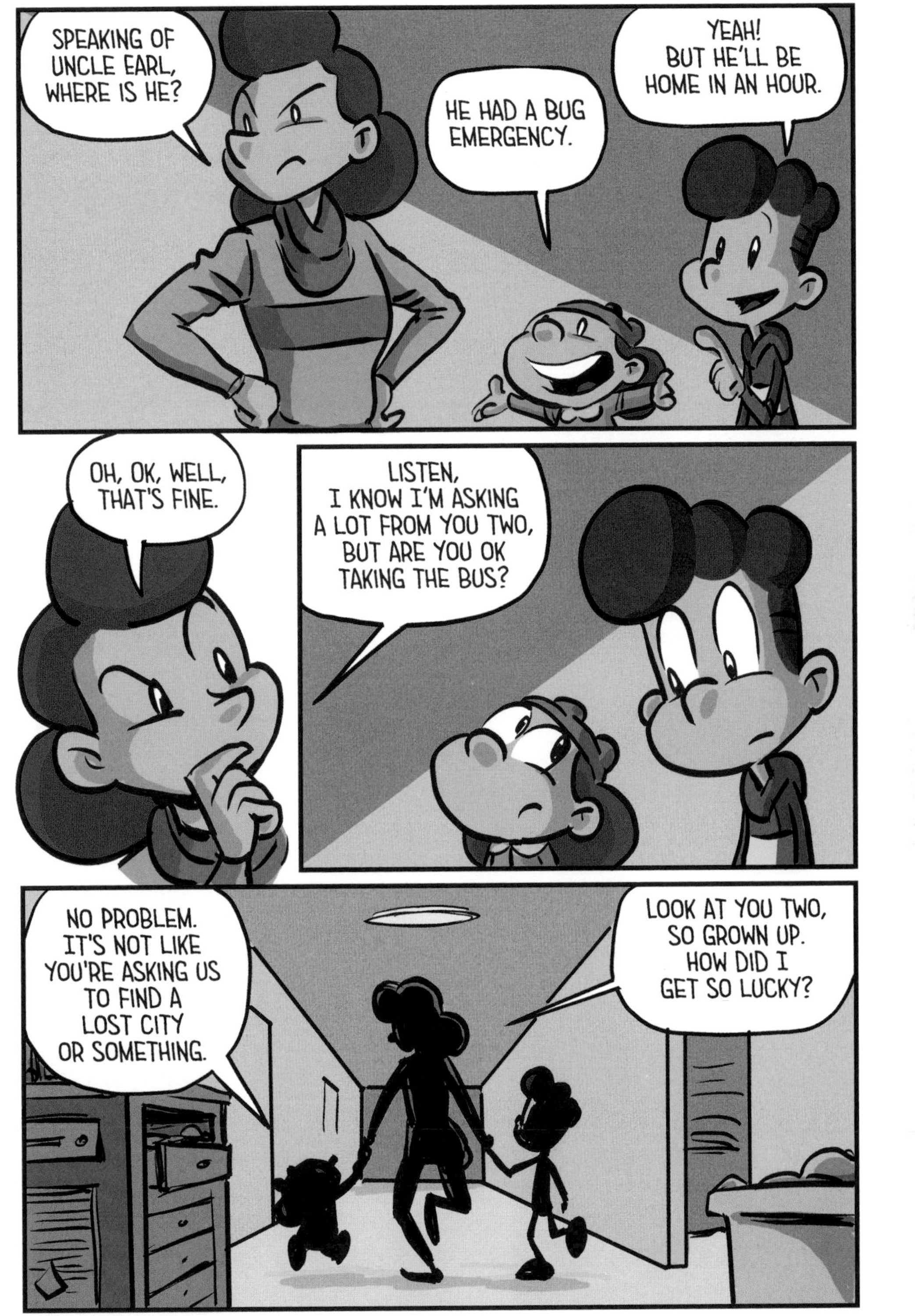
SPEAKING OF UNCLE EARL, WHERE IS HE?
HE HAD A BUG EMERGENCY.
YEAH! BUT HE'LL BE HOME IN AN HOUR.
OH, OK, WELL, THAT'S FINE.
LISTEN, I KNOW I'M ASKING A LOT FROM YOU TWO, BUT ARE YOU OK TAKING THE BUS?
NO PROBLEM. IT'S NOT LIKE YOU'RE ASKING US TO FIND A LOST CITY OR SOMETHING.
LOOK AT YOU TWO, SO GROWN UP. HOW DID I GET SO LUCKY?

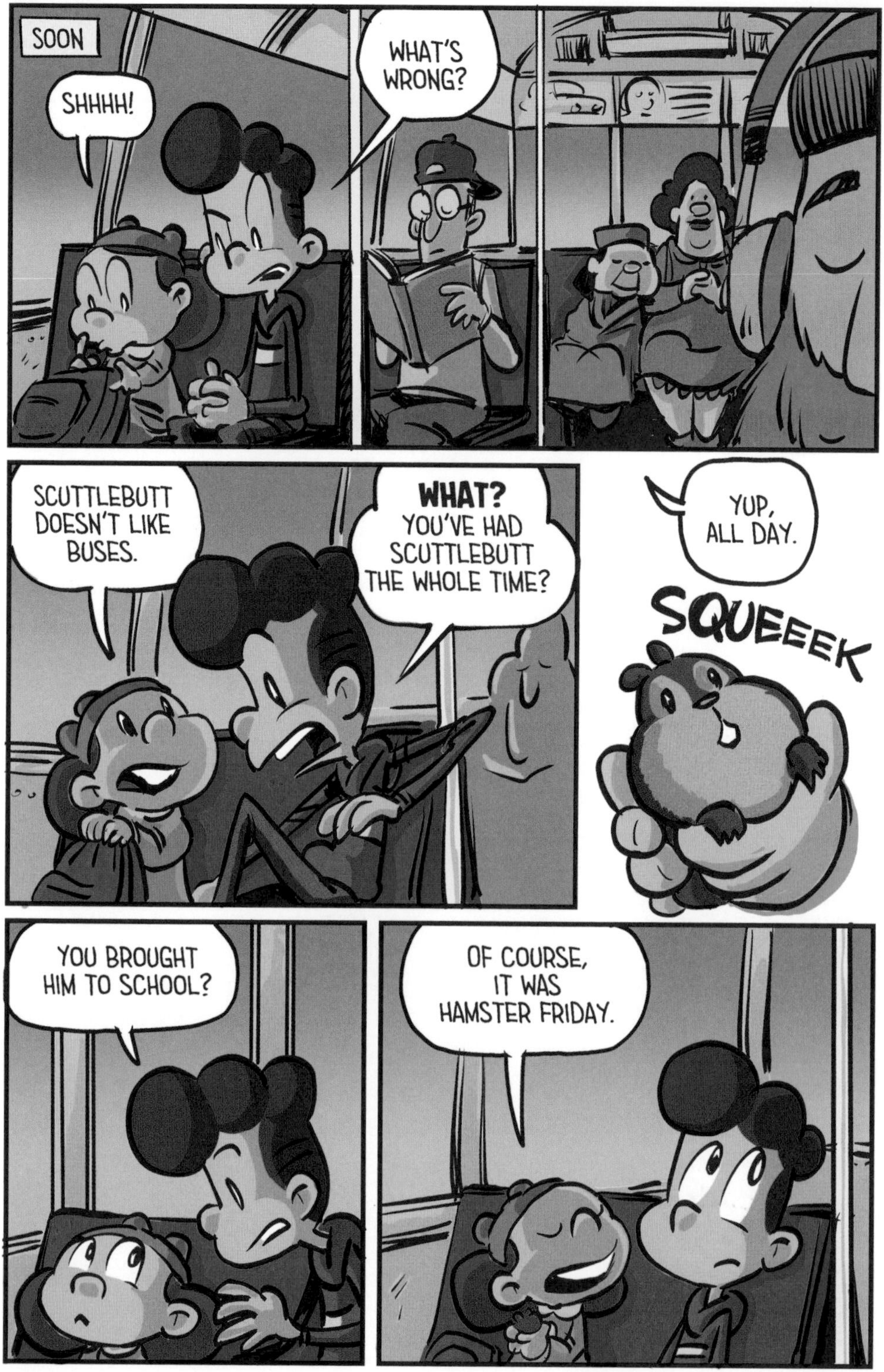
SOON
SHHHH!
WHAT'S WRONG?
SCUTTLEBUTT DOESN'T LIKE BUSES.
WHAT? YOU'VE HAD SCUTTLEBUTT THE WHOLE TIME?
YUP, ALL DAY.
SQUEEEEK
YOU BROUGHT HIM TO SCHOOL?
OF COURSE, IT WAS HAMSTER FRIDAY.

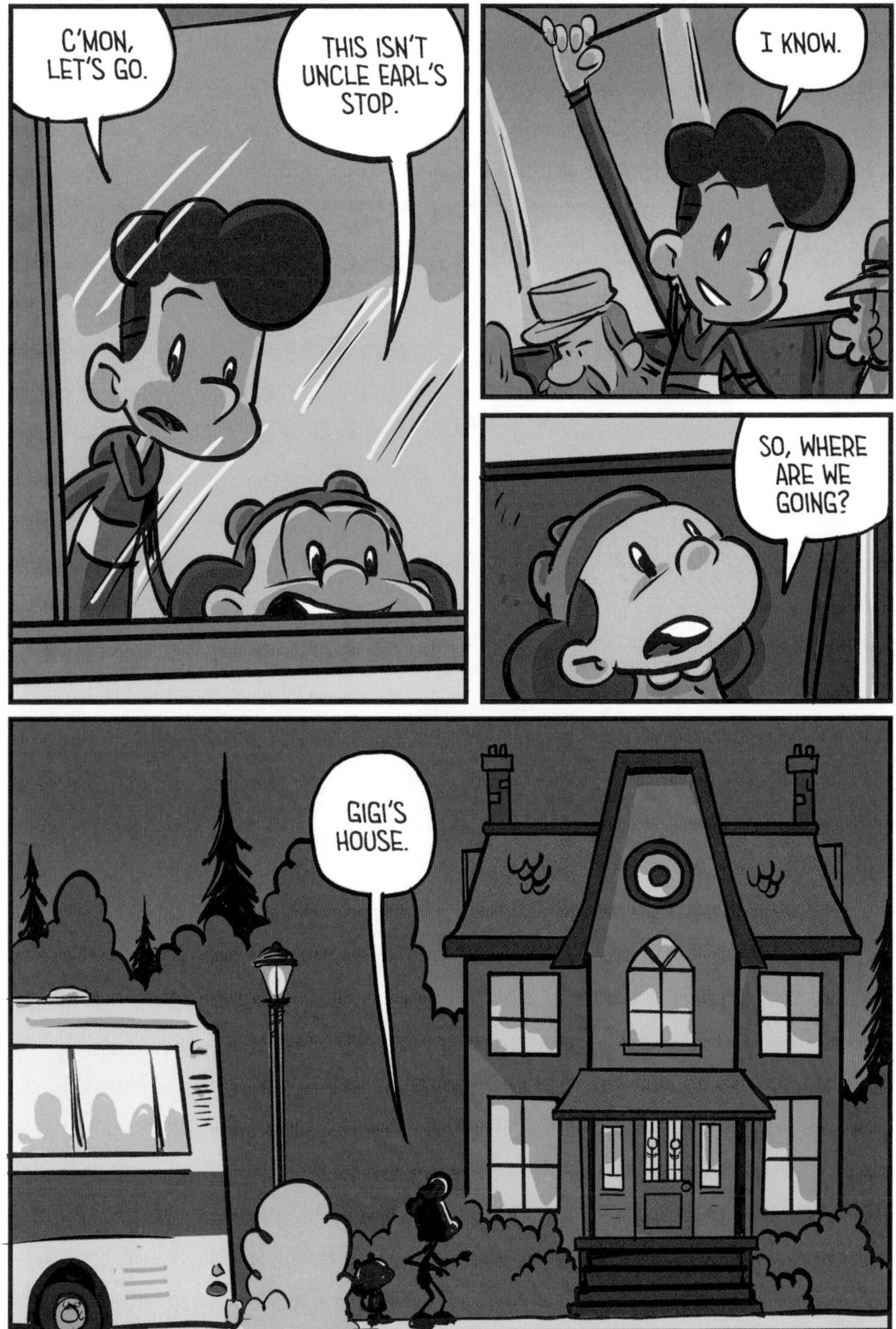
C'MON, LET'S GO.
THIS ISN'T UNCLE EARL'S STOP.
I KNOW.
SO, WHERE ARE WE GOING?
GIGI'S HOUSE.

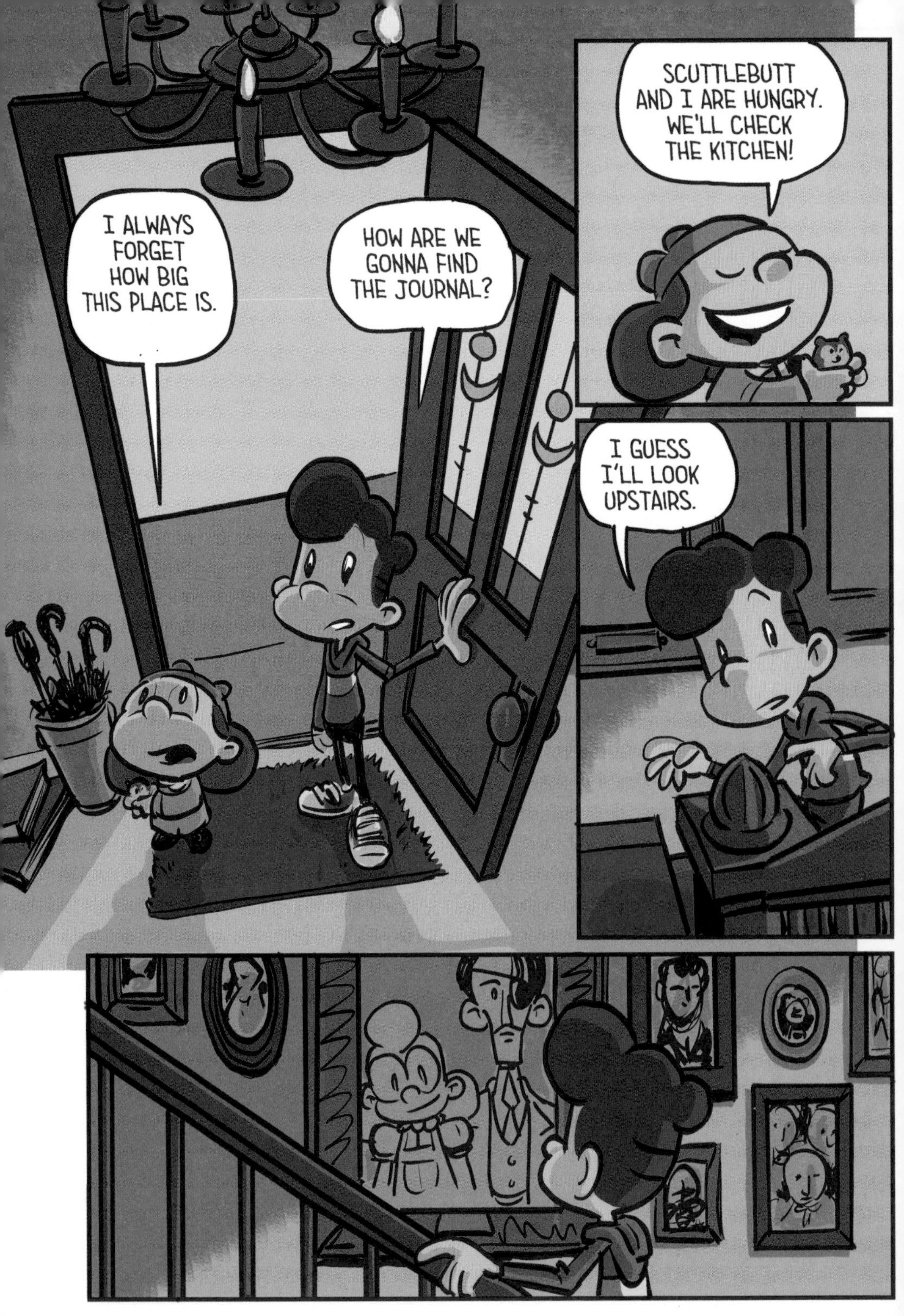
I ALWAYS FORGET HOW BIG THIS PLACE IS.
HOW ARE WE GONNA FIND THE JOURNAL?
SCUTTLEBUTT AND I ARE HUNGRY. WE'LL CHECK THE KITCHEN!
I GUESS I'LL LOOK UPSTAIRS.

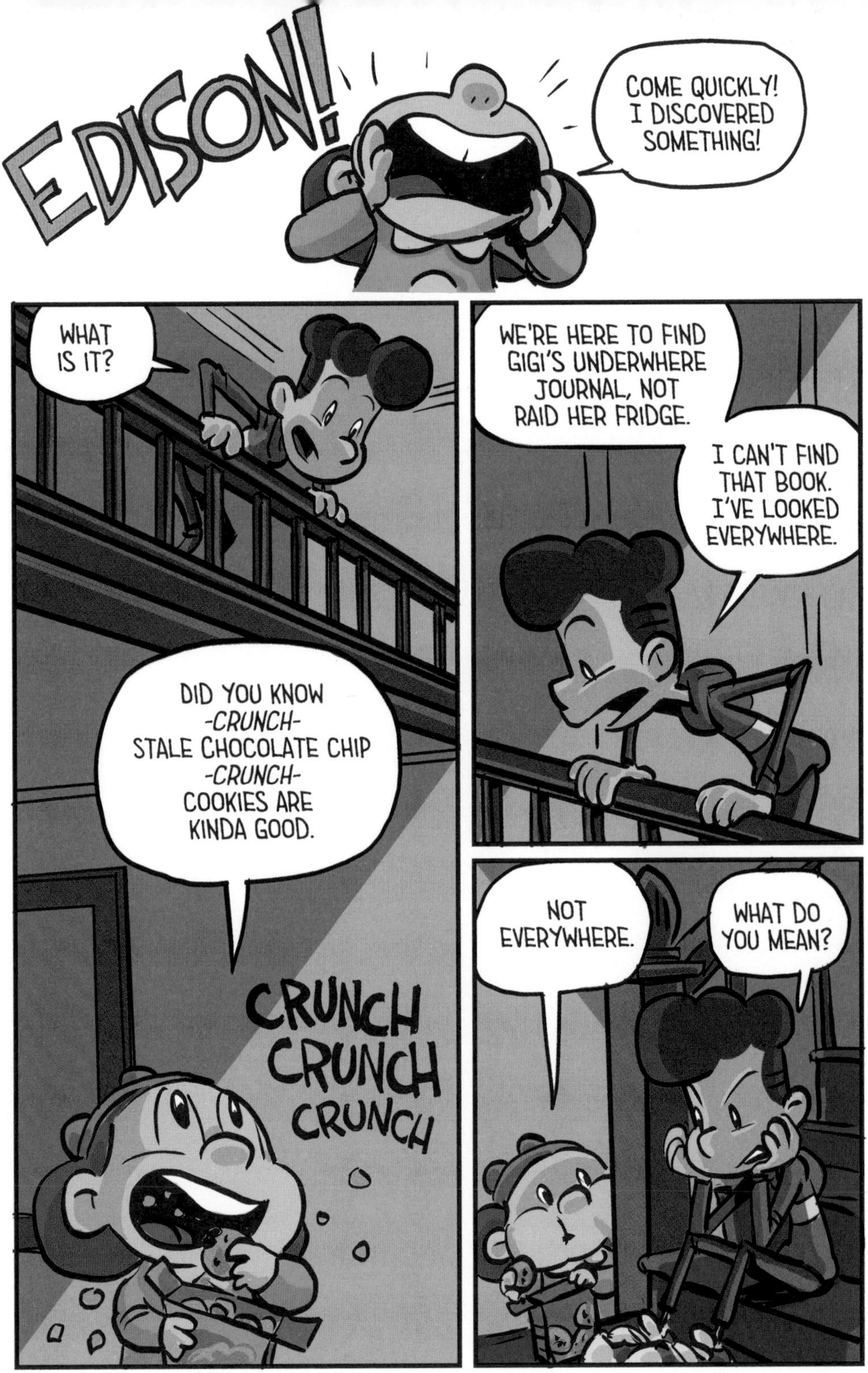
EDISON!
COME QUICKLY! I DISCOVERED SOMETHING!
WHAT IS IT?
WE'RE HERE TO FIND GIGI'S UNDERWHERE JOURNAL, NOT RAID HER FRIDGE.
I CAN'T FIND THAT BOOK. I'VE LOOKED EVERYWHERE.
DID YOU KNOW -CRUNCH- STALE CHOCOLATE CHIP -CRUNCH- COOKIES ARE KINDA GOOD.
CRUNCH CRUNCH CRUNCH
NOT EVERYWHERE.
WHAT DO YOU MEAN?

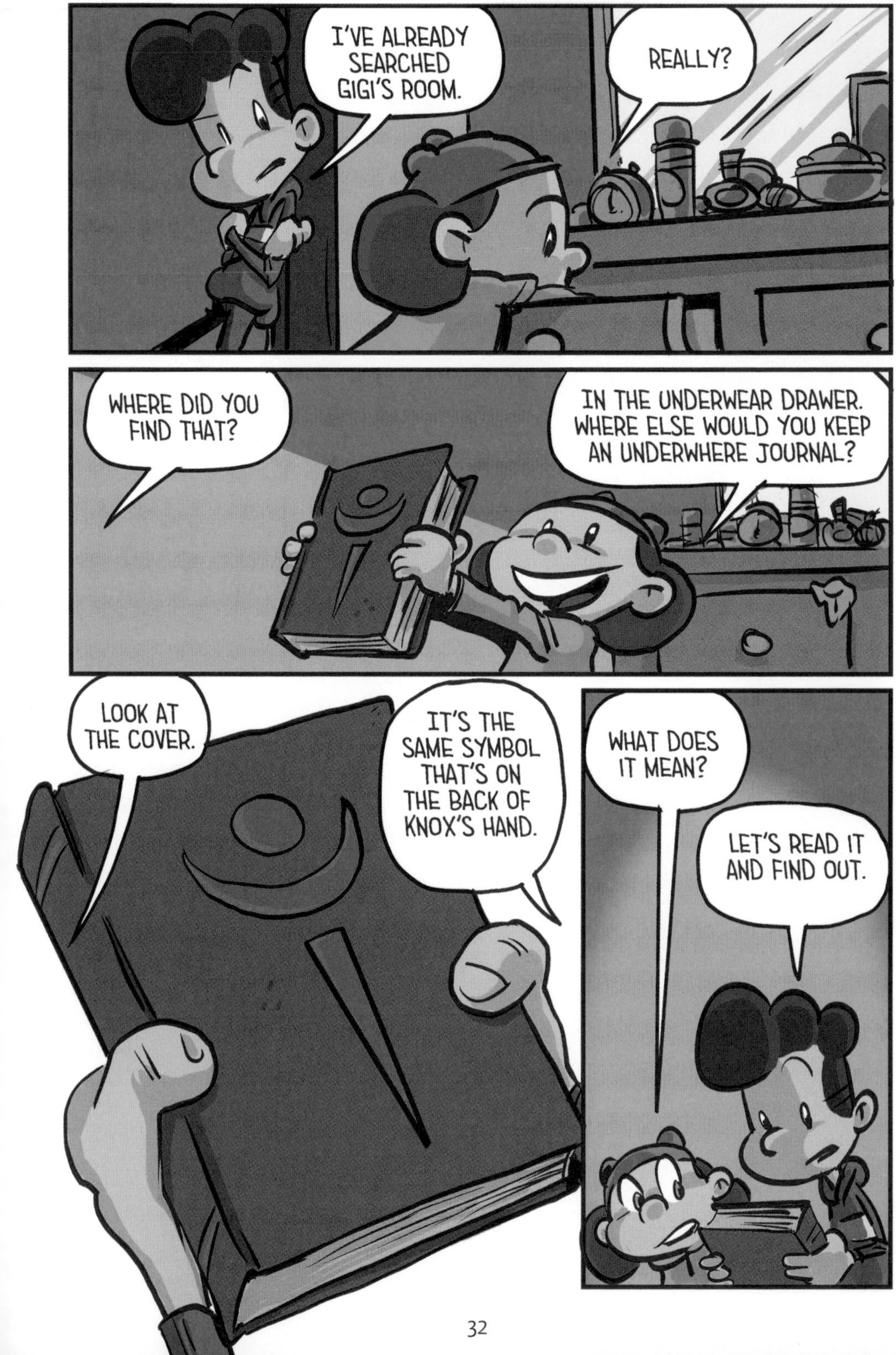
I'VE ALREADY SEARCHED GIGI'S ROOM.
REALLY?
WHERE DID YOU FIND THAT?
IN THE UNDERWEAR DRAWER. WHERE ELSE WOULD YOU KEEP AN UNDERWHERE JOURNAL?
LOOK AT THE COVER.
IT'S THE SAME SYMBOL THAT'S ON THE BACK OF KNOX'S HAND.
WHAT DOES IT MEAN?
LET'S READ IT AND FIND OUT.

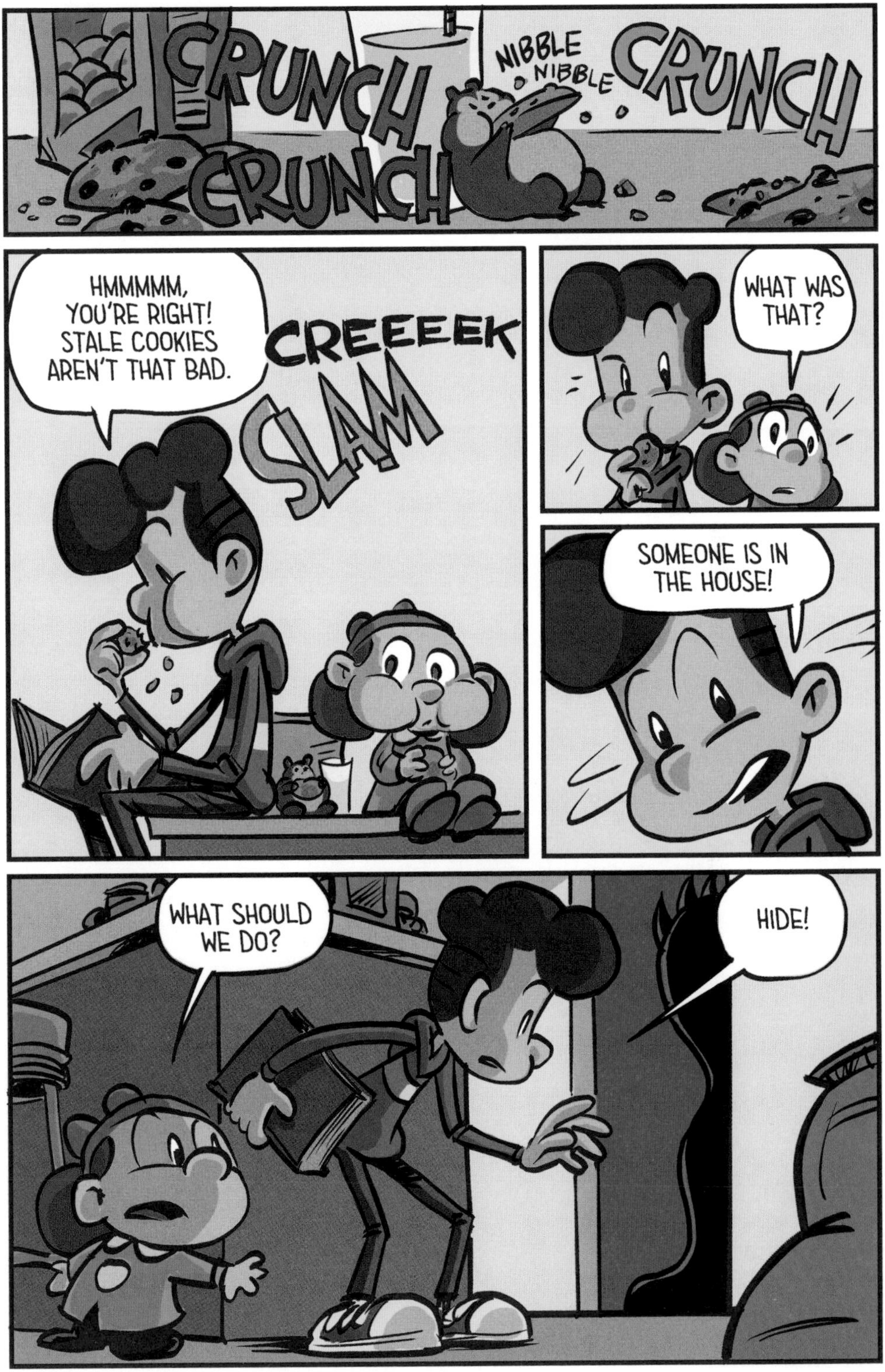
CRUNCH
CRUNCH
NIBBLE
NIBBLE
CRUNCH
HMMMMM, YOU'RE RIGHT! STALE COOKIES AREN'T THAT BAD.
CREEEEK
SLAM
WHAT WAS THAT?
SOMEONE IS IN THE HOUSE!
WHAT SHOULD WE DO?
HIDE!

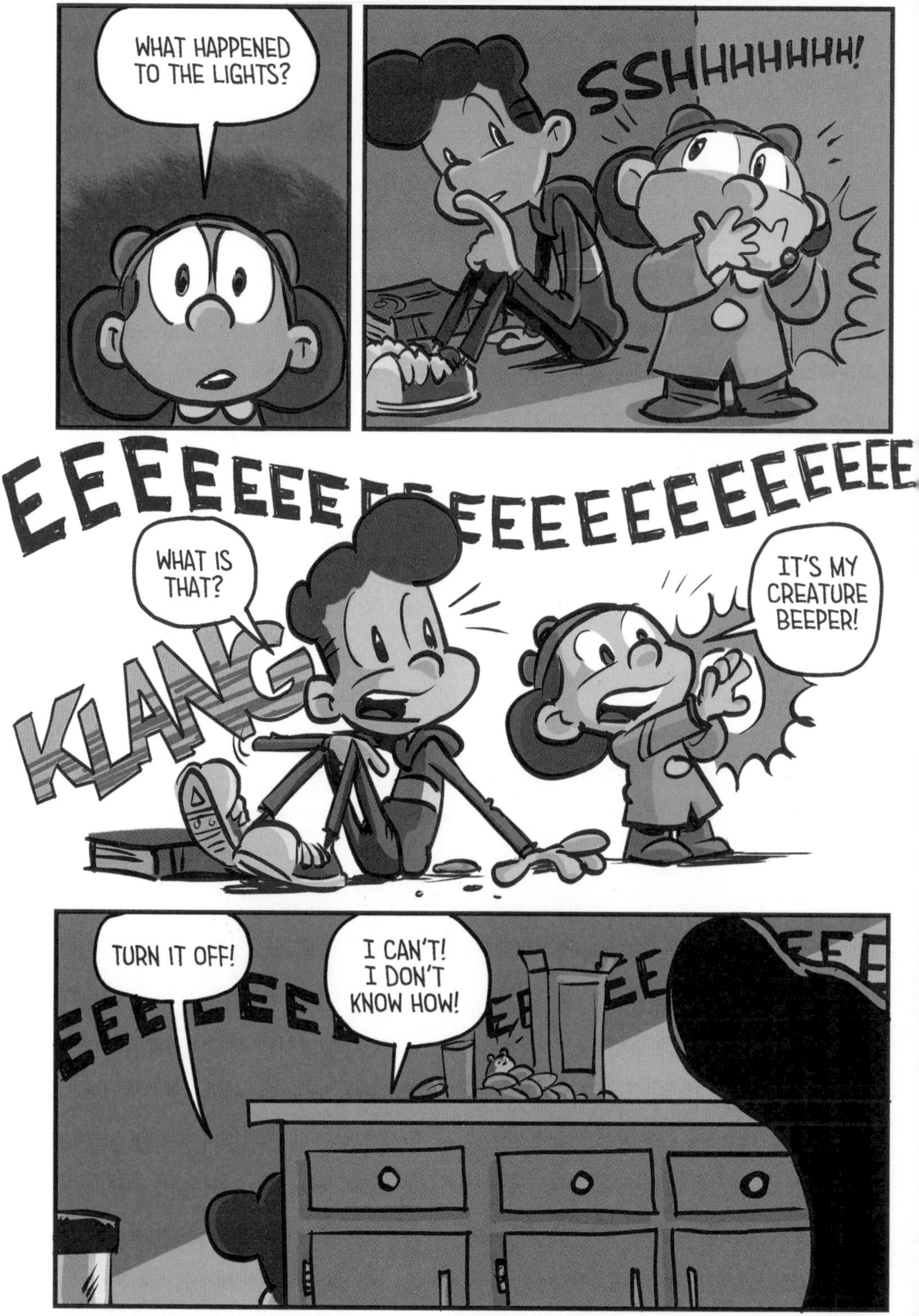
WHAT HAPPENED TO THE LIGHTS?
SSHHHHHHH!
EEEEEEEEEEEEEEEEEEEEE
WHAT IS THAT?
KLANG
IT'S MY CREATURE BEEPER!
TURN IT OFF!
I CAN'T! I DON'T KNOW HOW!

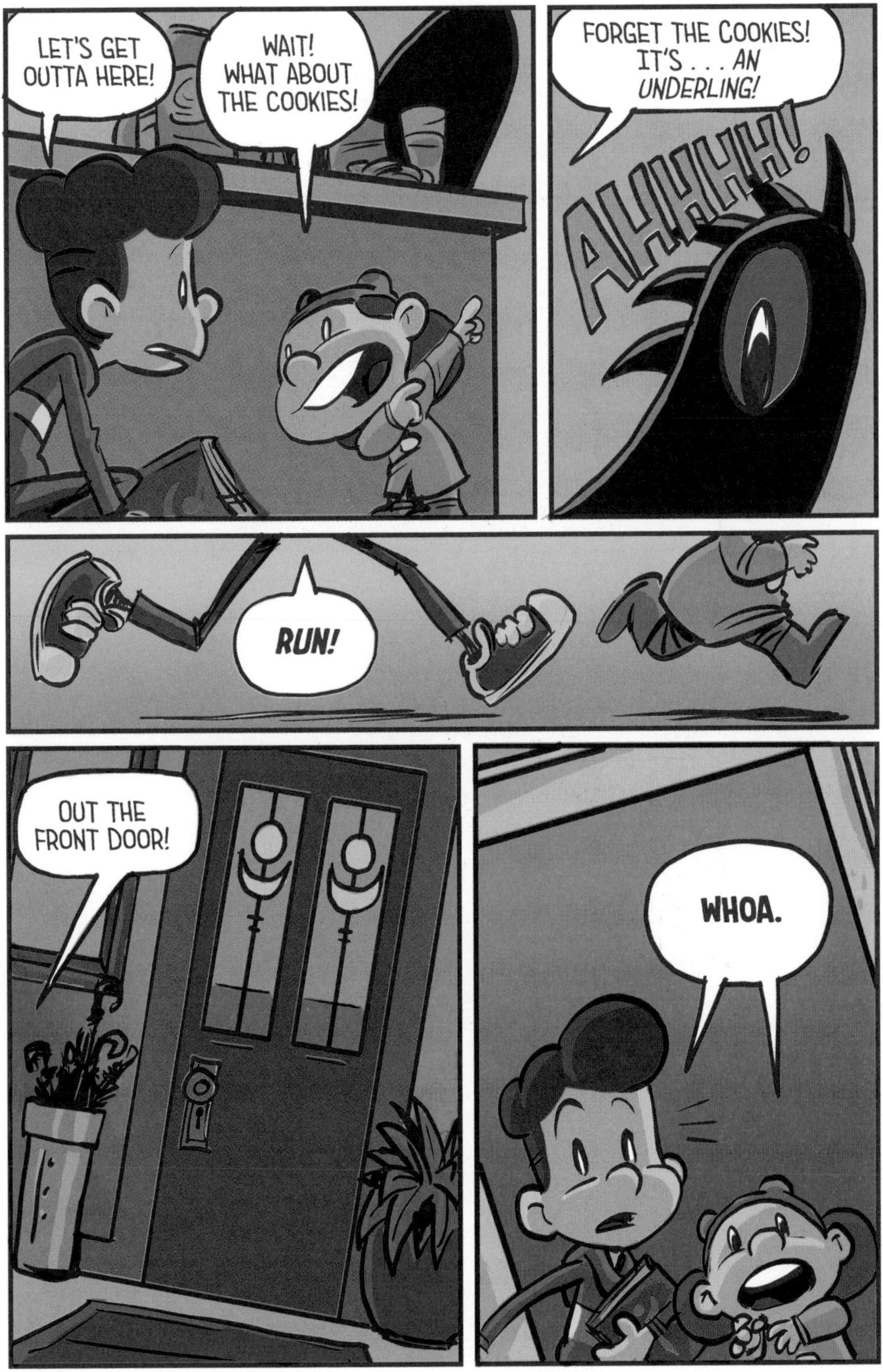
LET'S GET OUTTA HERE!
WAIT! WHAT ABOUT THE COOKIES!
FORGET THE COOKIES! IT'S . . . AN UNDERLING!
AHHHHH!
RUN!
OUT THE FRONT DOOR!
WHOA.

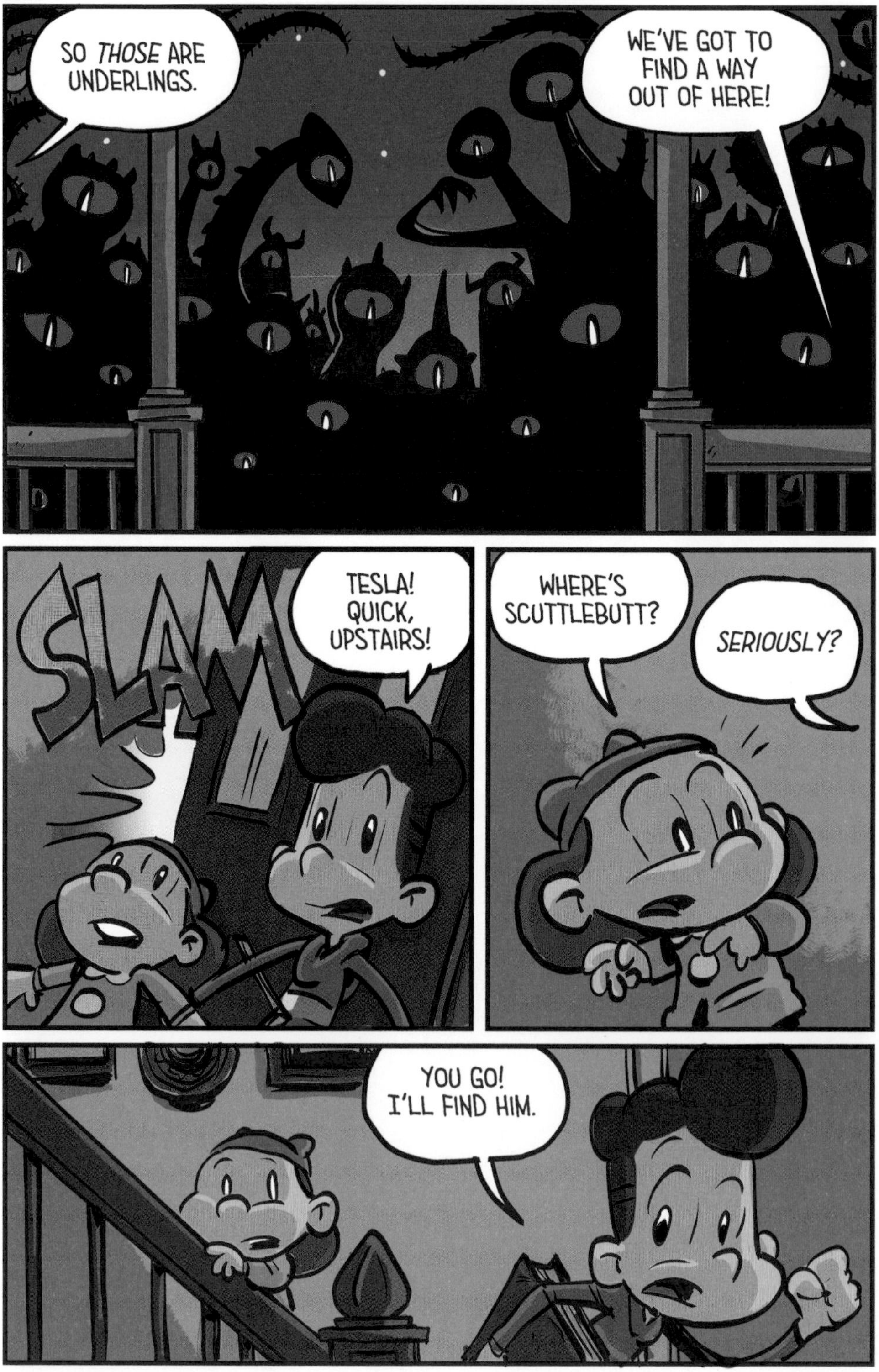
SO *THOSE* ARE UNDERLINGS.
WE'VE GOT TO FIND A WAY OUT OF HERE!
SLAM
TESLA! QUICK, UPSTAIRS!
WHERE'S SCUTTLEBUTT?
SERIOUSLY?
YOU GO! I'LL FIND HIM.

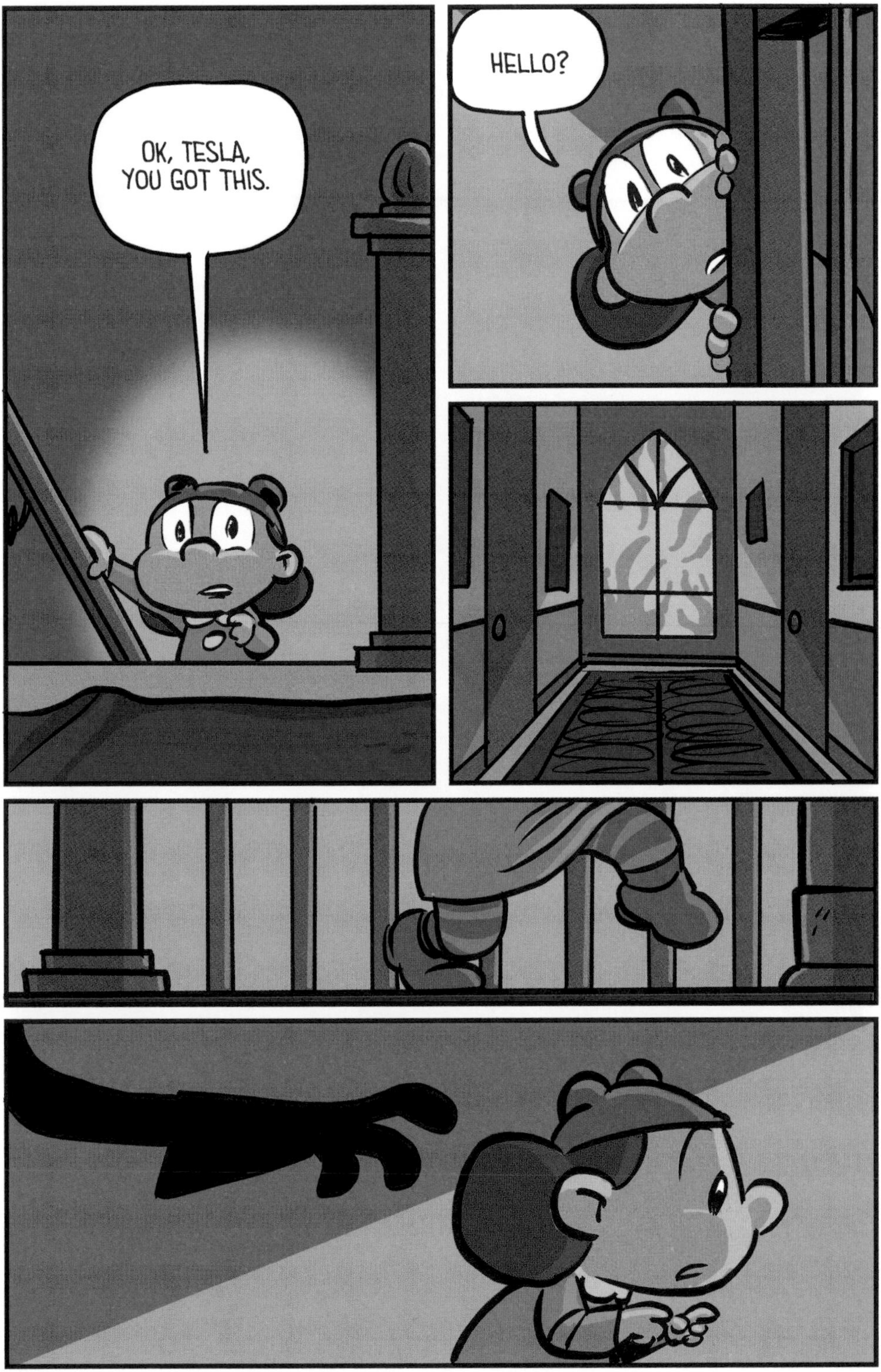
OK, TESLA, YOU GOT THIS.
HELLO?

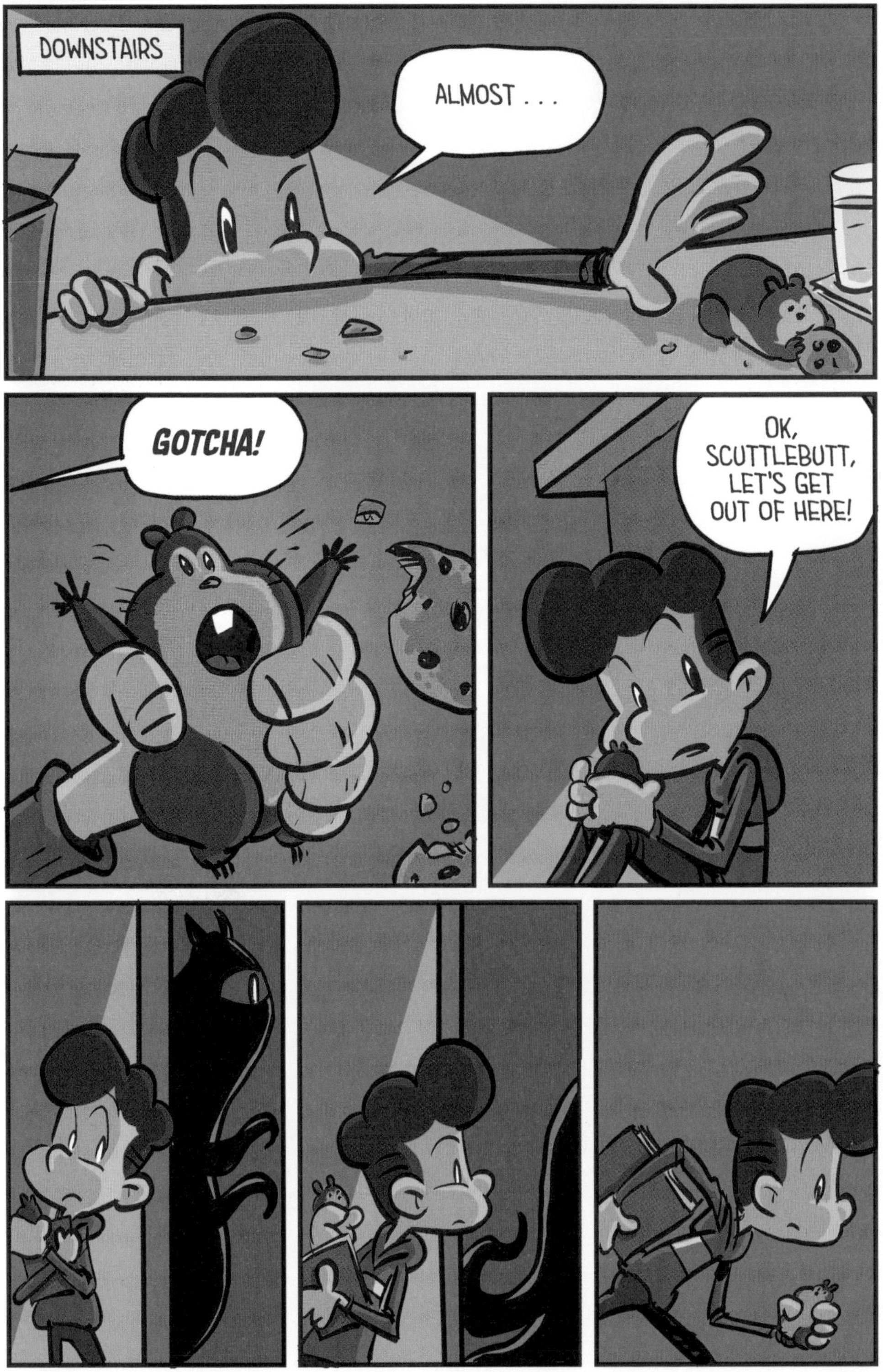
DOWNSTAIRS
ALMOST . . .
GOTCHA!
OK, SCUTTLEBUTT, LET'S GET OUT OF HERE!

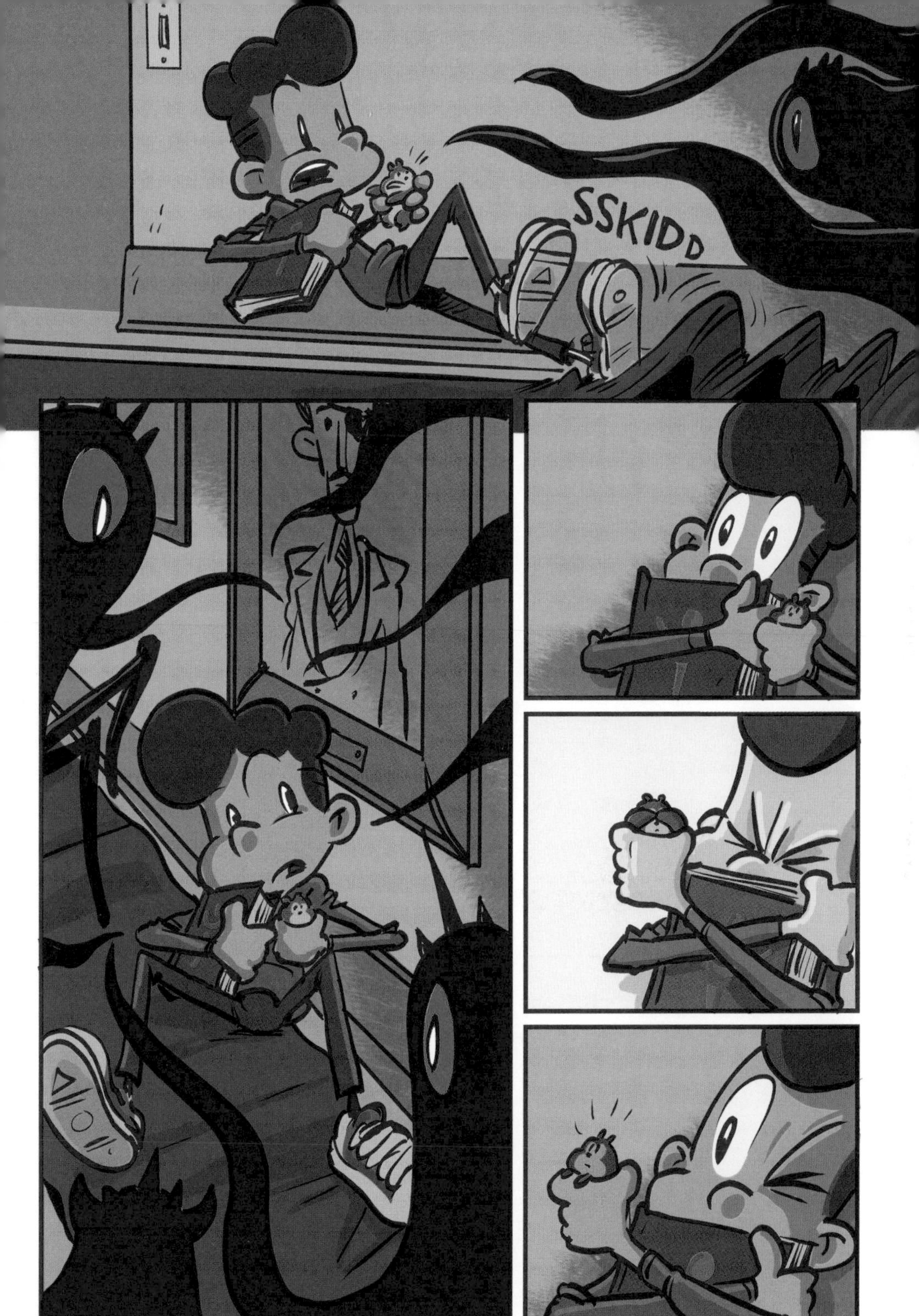
SSKIDD

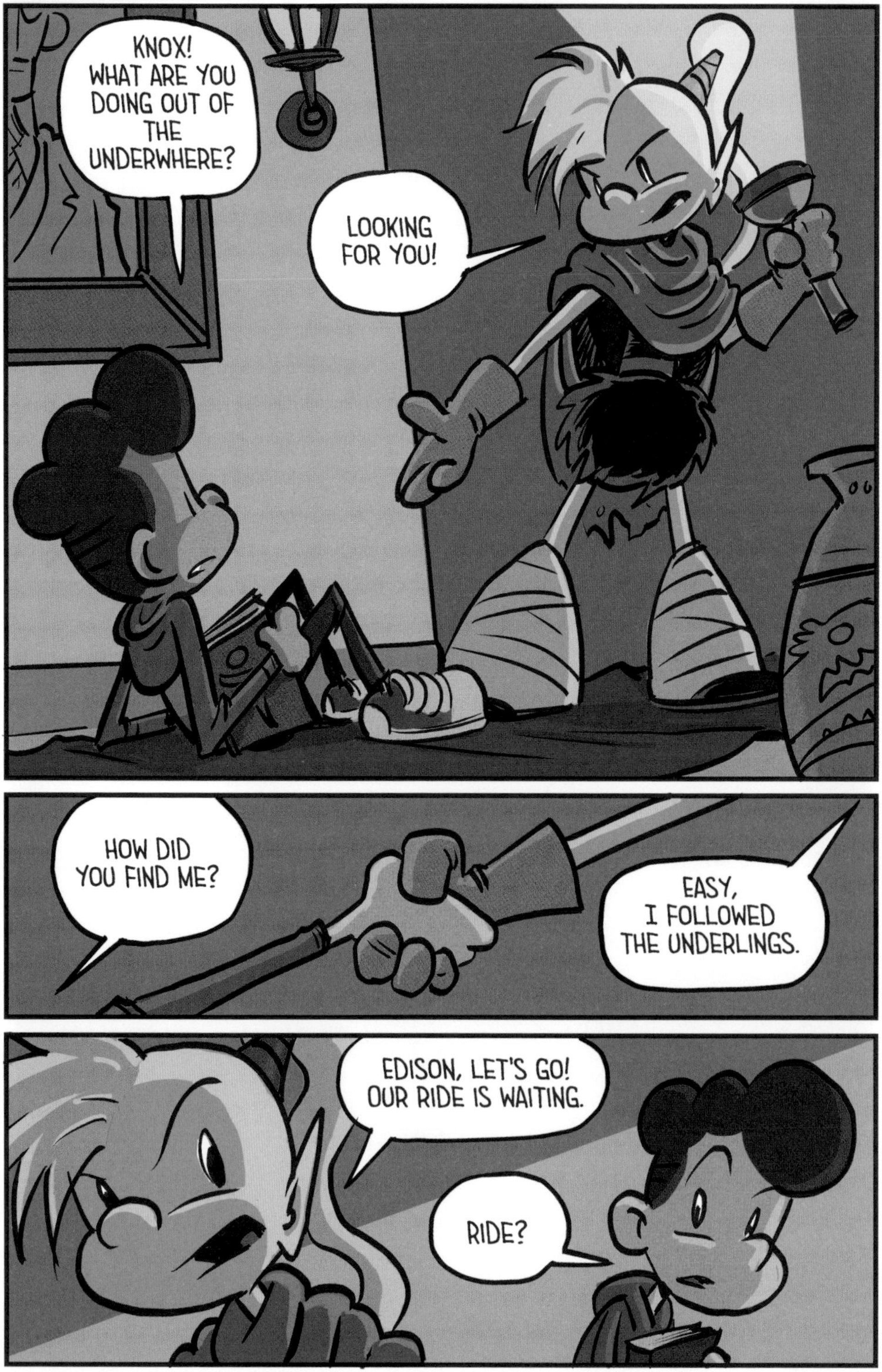
KNOX! WHAT ARE YOU DOING OUT OF THE UNDERWHERE?
LOOKING FOR YOU!
HOW DID YOU FIND ME?
EASY, I FOLLOWED THE UNDERLINGS.
EDISON, LET'S GO! OUR RIDE IS WAITING.
RIDE?

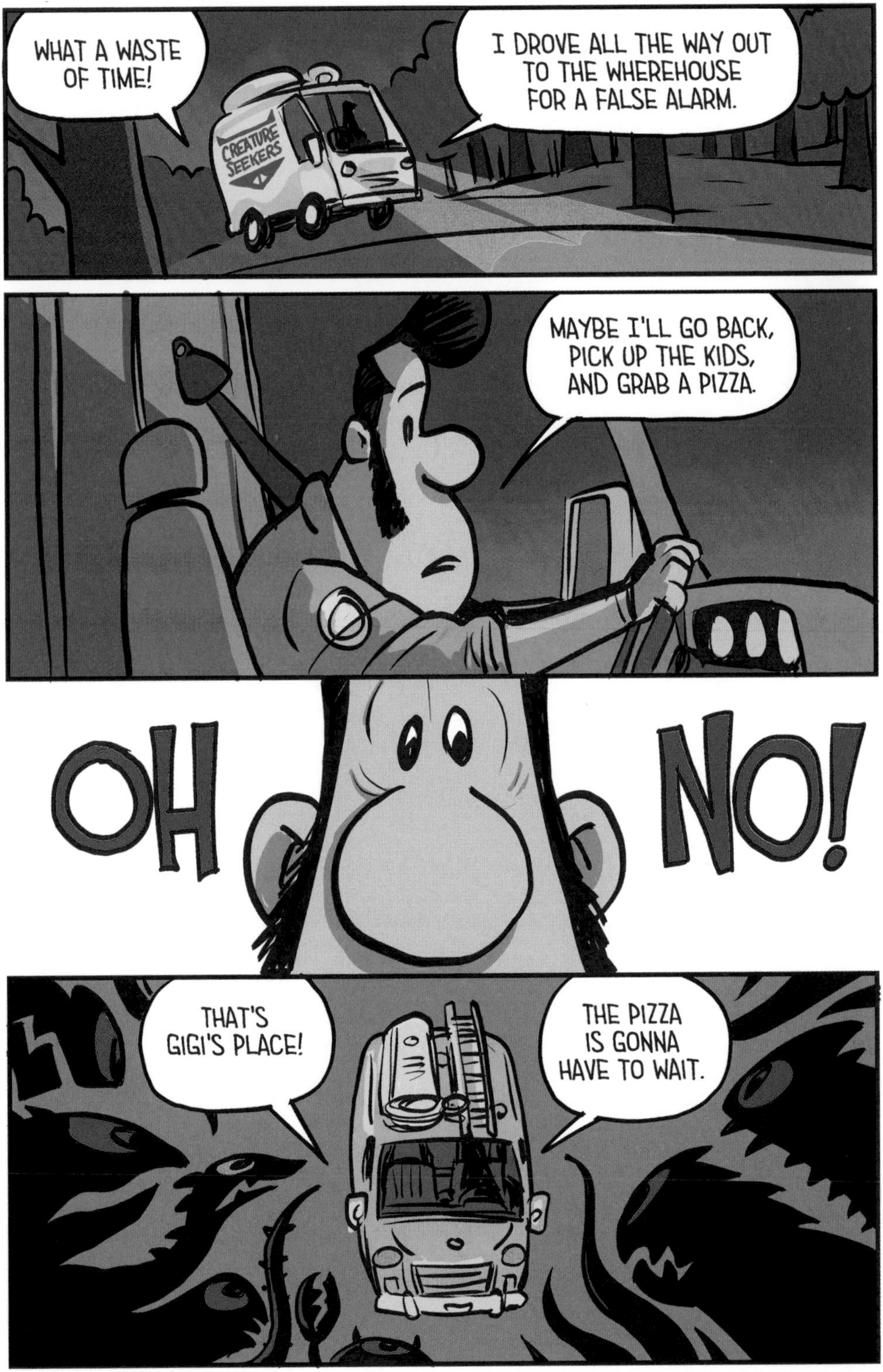
WHAT A WASTE OF TIME!
I DROVE ALL THE WAY OUT TO THE WHEREHOUSE FOR A FALSE ALARM.
CREATURE SEEKERS
MAYBE I'LL GO BACK, PICK UP THE KIDS, AND GRAB A PIZZA.
OH NO!
THAT'S GIGI'S PLACE!
THE PIZZA IS GONNA HAVE TO WAIT.

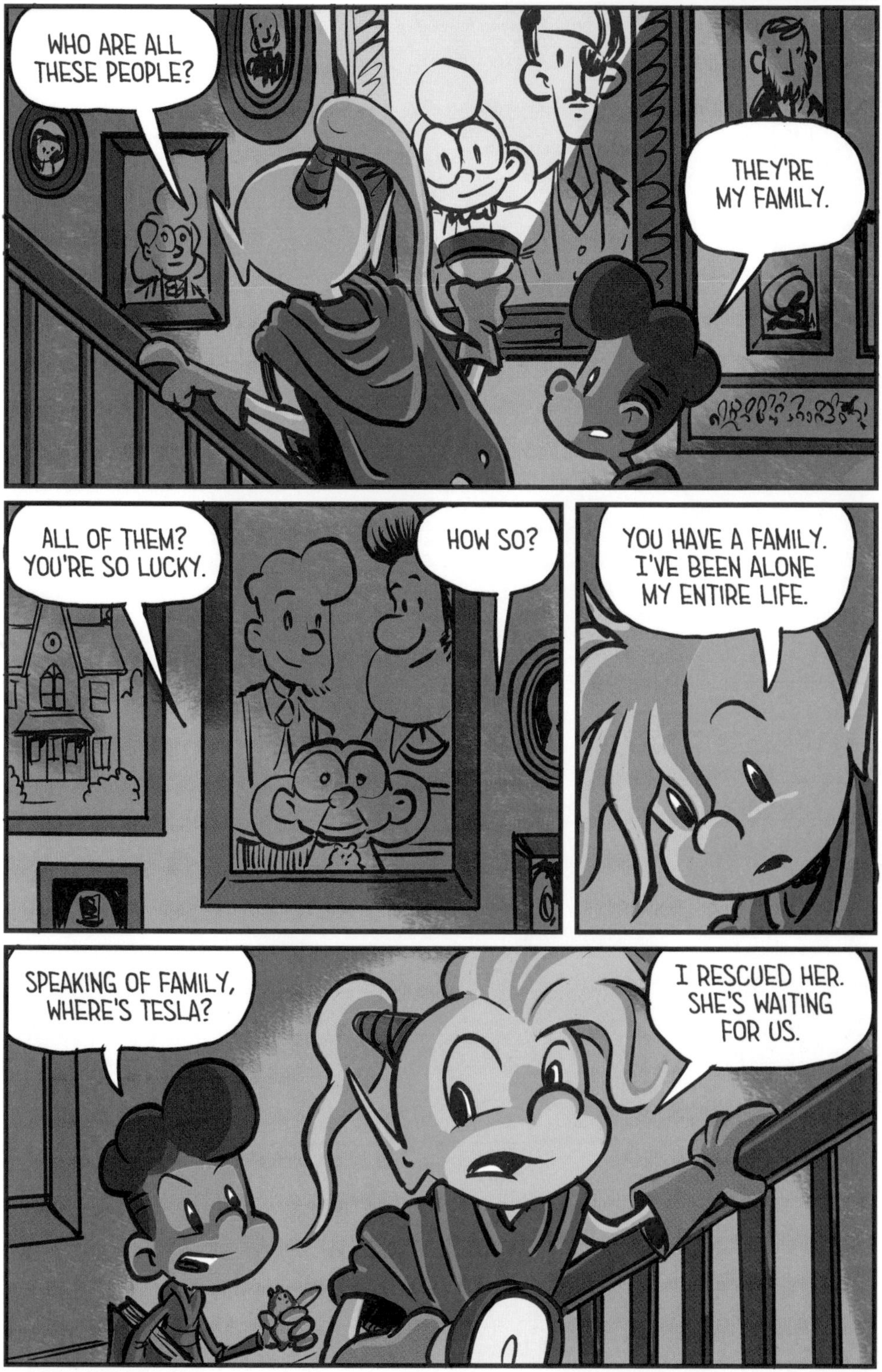
WHO ARE ALL THESE PEOPLE?
THEY'RE MY FAMILY.
ALL OF THEM? YOU'RE SO LUCKY.
HOW SO?
YOU HAVE A FAMILY. I'VE BEEN ALONE MY ENTIRE LIFE.
SPEAKING OF FAMILY, WHERE'S TESLA?
I RESCUED HER. SHE'S WAITING FOR US.

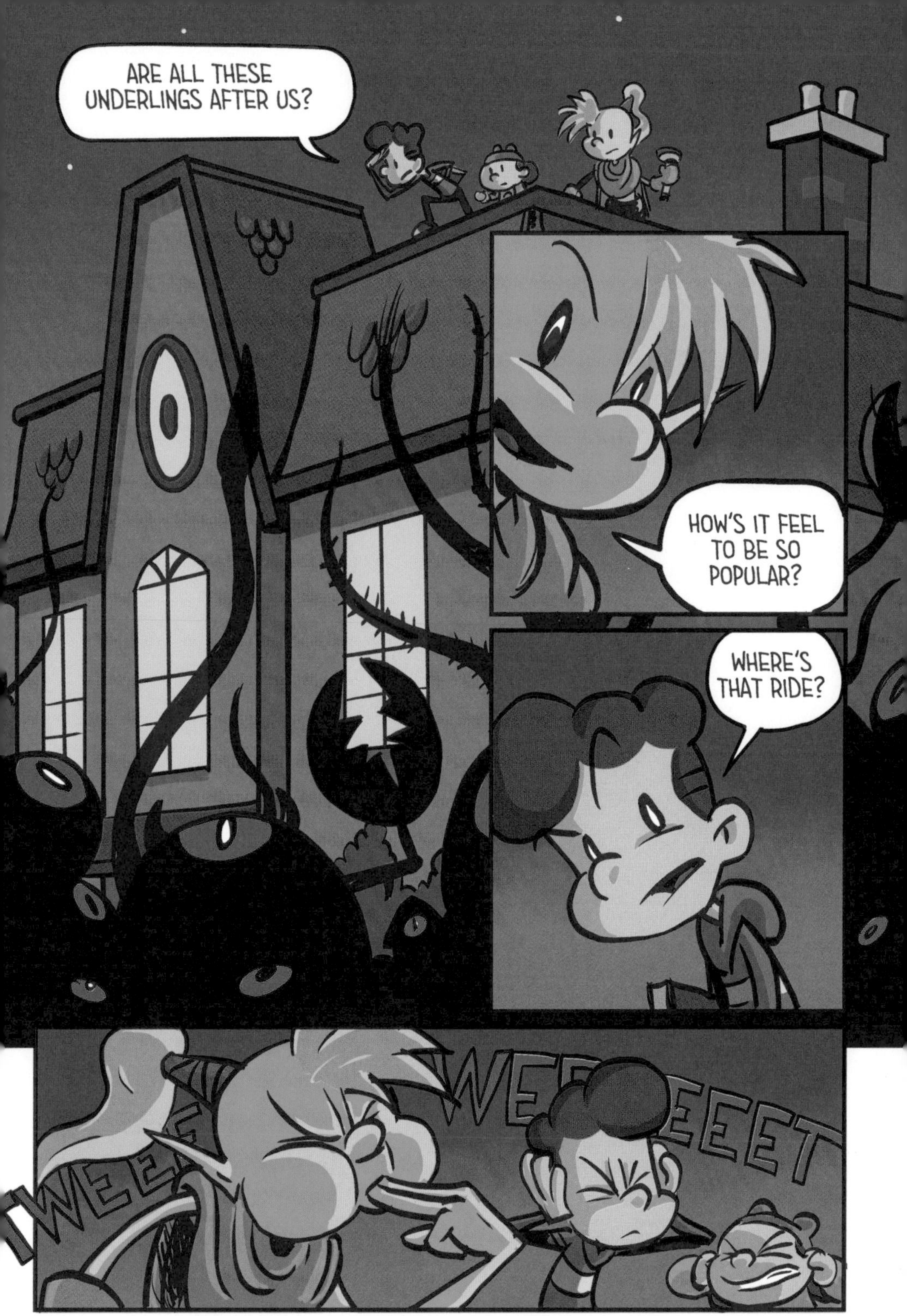
ARE ALL THESE UNDERLINGS AFTER US?
HOW'S IT FEEL TO BE SO POPULAR?
WHERE'S THAT RIDE?
WEEEEEEEEET

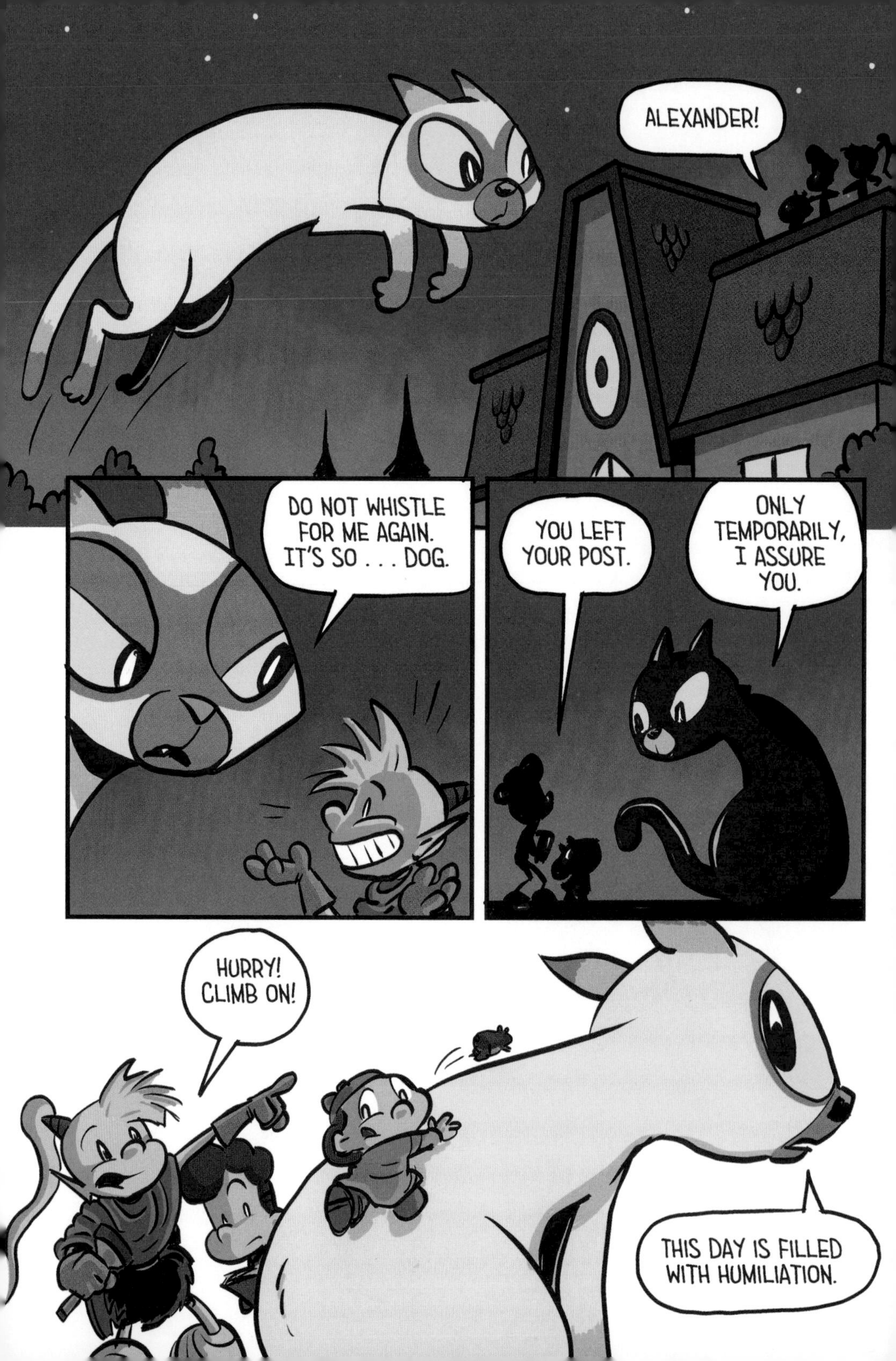
ALEXANDER!
DO NOT WHISTLE FOR ME AGAIN. IT'S SO . . . DOG.
YOU LEFT YOUR POST.
ONLY TEMPORARILY, I ASSURE YOU.
HURRY! CLIMB ON!
THIS DAY IS FILLED WITH HUMILIATION.

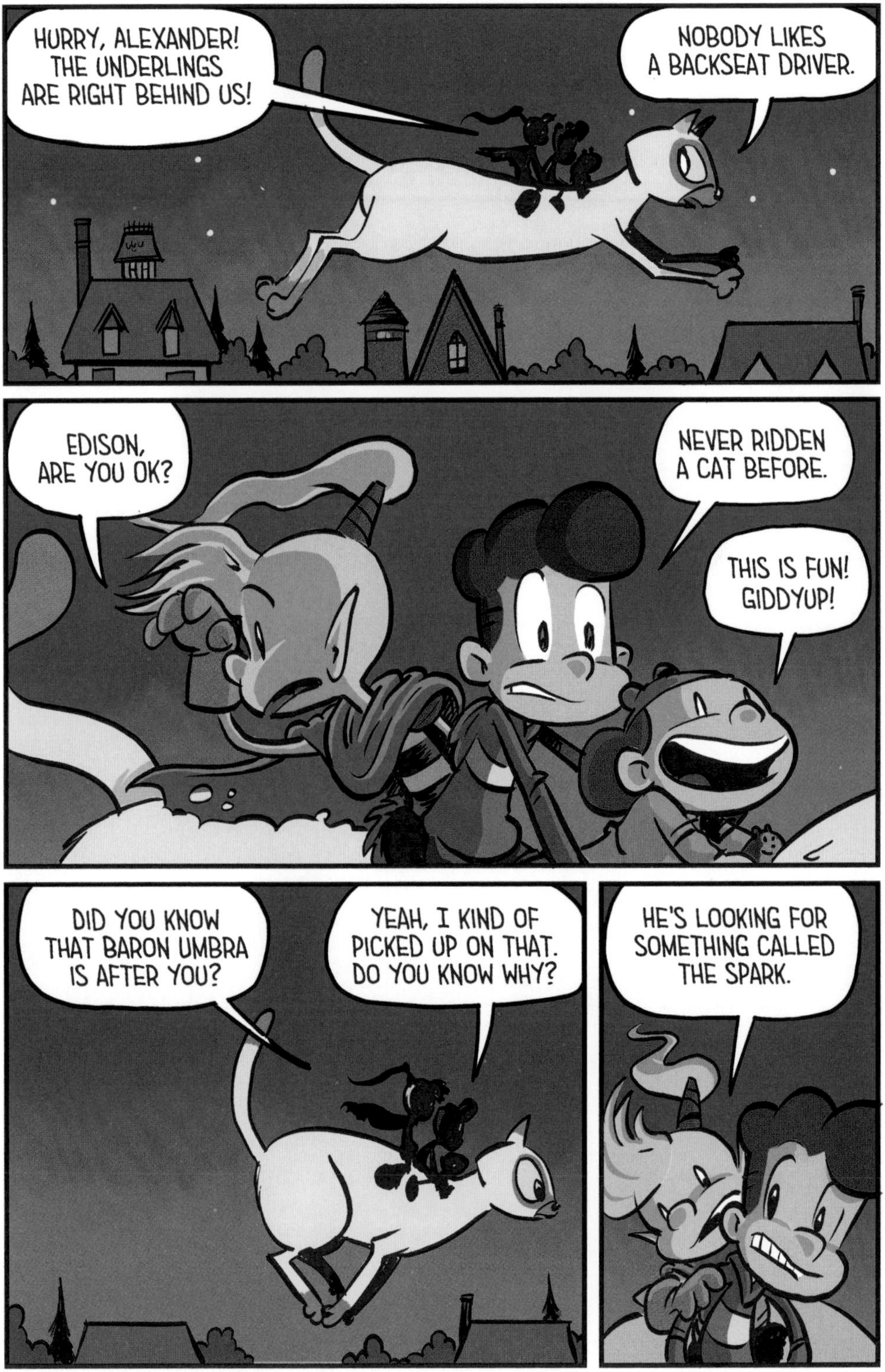
HURRY, ALEXANDER! THE UNDERLINGS ARE RIGHT BEHIND US!
NOBODY LIKES A BACKSEAT DRIVER.
EDISON, ARE YOU OK?
NEVER RIDDEN A CAT BEFORE.
THIS IS FUN! GIDDYUP!
DID YOU KNOW THAT BARON UMBRA IS AFTER YOU?
YEAH, I KIND OF PICKED UP ON THAT. DO YOU KNOW WHY?
HE'S LOOKING FOR SOMETHING CALLED THE SPARK.

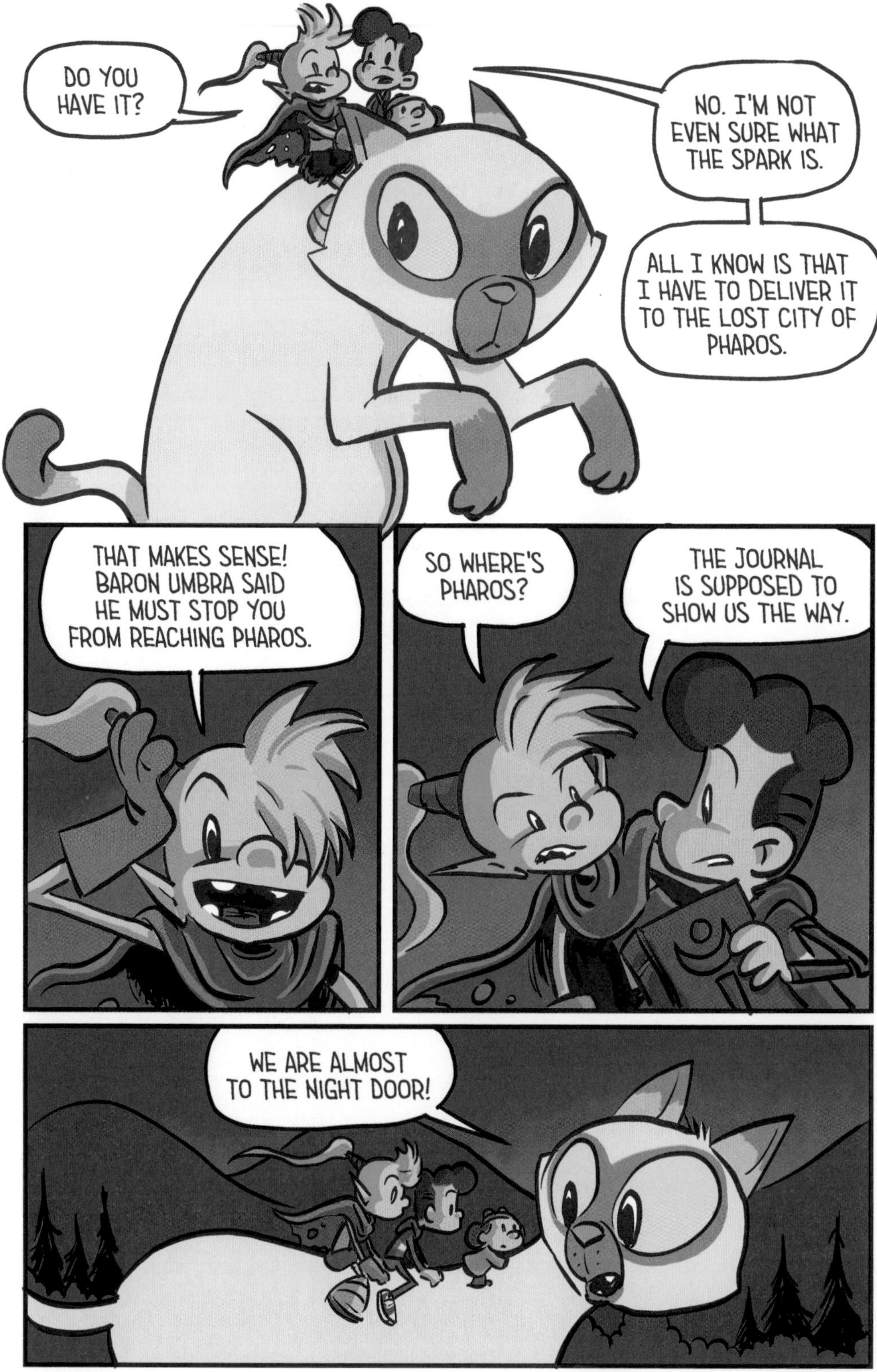
DO YOU HAVE IT?
NO. I'M NOT EVEN SURE WHAT THE SPARK IS.
ALL I KNOW IS THAT I HAVE TO DELIVER IT TO THE LOST CITY OF PHAROS.
THAT MAKES SENSE! BARON UMBRA SAID HE MUST STOP YOU FROM REACHING PHAROS.
SO WHERE'S PHAROS?
THE JOURNAL IS SUPPOSED TO SHOW US THE WAY.
WE ARE ALMOST TO THE NIGHT DOOR!

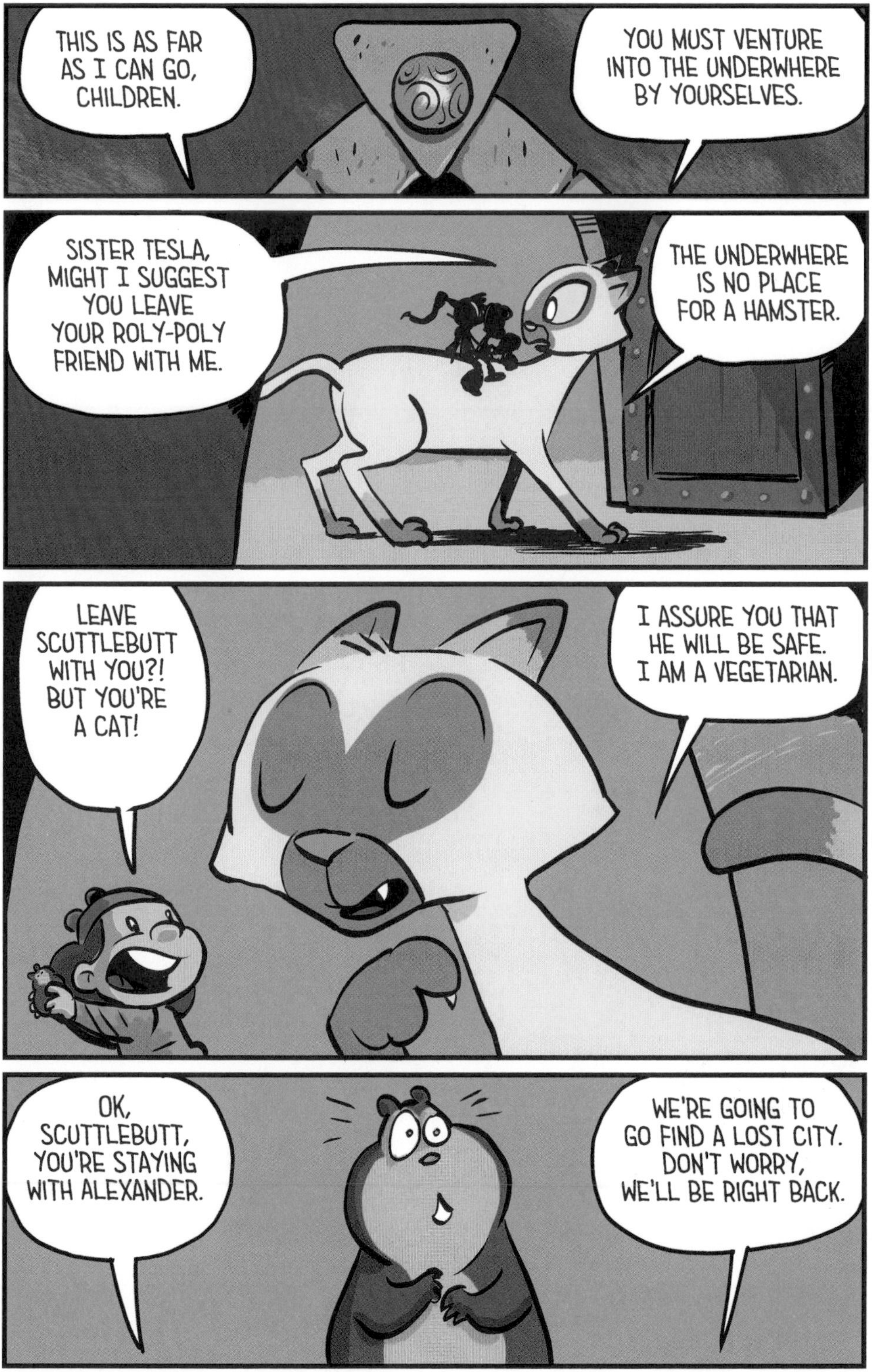
THIS IS AS FAR AS I CAN GO, CHILDREN.
YOU MUST VENTURE INTO THE UNDERWHERE BY YOURSELVES.
SISTER TESLA, MIGHT I SUGGEST YOU LEAVE YOUR ROLY-POLY FRIEND WITH ME.
THE UNDERWHERE IS NO PLACE FOR A HAMSTER.
LEAVE SCUTTLEBUTT WITH YOU?! BUT YOU'RE A CAT!
I ASSURE YOU THAT HE WILL BE SAFE. I AM A VEGETARIAN.
OK, SCUTTLEBUTT, YOU'RE STAYING WITH ALEXANDER.
WE'RE GOING TO GO FIND A LOST CITY. DON'T WORRY, WE'LL BE RIGHT BACK.

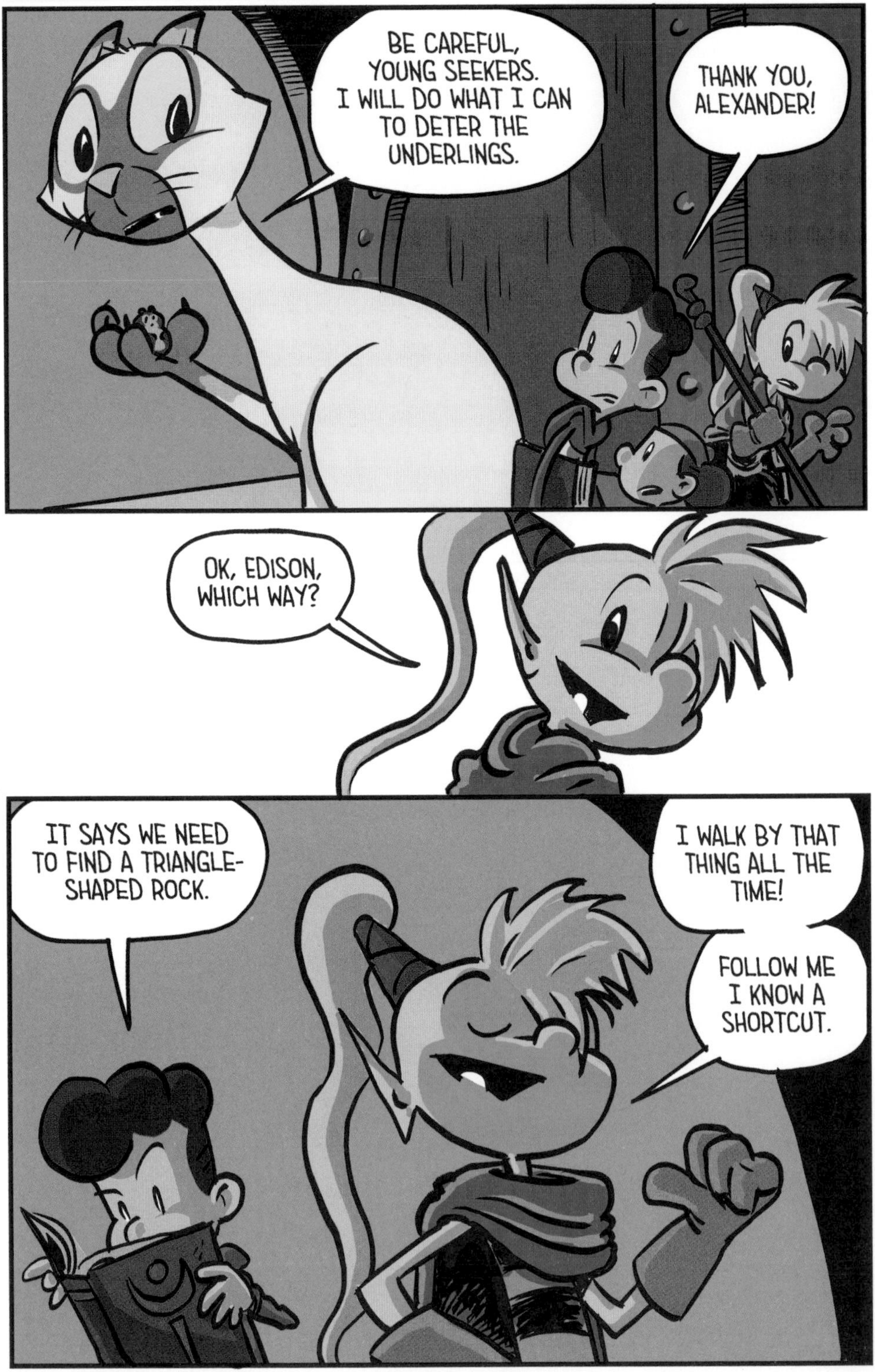
BE CAREFUL, YOUNG SEEKERS. I WILL DO WHAT I CAN TO DETER THE UNDERLINGS.
THANK YOU, ALEXANDER!
OK, EDISON, WHICH WAY?
IT SAYS WE NEED TO FIND A TRIANGLE-SHAPED ROCK.
I WALK BY THAT THING ALL THE TIME!
FOLLOW ME I KNOW A SHORTCUT.

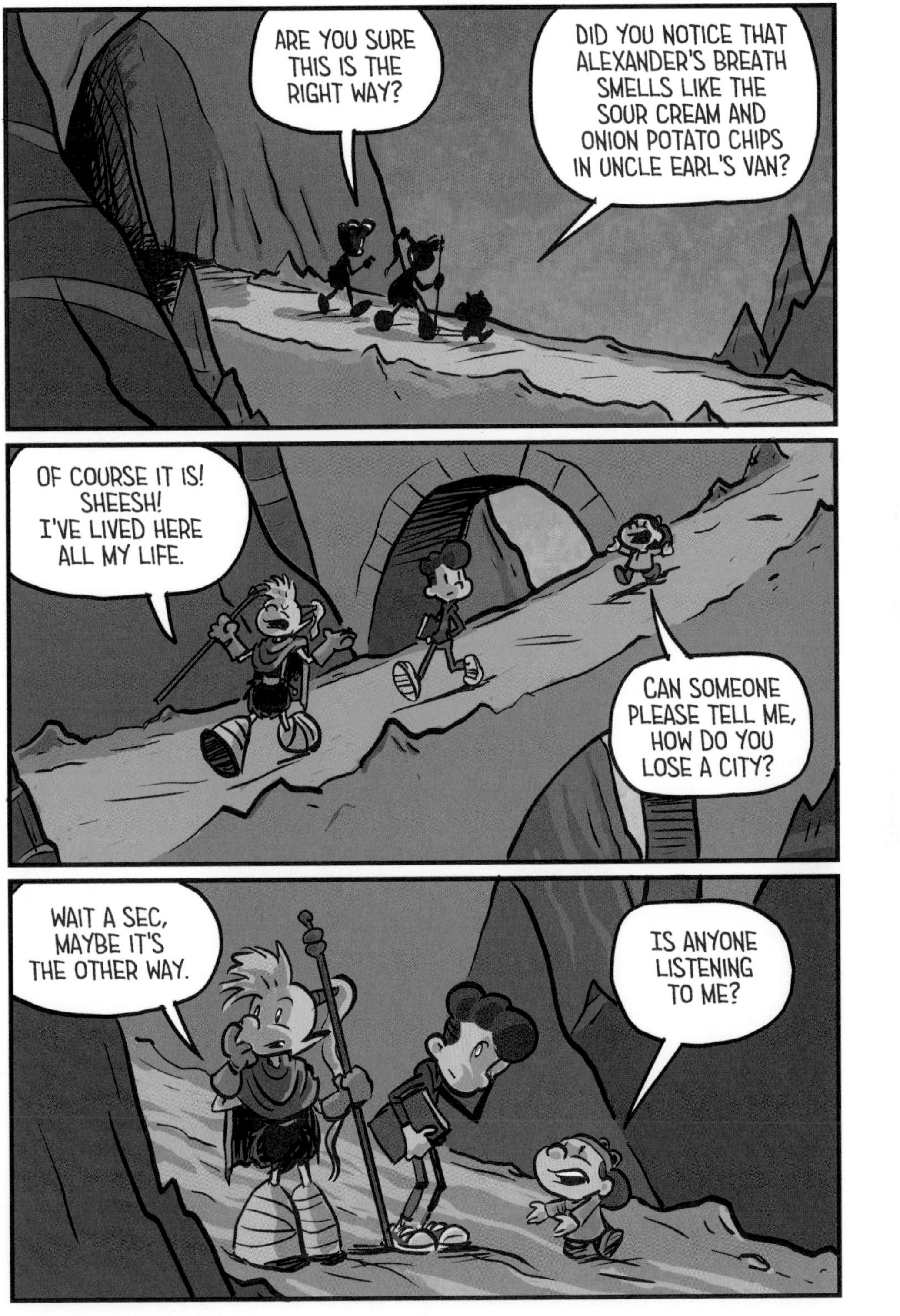
ARE YOU SURE THIS IS THE RIGHT WAY?
DID YOU NOTICE THAT ALEXANDER'S BREATH SMELLS LIKE THE SOUR CREAM AND ONION POTATO CHIPS IN UNCLE EARL'S VAN?
OF COURSE IT IS! SHEESH! I'VE LIVED HERE ALL MY LIFE.
CAN SOMEONE PLEASE TELL ME, HOW DO YOU LOSE A CITY?
WAIT A SEC, MAYBE IT'S THE OTHER WAY.
IS ANYONE LISTENING TO ME?

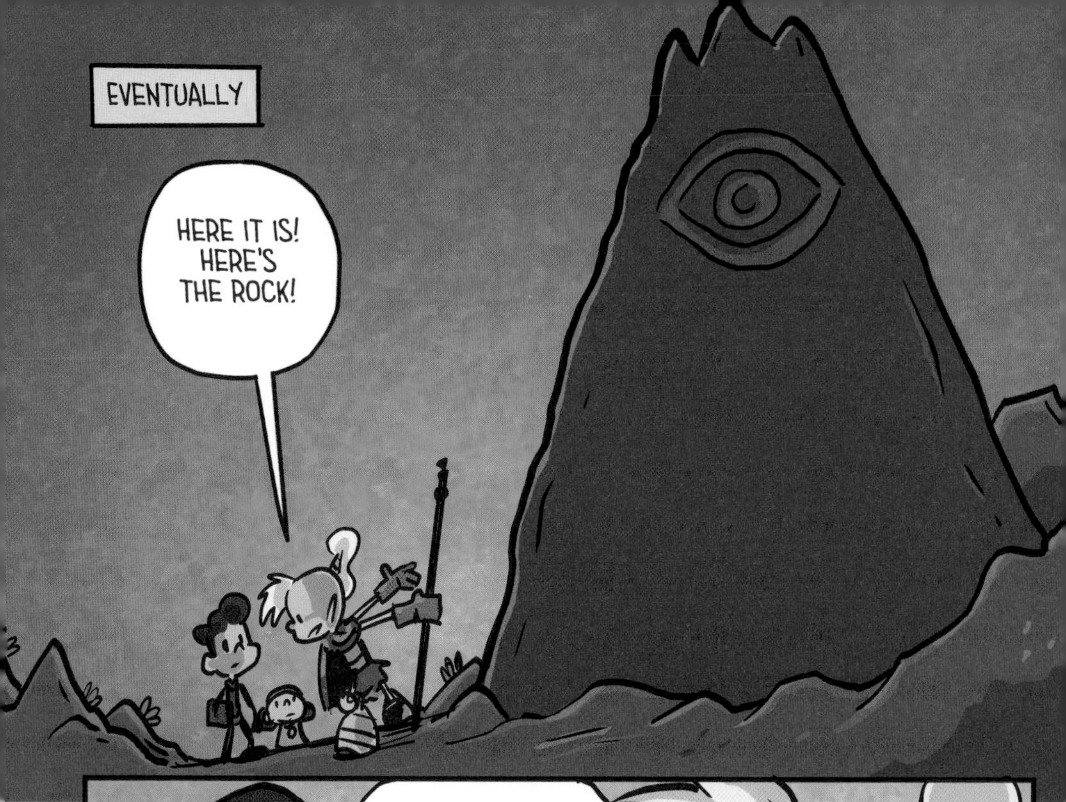
EVENTUALLY
HERE IT IS! HERE'S THE ROCK!
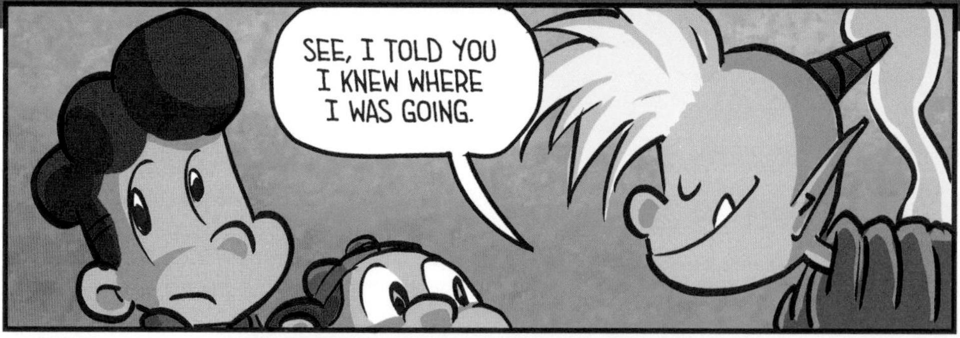
SEE, I TOLD YOU I KNEW WHERE I WAS GOING.
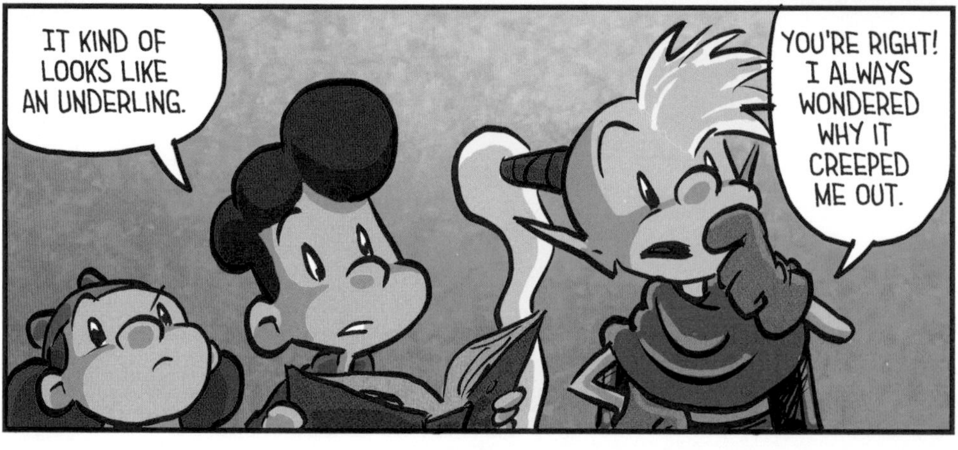
IT KIND OF LOOKS LIKE AN UNDERLING.
YOU'RE RIGHT! I ALWAYS WONDERED WHY IT CREEPED ME OUT.

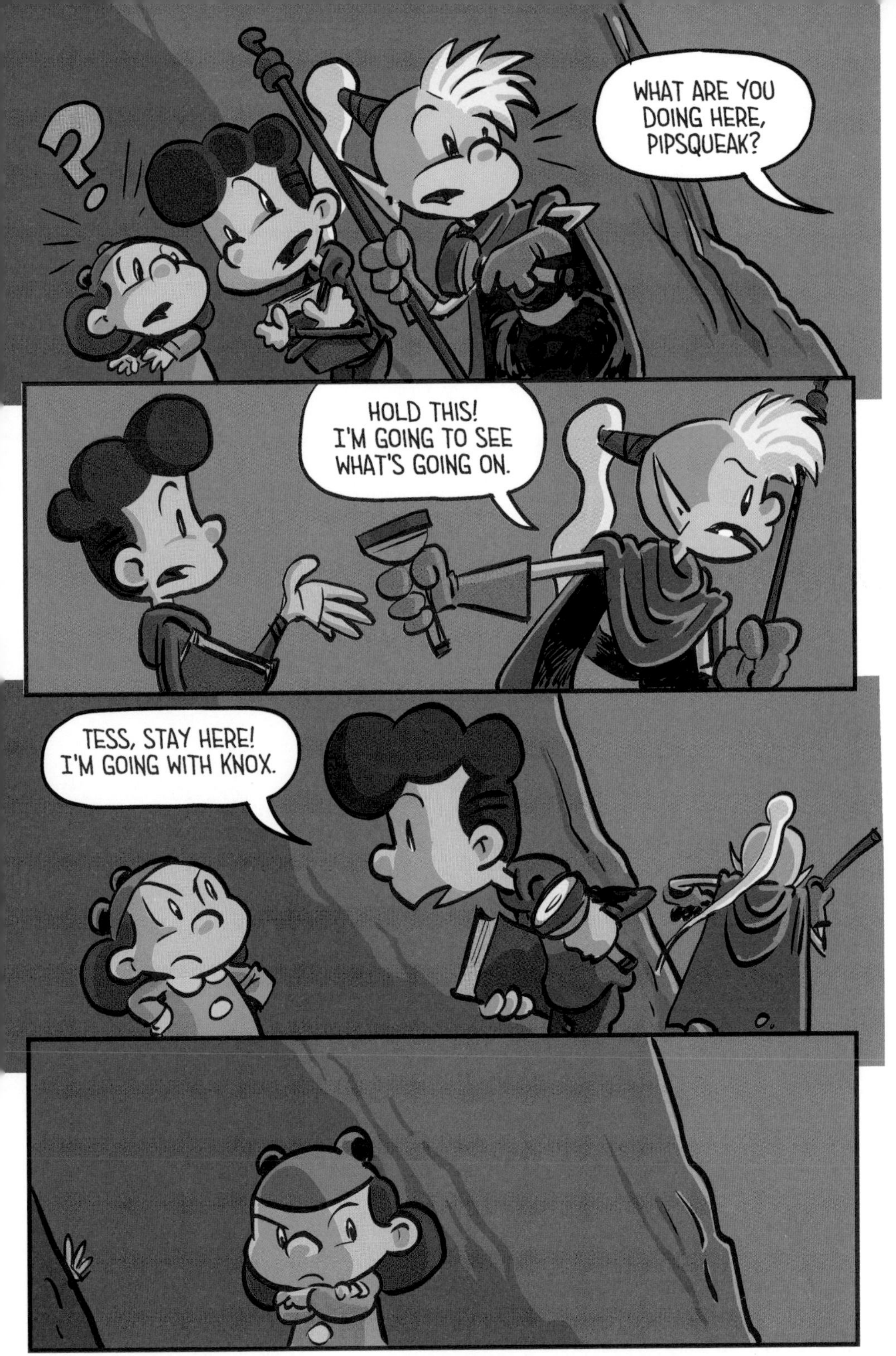
?
WHAT ARE YOU DOING HERE, PIPSQUEAK?
HOLD THIS! I'M GOING TO SEE WHAT'S GOING ON.
TESS, STAY HERE! I'M GOING WITH KNOX.

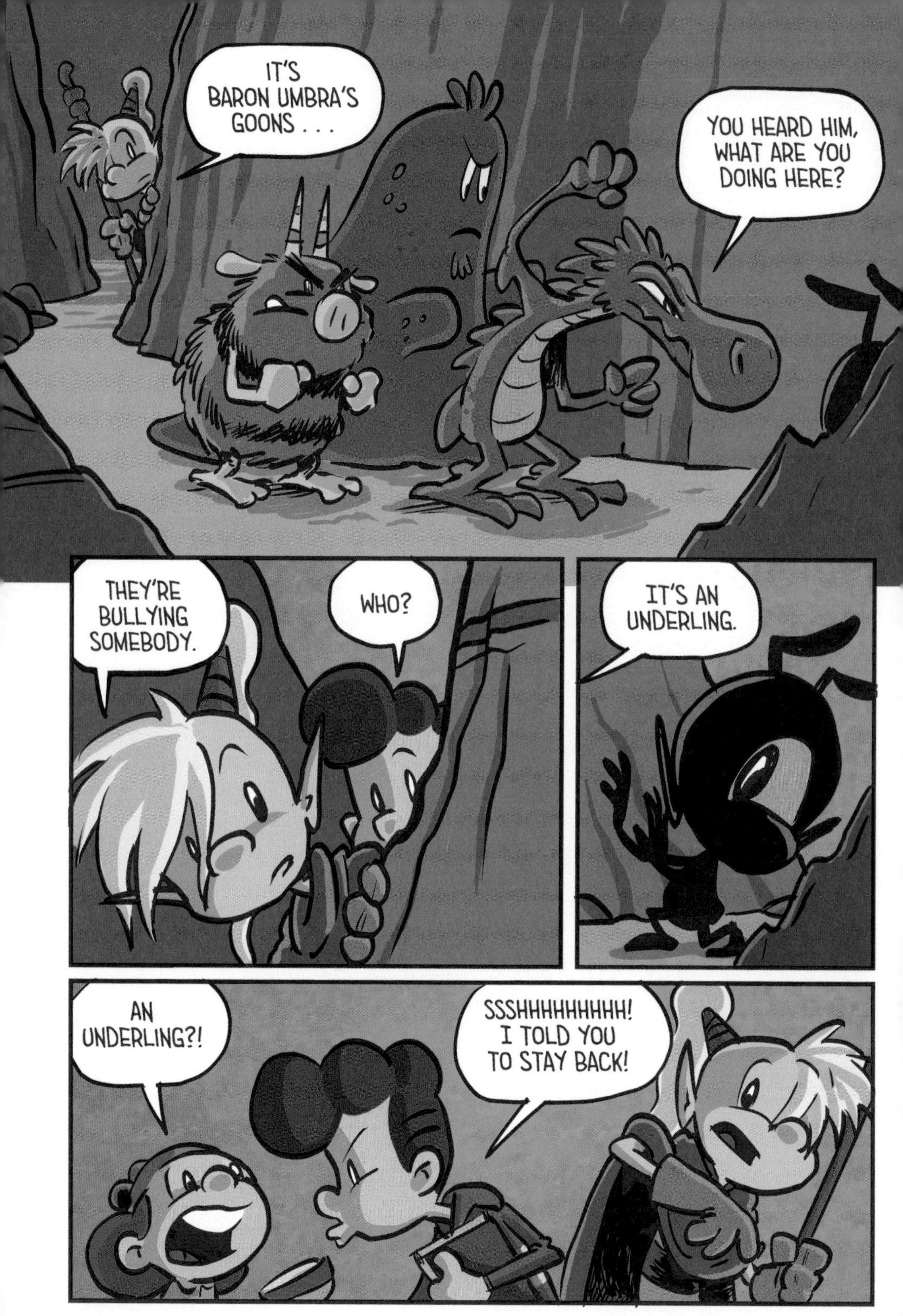
IT'S BARON UMBRA'S GOONS . . .
YOU HEARD HIM, WHAT ARE YOU DOING HERE?
THEY'RE BULLYING SOMEBODY.
WHO?
IT'S AN UNDERLING.
AN UNDERLING?!
SSSHHHHHHHHH! I TOLD YOU TO STAY BACK!

54

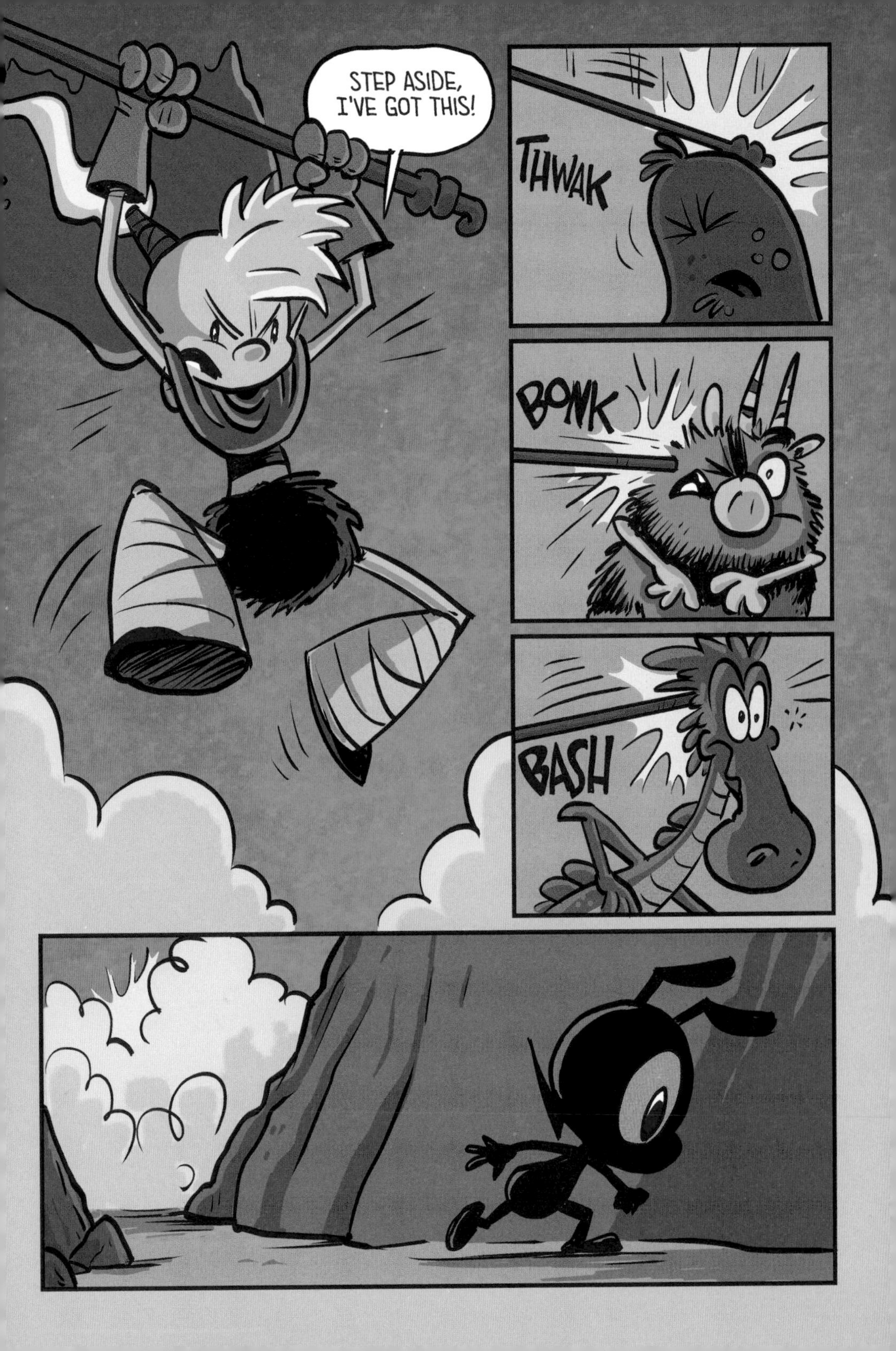
STEP ASIDE, I'VE GOT THIS!
THWAK
BONK
BASH

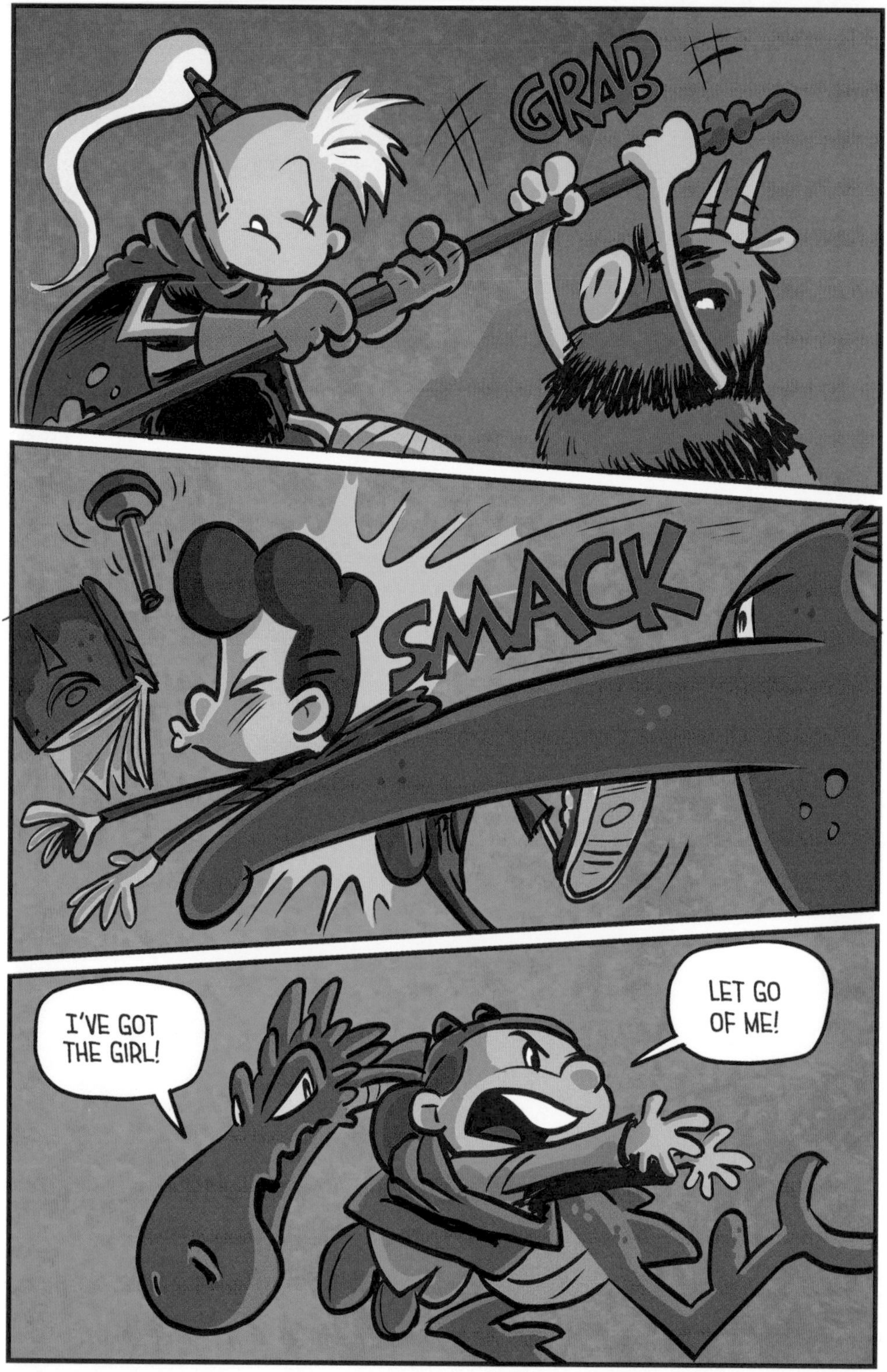
GRAB
SMACK
I'VE GOT THE GIRL!
LET GO OF ME!

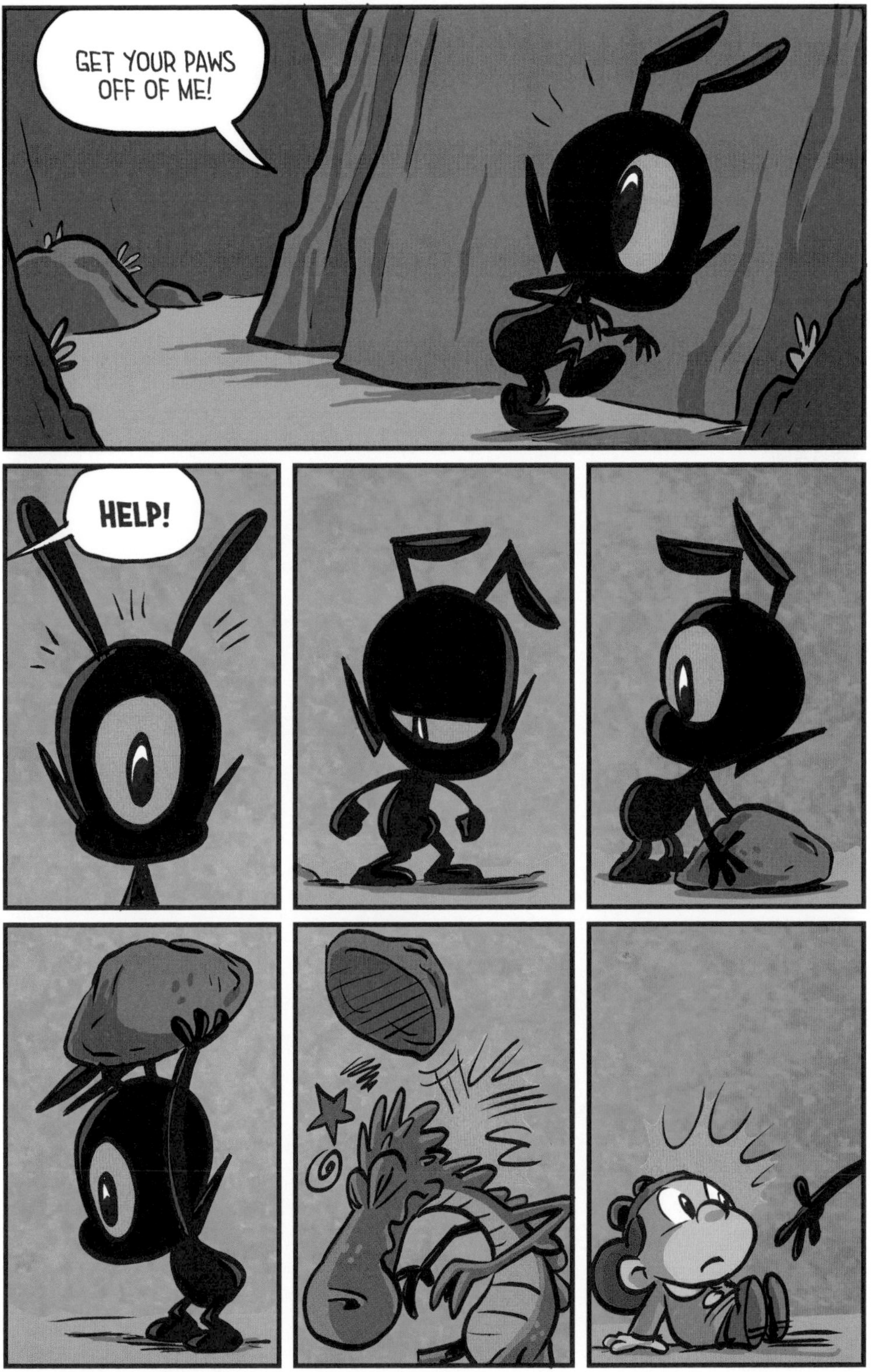
GET YOUR PAWS OFF OF ME!
HELP!

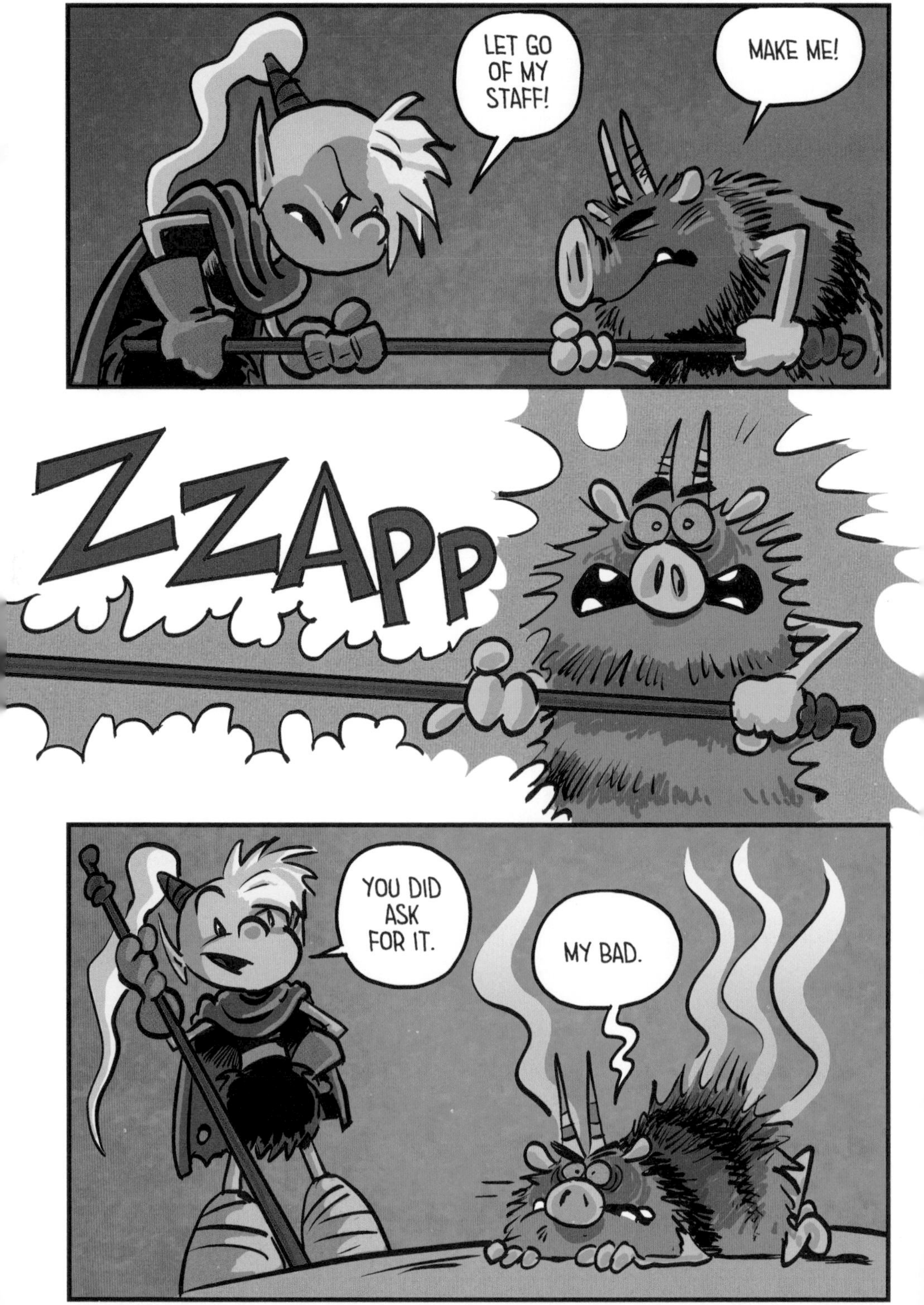
LET GO OF MY STAFF!
MAKE ME!
ZZAPP
YOU DID ASK FOR IT.
MY BAD.

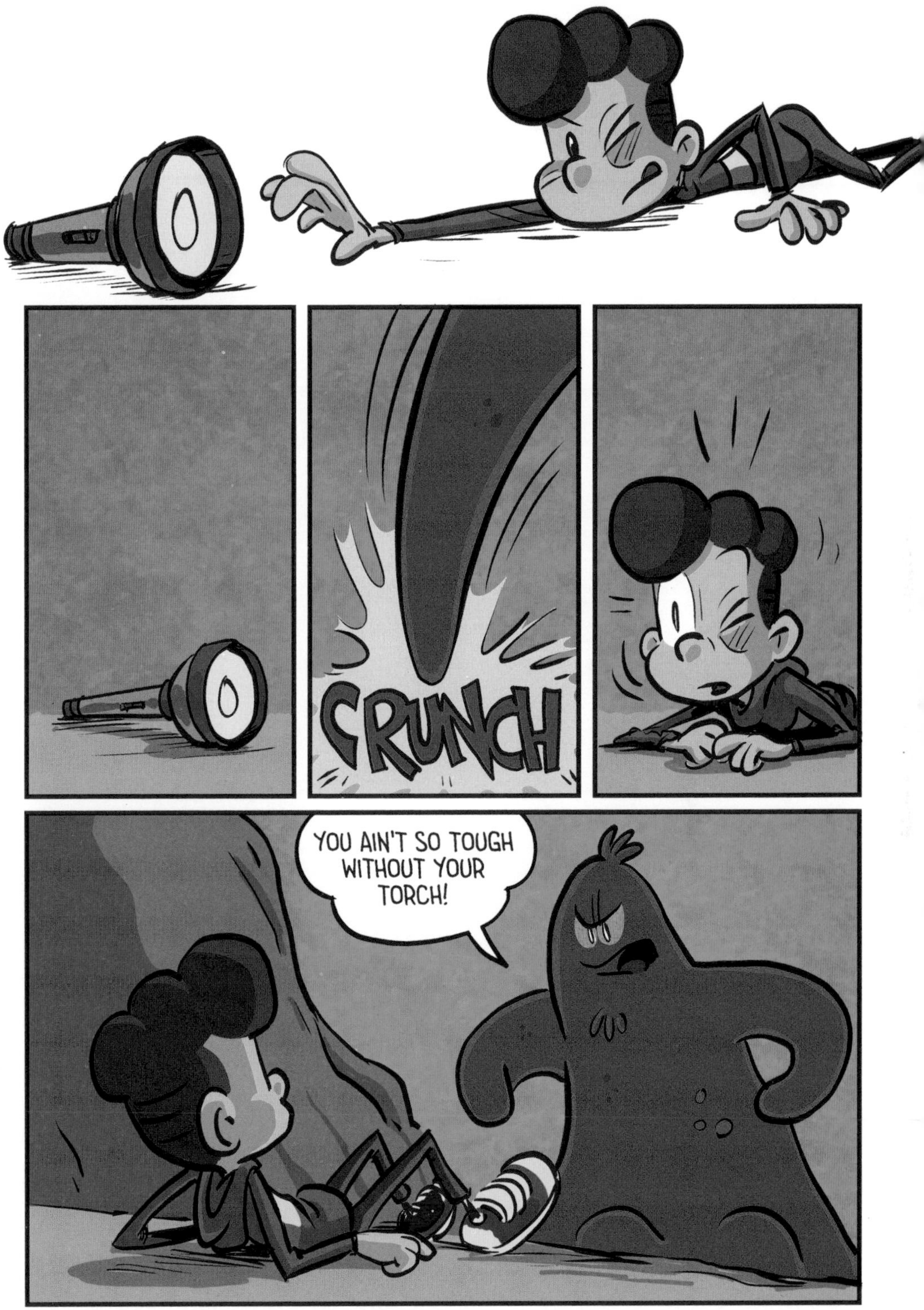
CRUNCH
YOU AIN'T SO TOUGH WITHOUT YOUR TORCH!

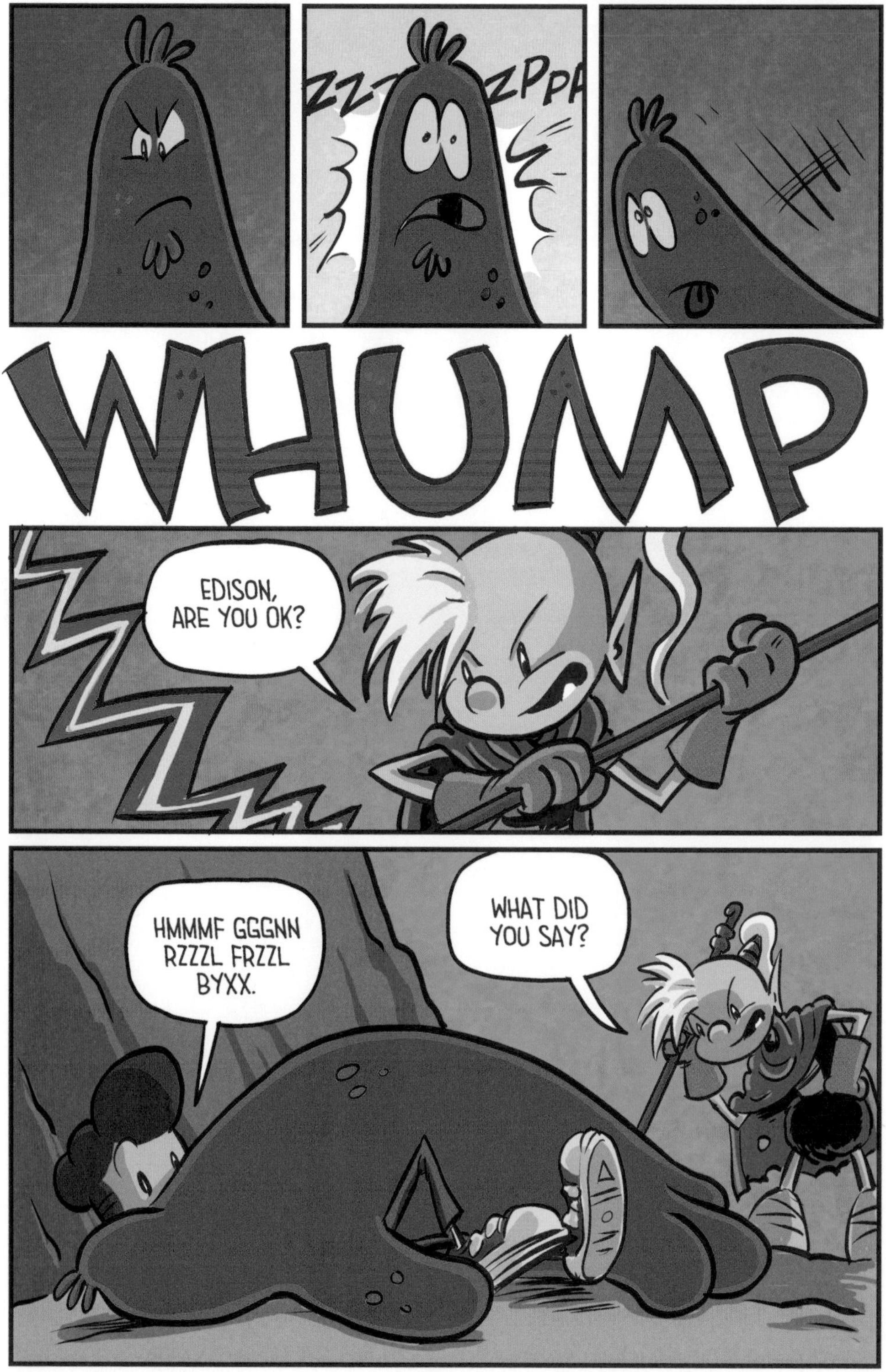
ZZZT
ZPPA
WHUMP
EDISON, ARE YOU OK?
HMMMF GGGNN RZZZL FRZZL BYXX.
WHAT DID YOU SAY?

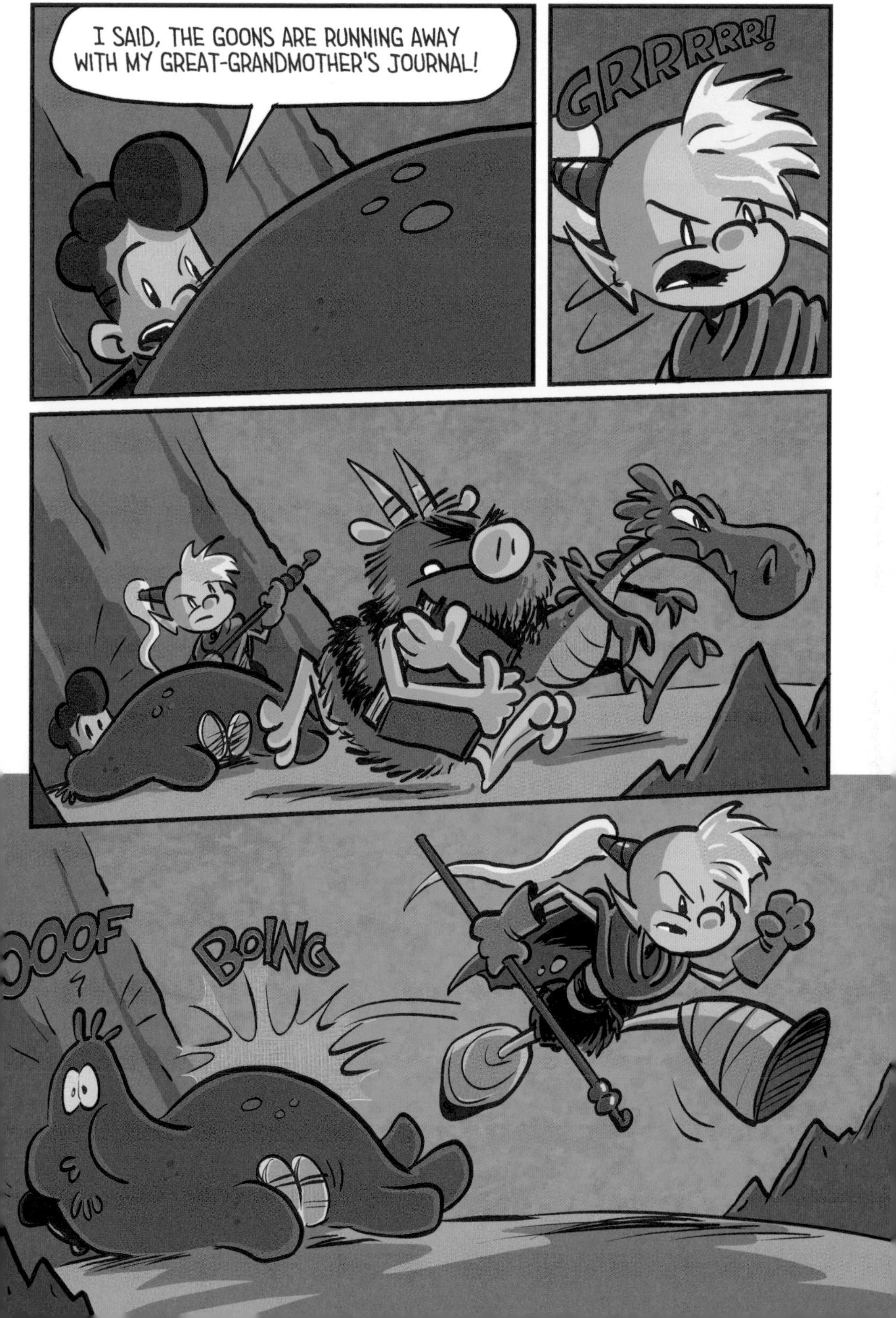
I SAID, THE GOONS ARE RUNNING AWAY WITH MY GREAT-GRANDMOTHER'S JOURNAL!
GRRRRRR!
OOOF
BOING

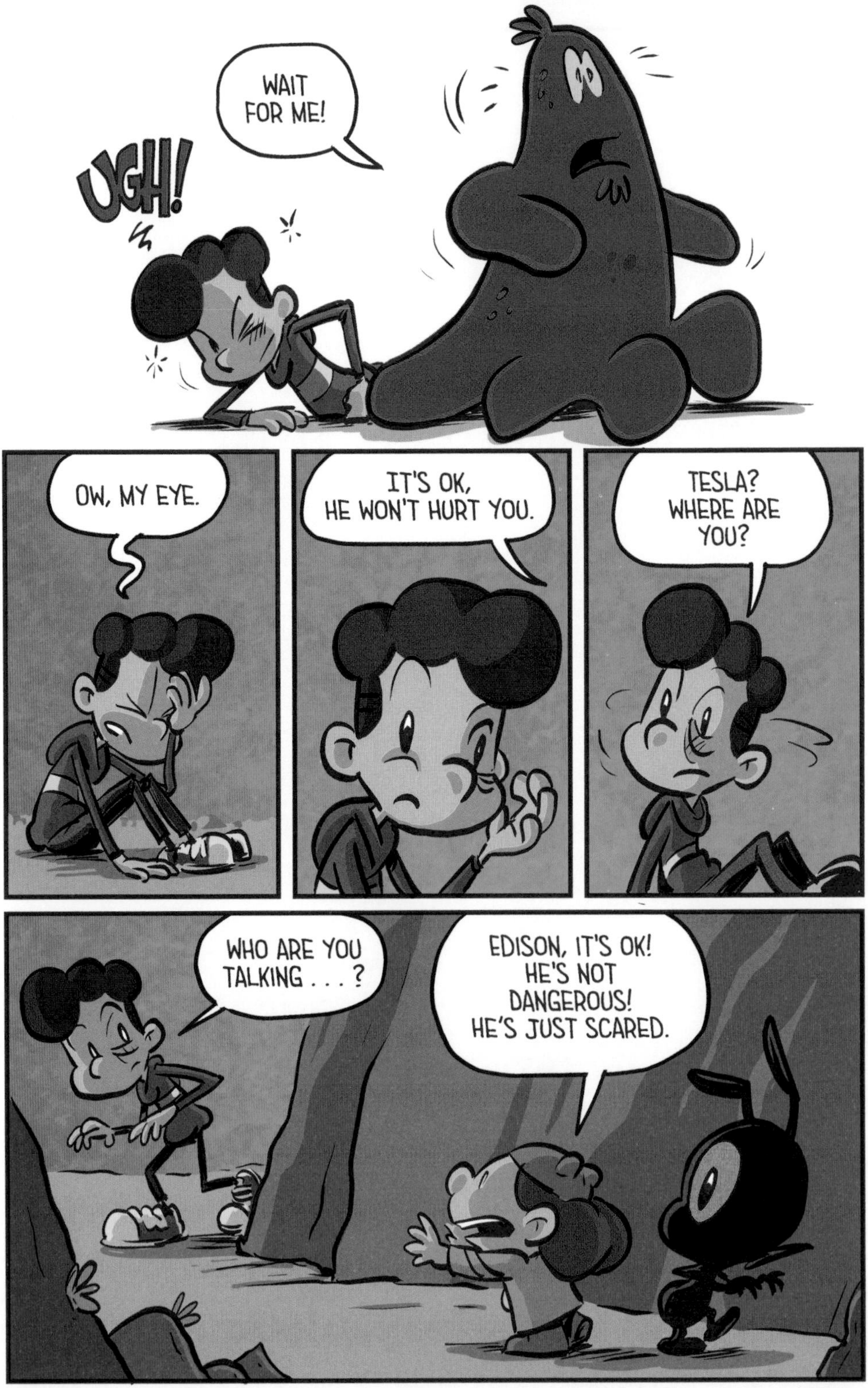
UGH!
WAIT FOR ME!
OW, MY EYE.
IT'S OK, HE WON'T HURT YOU.
TESLA? WHERE ARE YOU?
WHO ARE YOU TALKING . . . ?
EDISON, IT'S OK! HE'S NOT DANGEROUS! HE'S JUST SCARED.

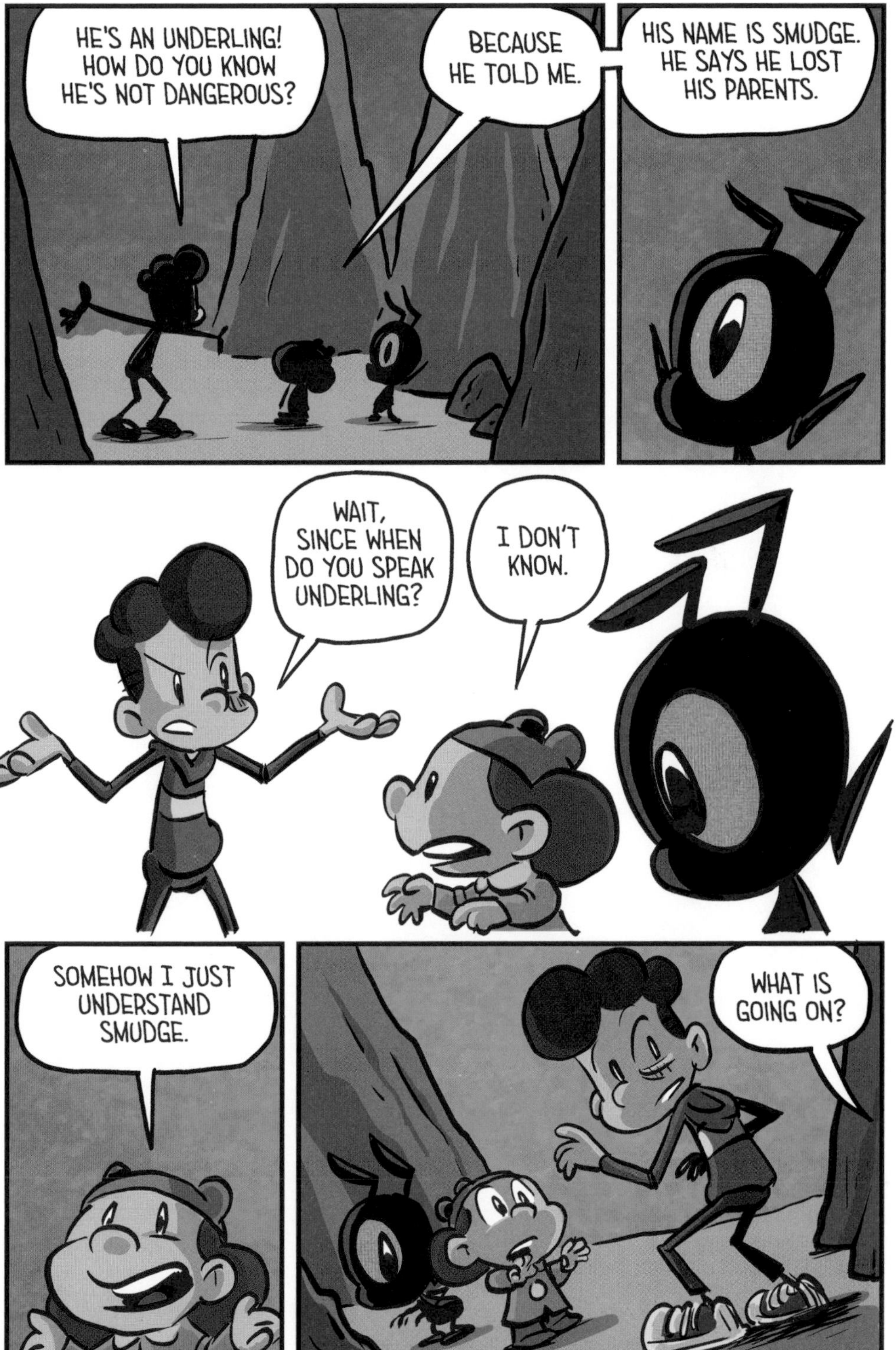
HE'S AN UNDERLING! HOW DO YOU KNOW HE'S NOT DANGEROUS?
BECAUSE HE TOLD ME.
HIS NAME IS SMUDGE. HE SAYS HE LOST HIS PARENTS.
WAIT, SINCE WHEN DO YOU SPEAK UNDERLING?
I DON'T KNOW.
SOMEHOW I JUST UNDERSTAND SMUDGE.
WHAT IS GOING ON?

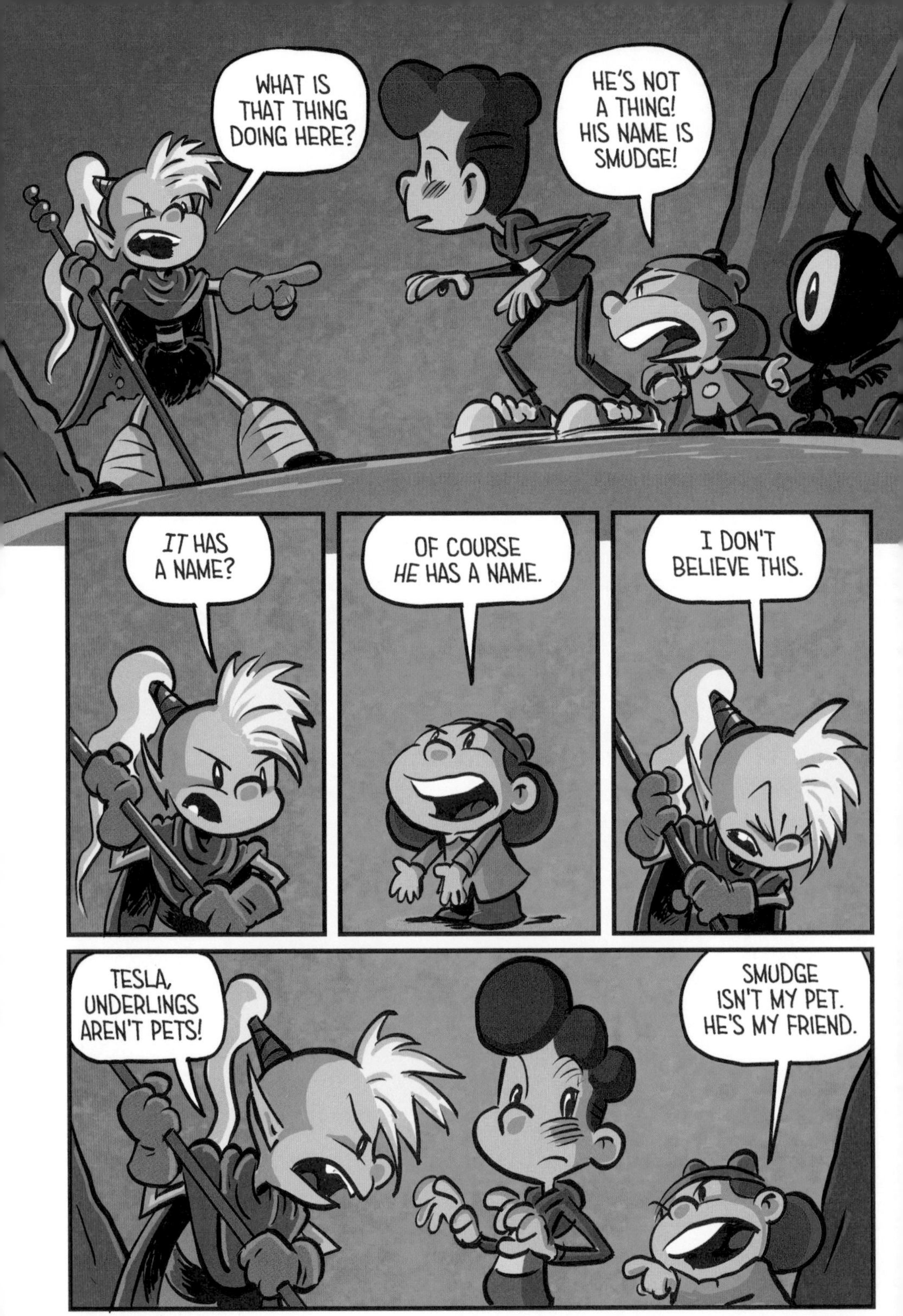
WHAT IS THAT THING DOING HERE?
HE'S NOT A THING! HIS NAME IS SMUDGE!
IT HAS A NAME?
OF COURSE *HE* HAS A NAME.
I DON'T BELIEVE THIS.
TESLA, UNDERLINGS AREN'T PETS!
SMUDGE ISN'T MY PET. HE'S MY FRIEND.

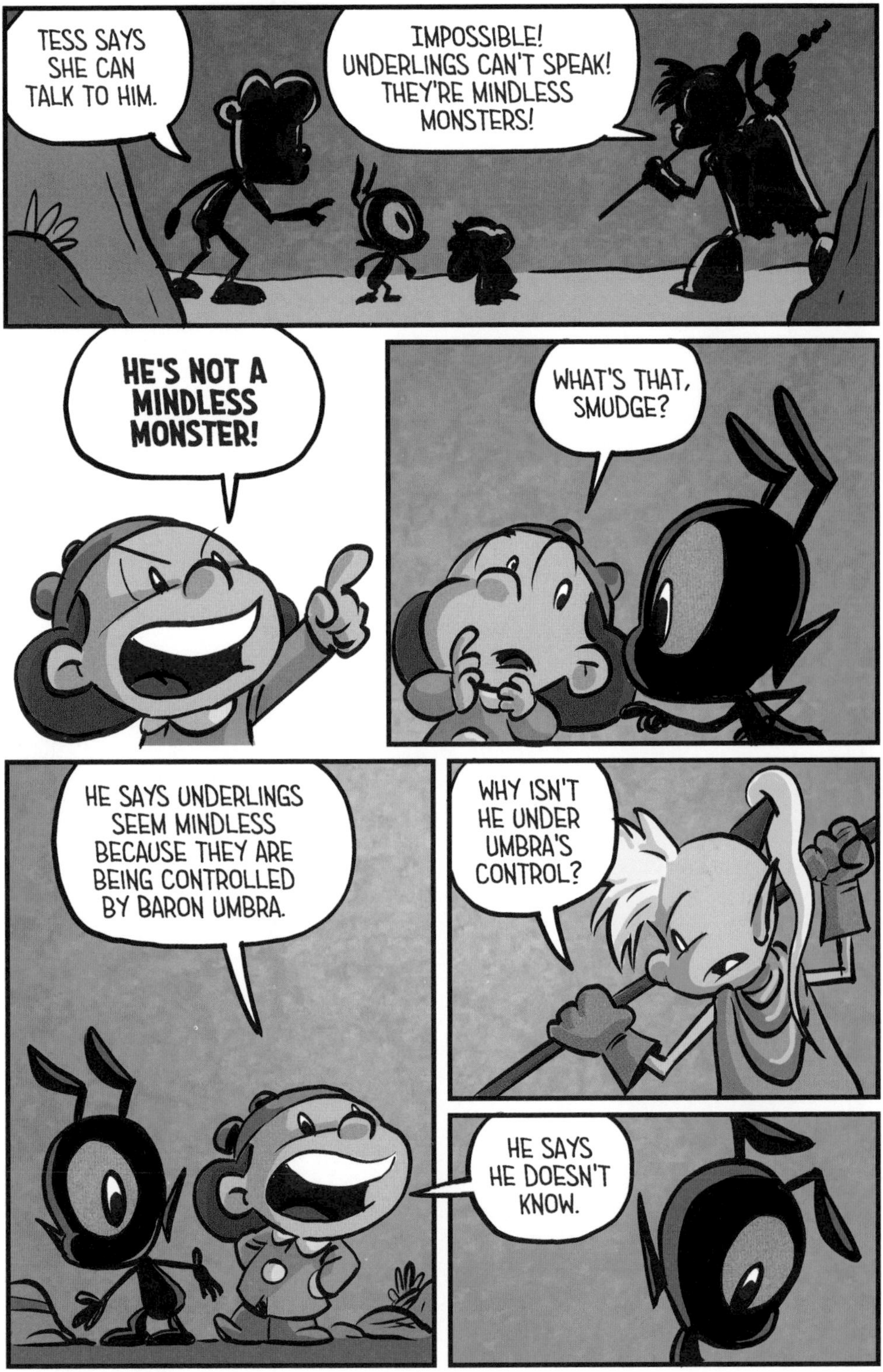
TESS SAYS SHE CAN TALK TO HIM.
IMPOSSIBLE! UNDERLINGS CAN'T SPEAK! THEY'RE MINDLESS MONSTERS!
HE'S NOT A MINDLESS MONSTER!
WHAT'S THAT, SMUDGE?
HE SAYS UNDERLINGS SEEM MINDLESS BECAUSE THEY ARE BEING CONTROLLED BY BARON UMBRA.
WHY ISN'T HE UNDER UMBRA'S CONTROL?
HE SAYS HE DOESN'T KNOW.

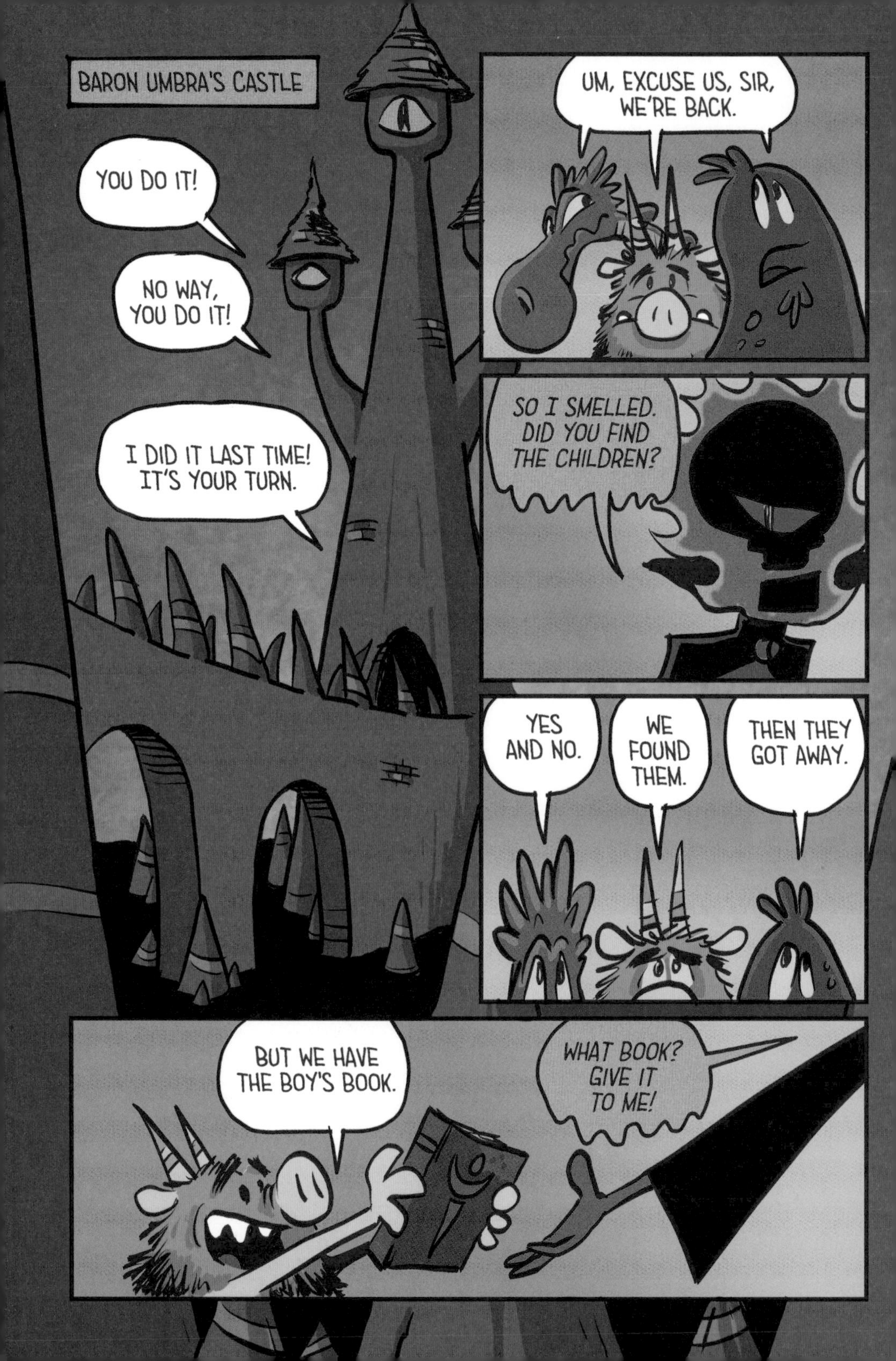
BARON UMBRA'S CASTLE
YOU DO IT!
NO WAY, YOU DO IT!
I DID IT LAST TIME! IT'S YOUR TURN.
UM, EXCUSE US, SIR, WE'RE BACK.
SO I SMELLED. DID YOU FIND THE CHILDREN?
YES AND NO.
WE FOUND THEM.
THEN THEY GOT AWAY.
BUT WE HAVE THE BOY'S BOOK.
WHAT BOOK? GIVE IT TO ME!

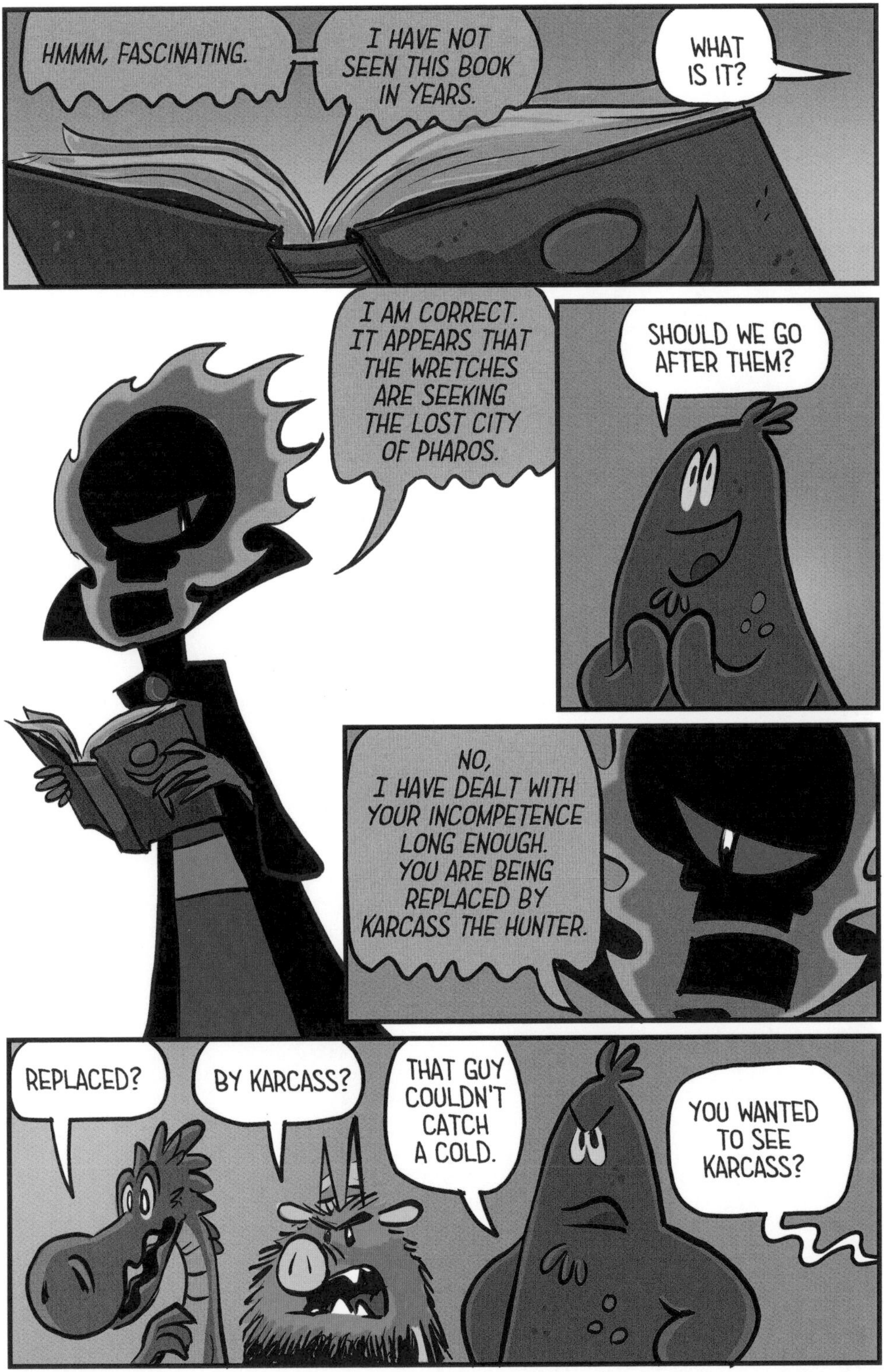
HMMM, FASCINATING.
I HAVE NOT SEEN THIS BOOK IN YEARS.
WHAT IS IT?
I AM CORRECT. IT APPEARS THAT THE WRETCHES ARE SEEKING THE LOST CITY OF PHAROS.
SHOULD WE GO AFTER THEM?
NO, I HAVE DEALT WITH YOUR INCOMPETENCE LONG ENOUGH. YOU ARE BEING REPLACED BY KARCASS THE HUNTER.
REPLACED?
BY KARCASS?
THAT GUY COULDN'T CATCH A COLD.
YOU WANTED TO SEE KARCASS?

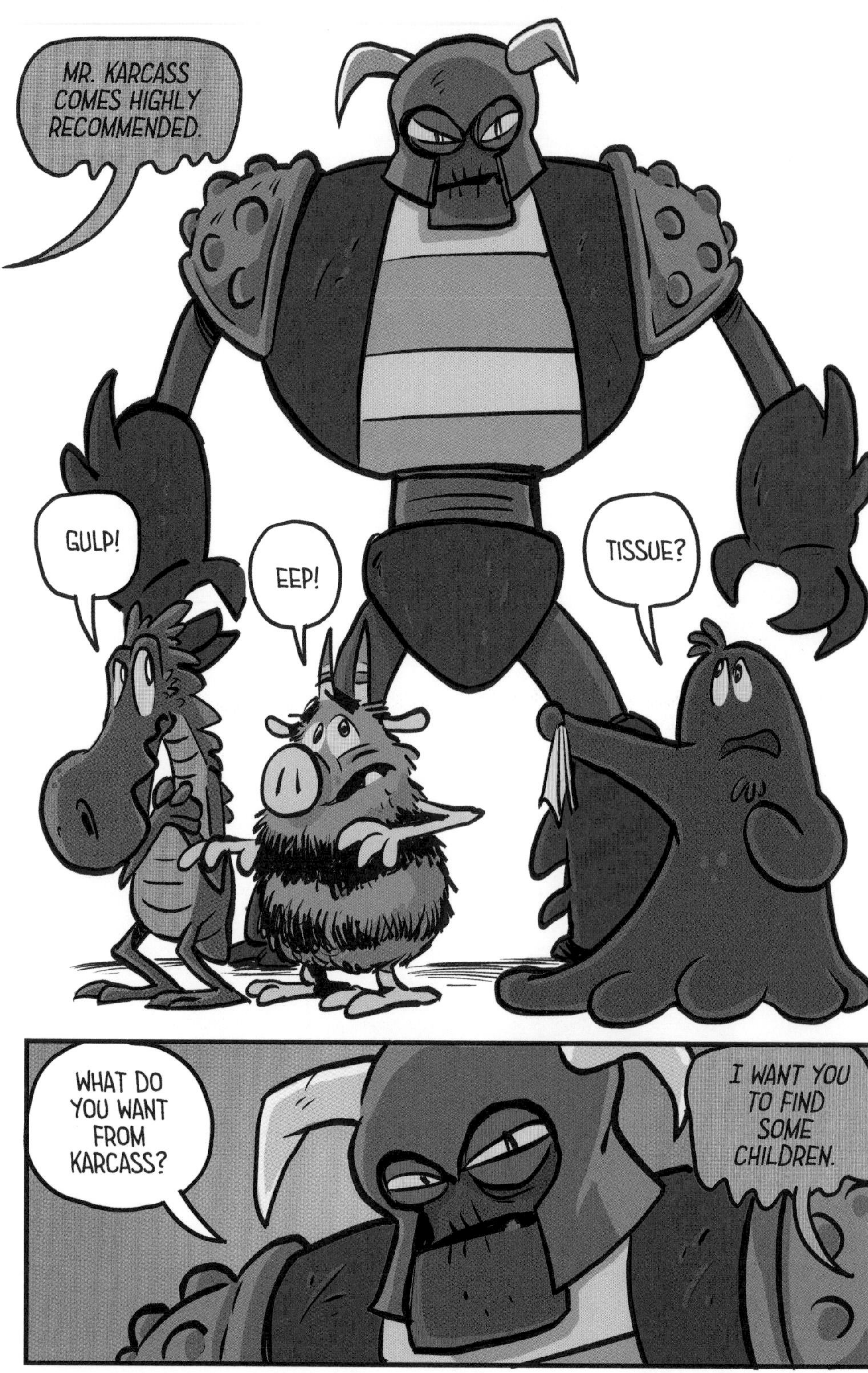
MR. KARCASS COMES HIGHLY RECOMMENDED.
GULP!
EEP!
TISSUE?
WHAT DO YOU WANT FROM KARCASS?
I WANT YOU TO FIND SOME CHILDREN.

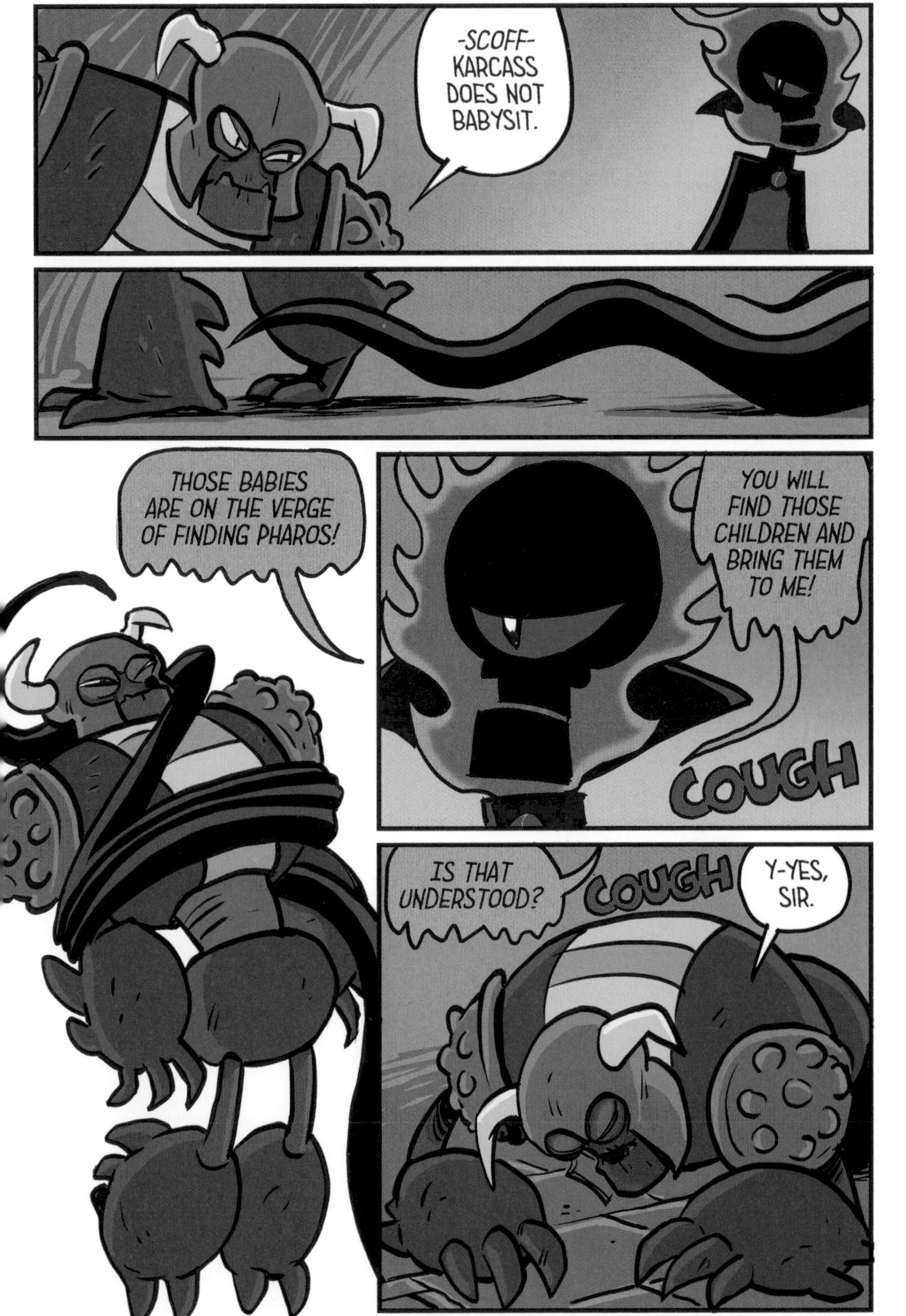
-SCOFF-
KARCASS DOES NOT BABYSIT.
THOSE BABIES ARE ON THE VERGE OF FINDING PHAROS!
YOU WILL FIND THOSE CHILDREN AND BRING THEM TO ME!
COUGH
IS THAT UNDERSTOOD?
COUGH
Y-YES, SIR.

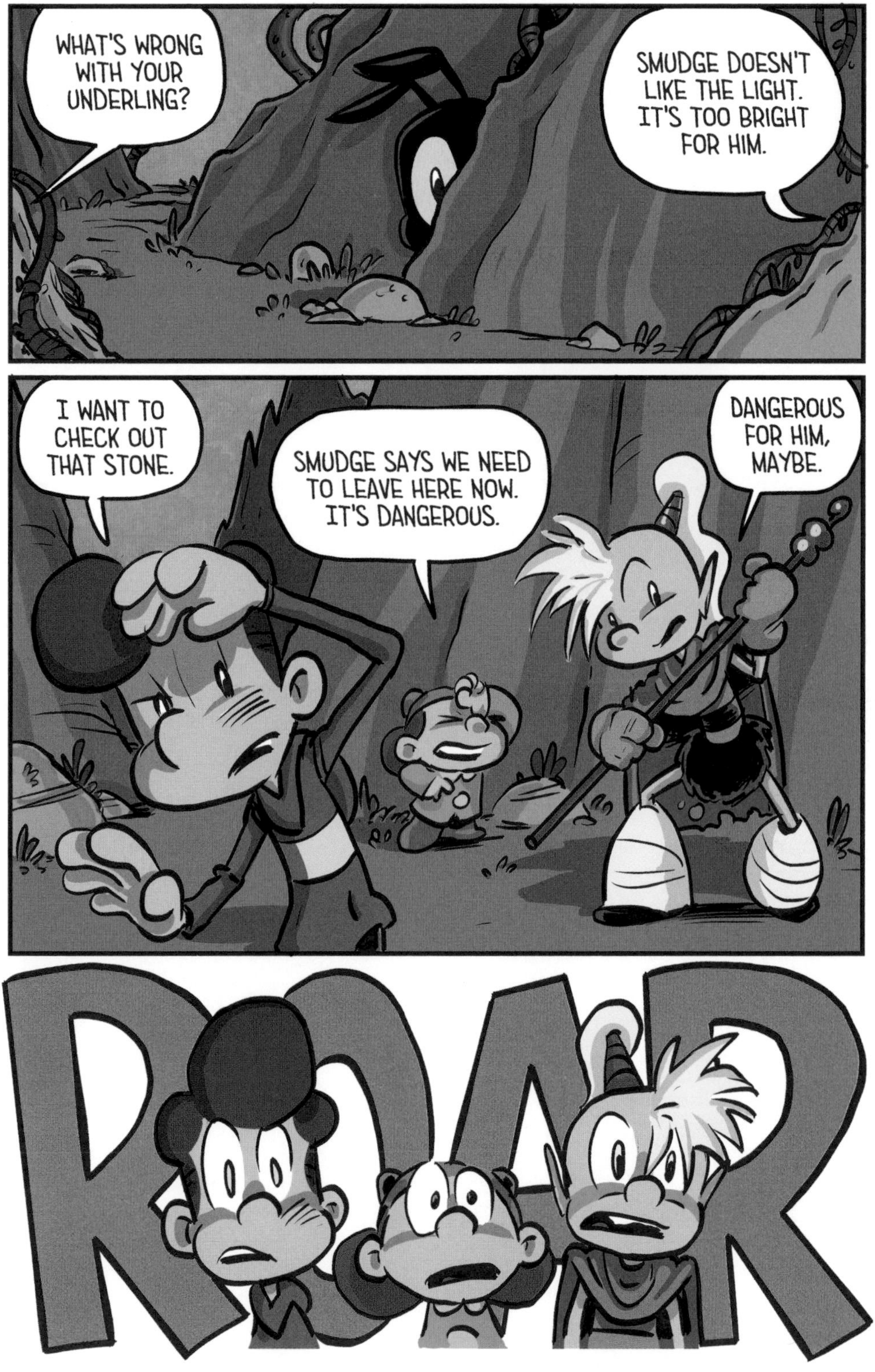
WHAT'S WRONG WITH YOUR UNDERLING?
SMUDGE DOESN'T LIKE THE LIGHT. IT'S TOO BRIGHT FOR HIM.
I WANT TO CHECK OUT THAT STONE.
SMUDGE SAYS WE NEED TO LEAVE HERE NOW. IT'S DANGEROUS.
DANGEROUS FOR HIM, MAYBE.
ROAR

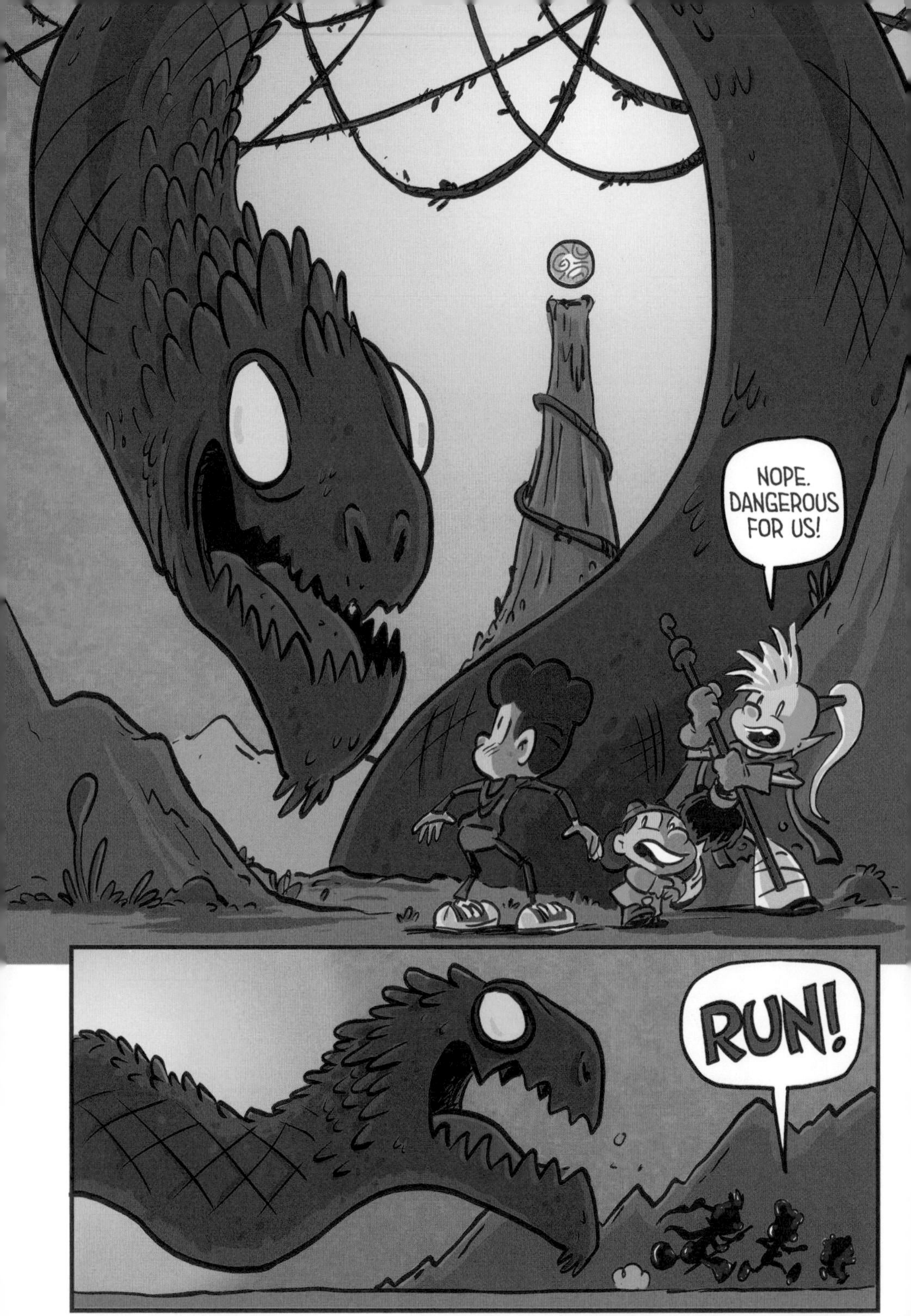
NOPE. DANGEROUS FOR US!
RUN!

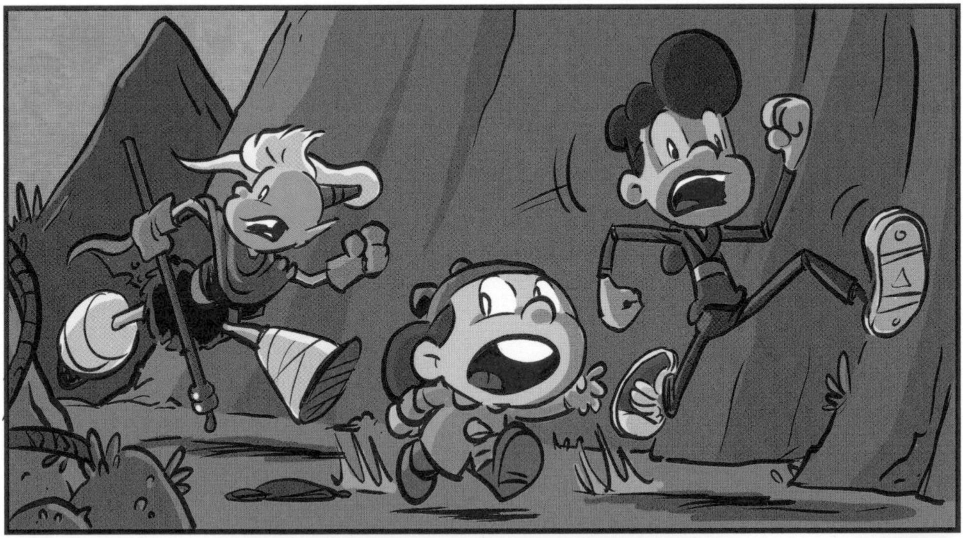

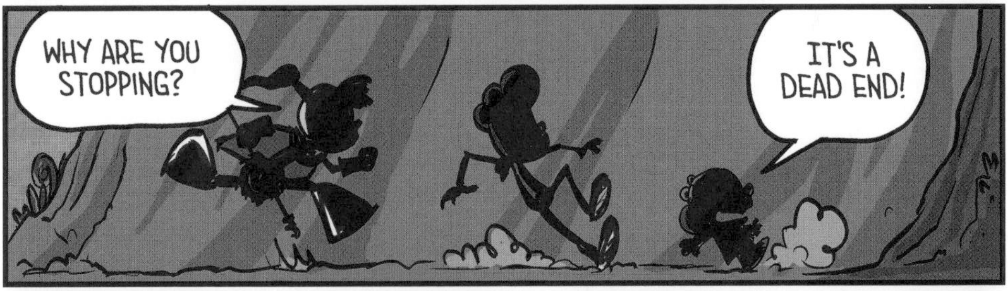
WHY ARE YOU STOPPING?
IT'S A DEAD END!

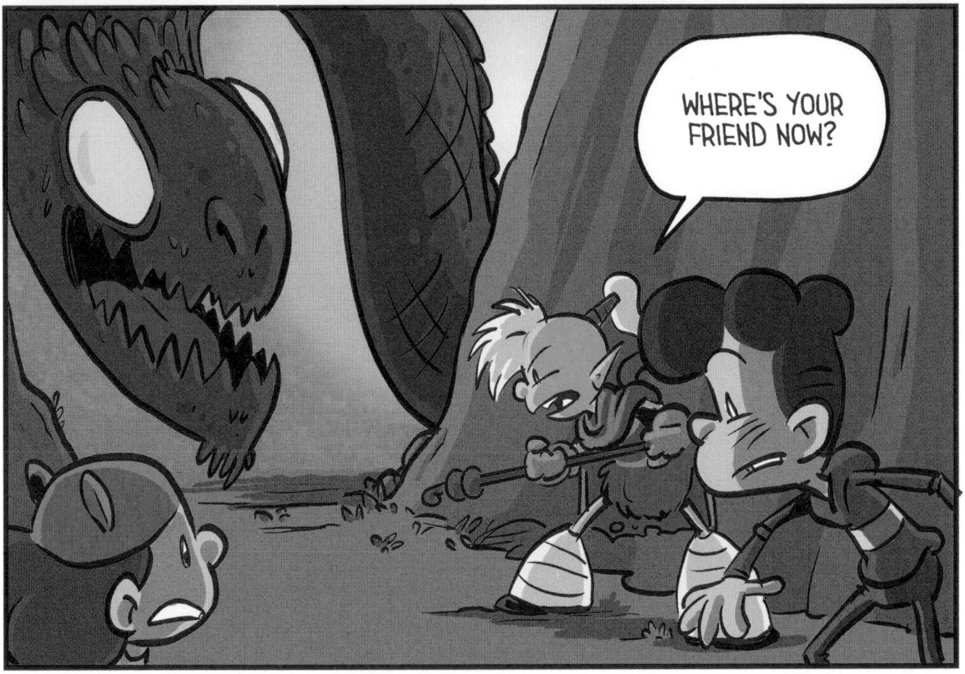
WHERE'S YOUR FRIEND NOW?

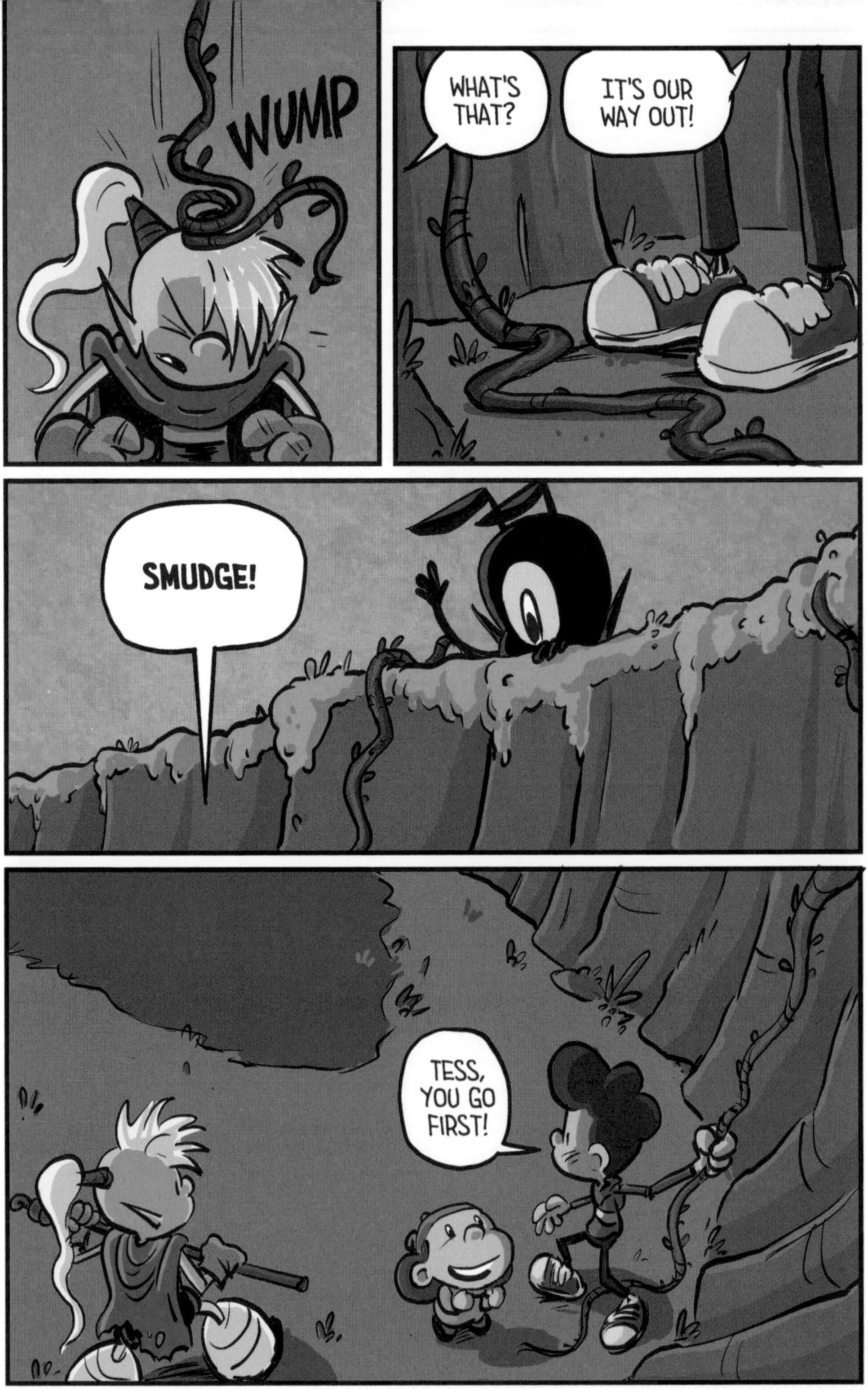
WUMP
WHAT'S THAT?
IT'S OUR WAY OUT!
SMUDGE!
TESS, YOU GO FIRST!

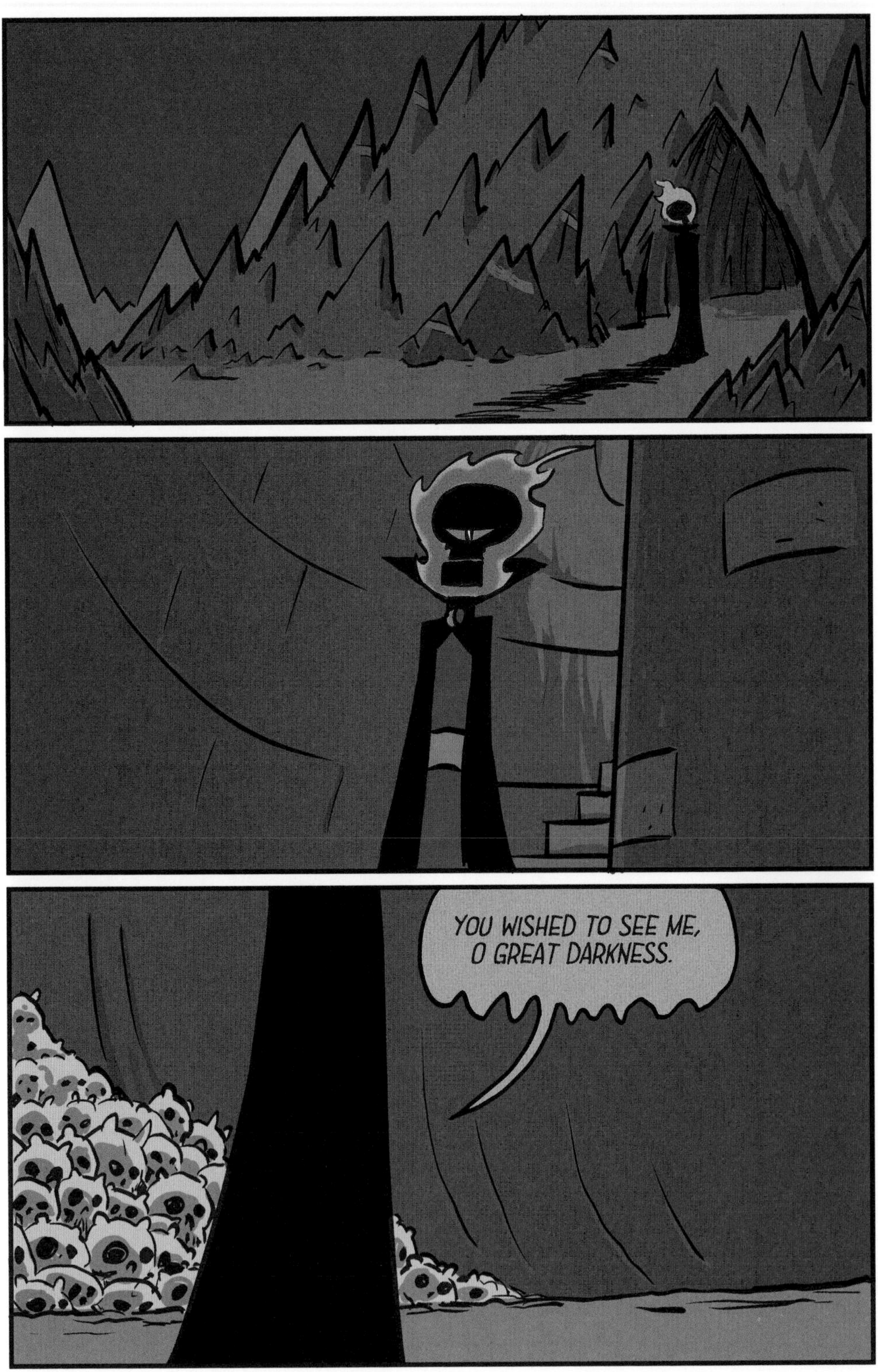
YOU WISHED TO SEE ME, O GREAT DARKNESS.

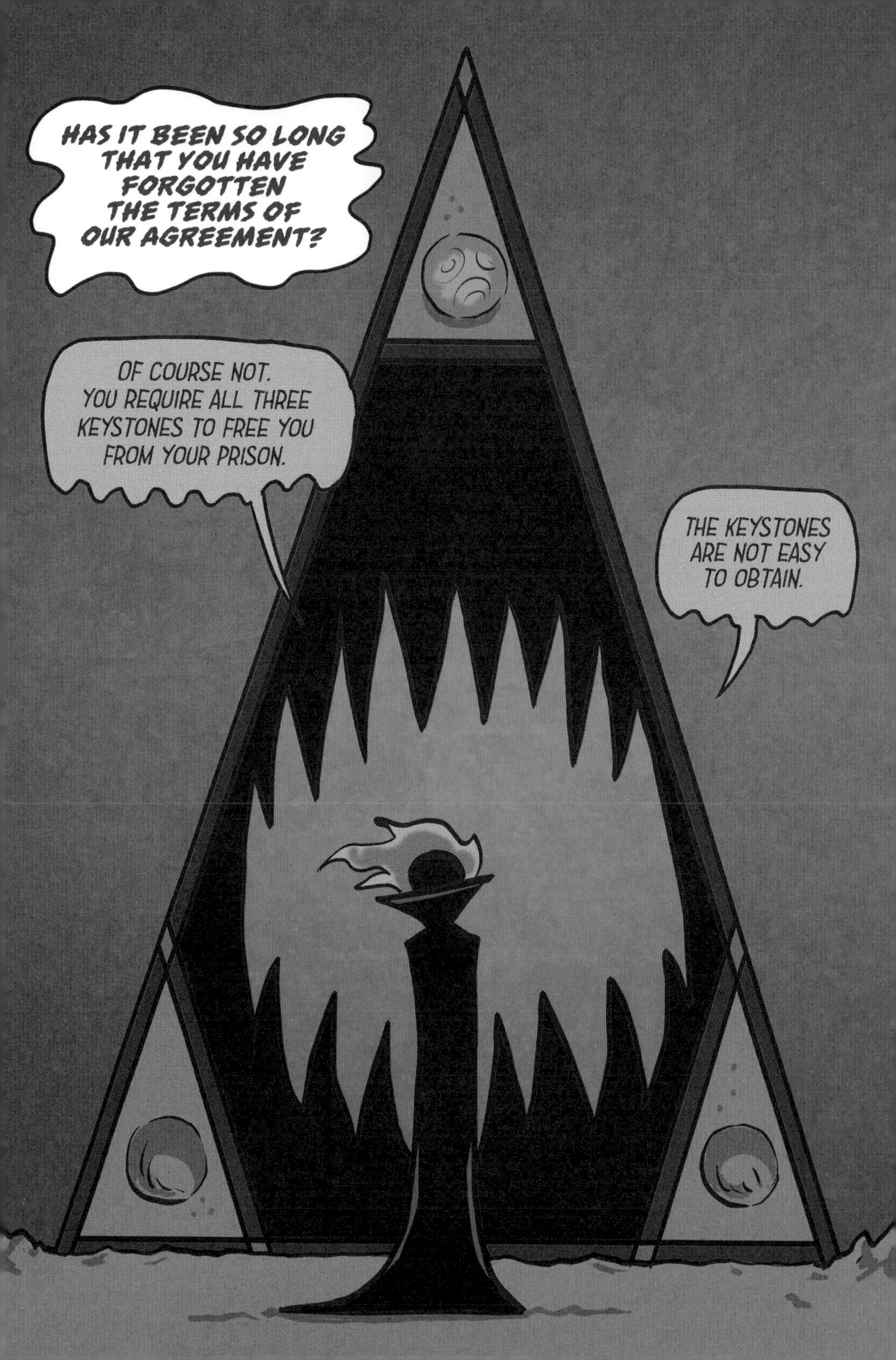
HAS IT BEEN SO LONG THAT YOU HAVE FORGOTTEN THE TERMS OF OUR AGREEMENT?
OF COURSE NOT. YOU REQUIRE ALL THREE KEYSTONES TO FREE YOU FROM YOUR PRISON.
THE KEYSTONES ARE NOT EASY TO OBTAIN.

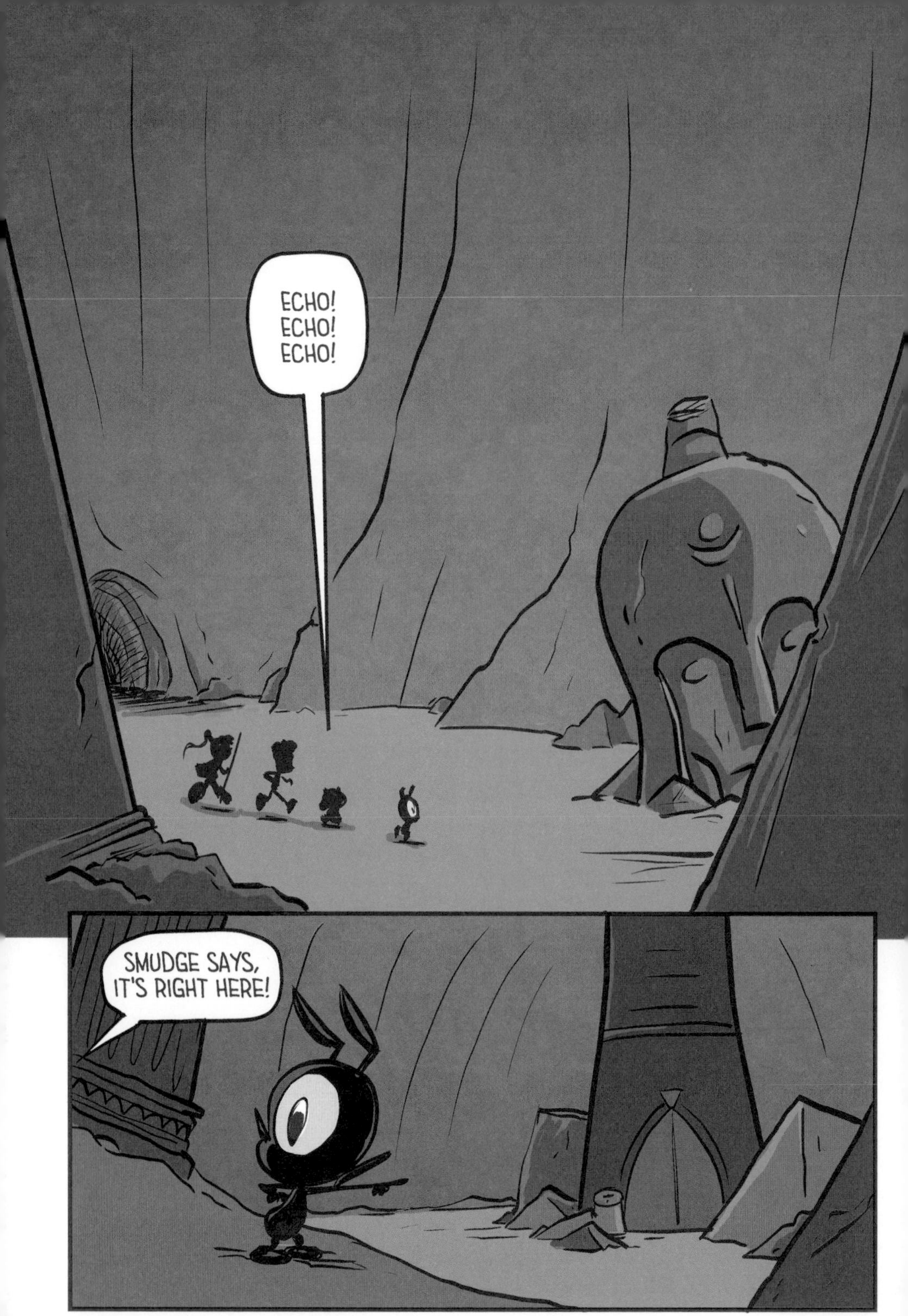
ECHO! ECHO! ECHO!
SMUDGE SAYS, IT'S RIGHT HERE!

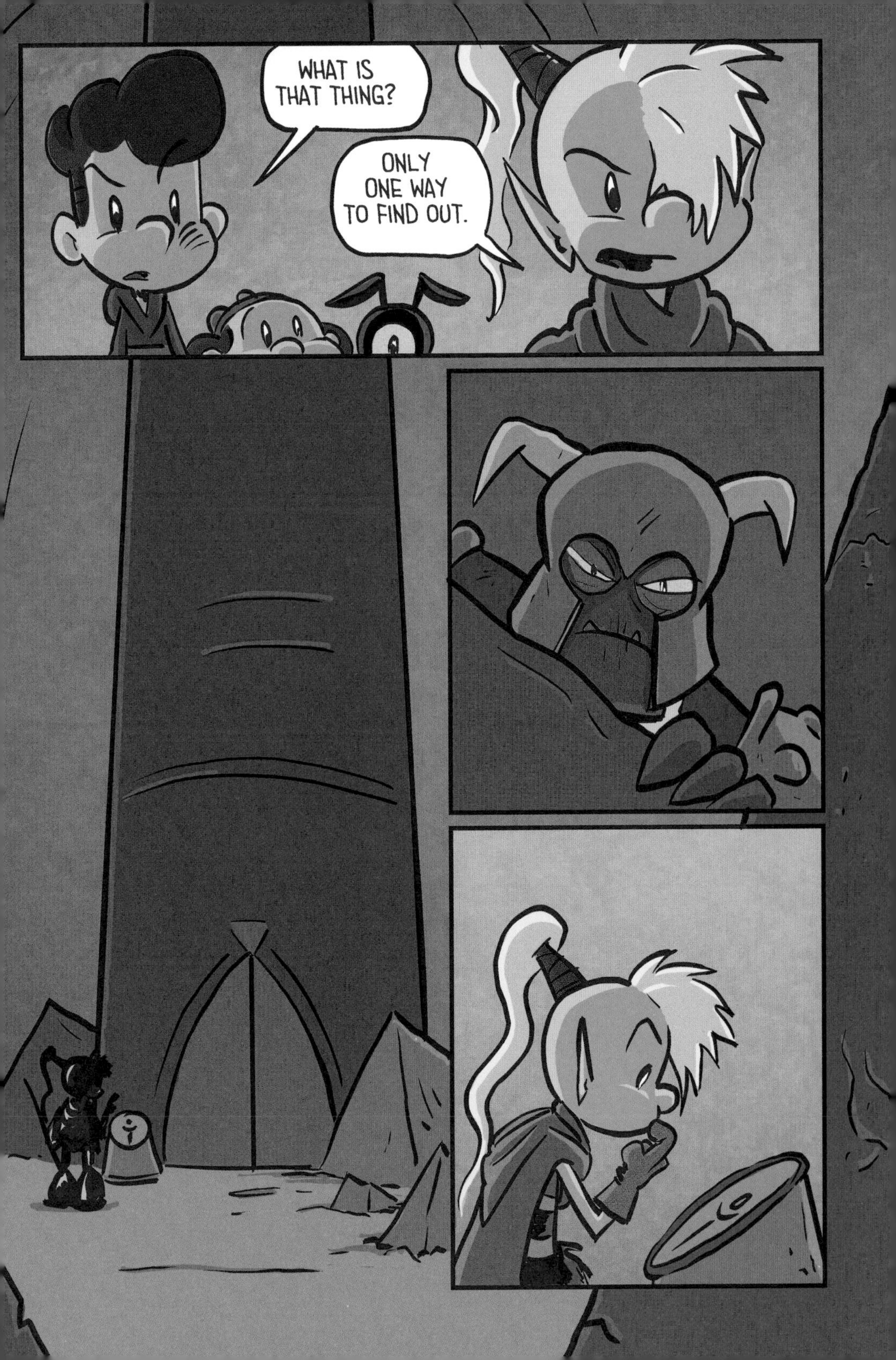
WHAT IS THAT THING?
ONLY ONE WAY TO FIND OUT.

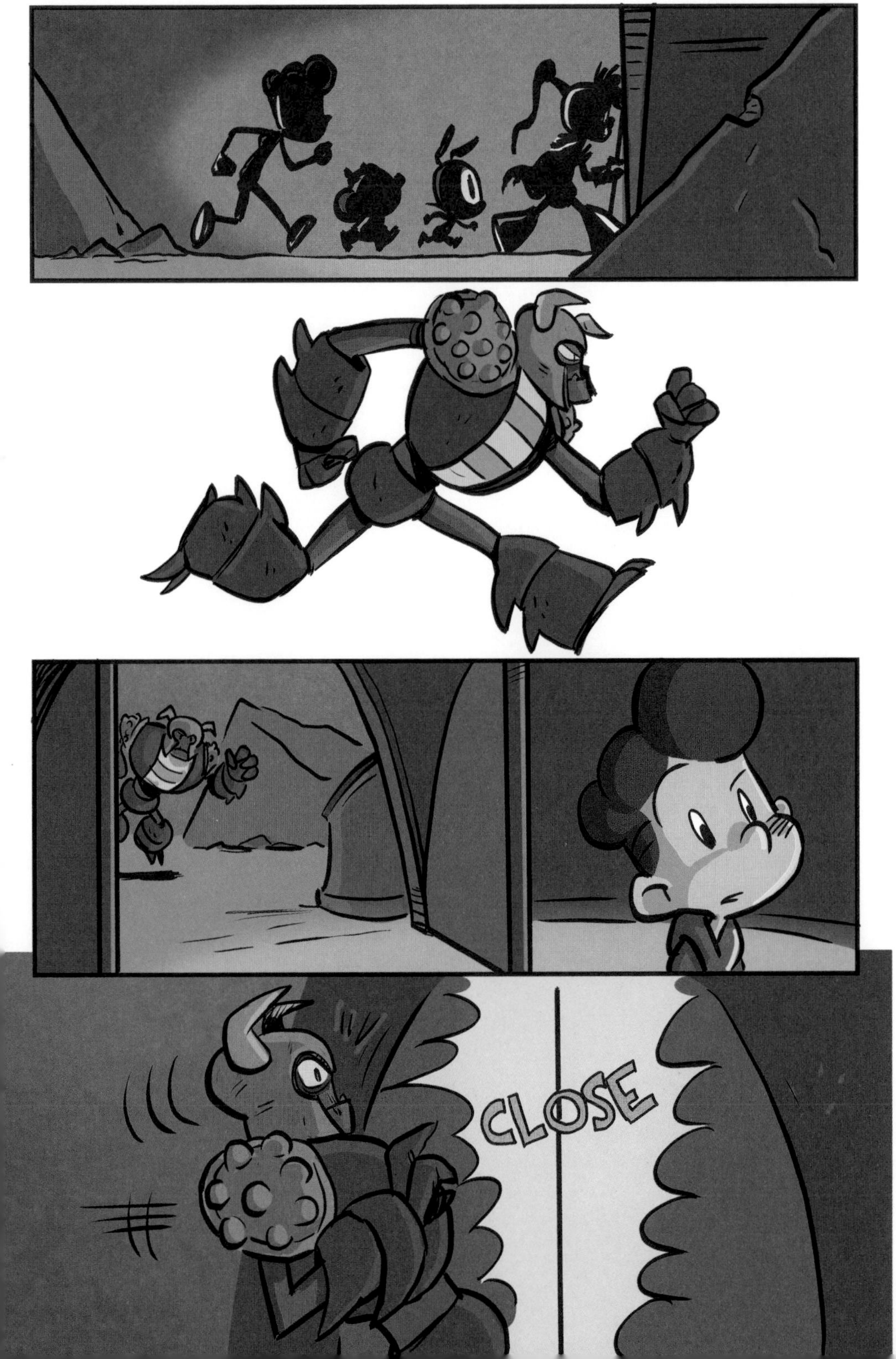
CLOSE

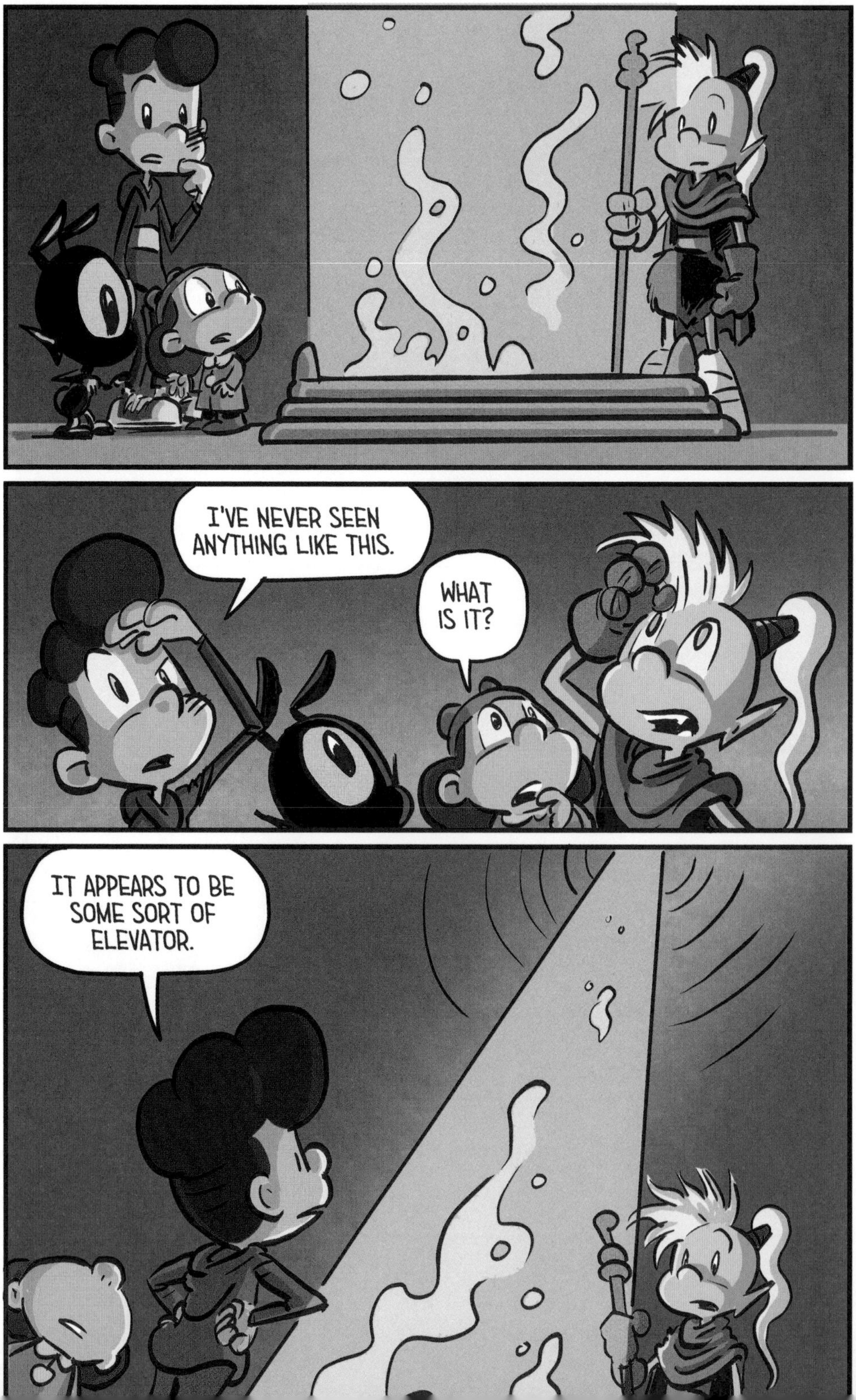
I'VE NEVER SEEN ANYTHING LIKE THIS.
WHAT IS IT?
IT APPEARS TO BE SOME SORT OF ELEVATOR.

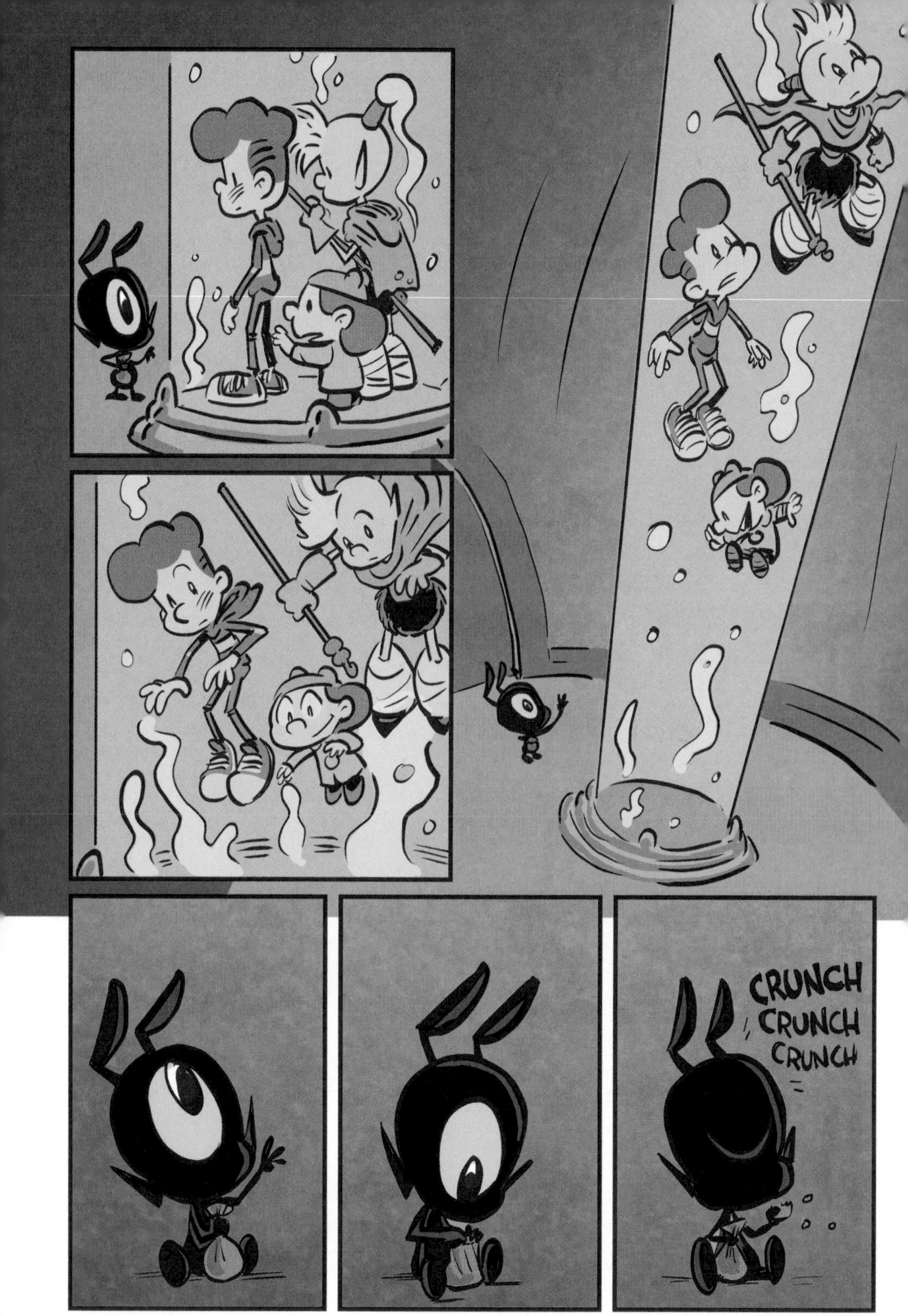
CRUNCH
CRUNCH
CRUNCH

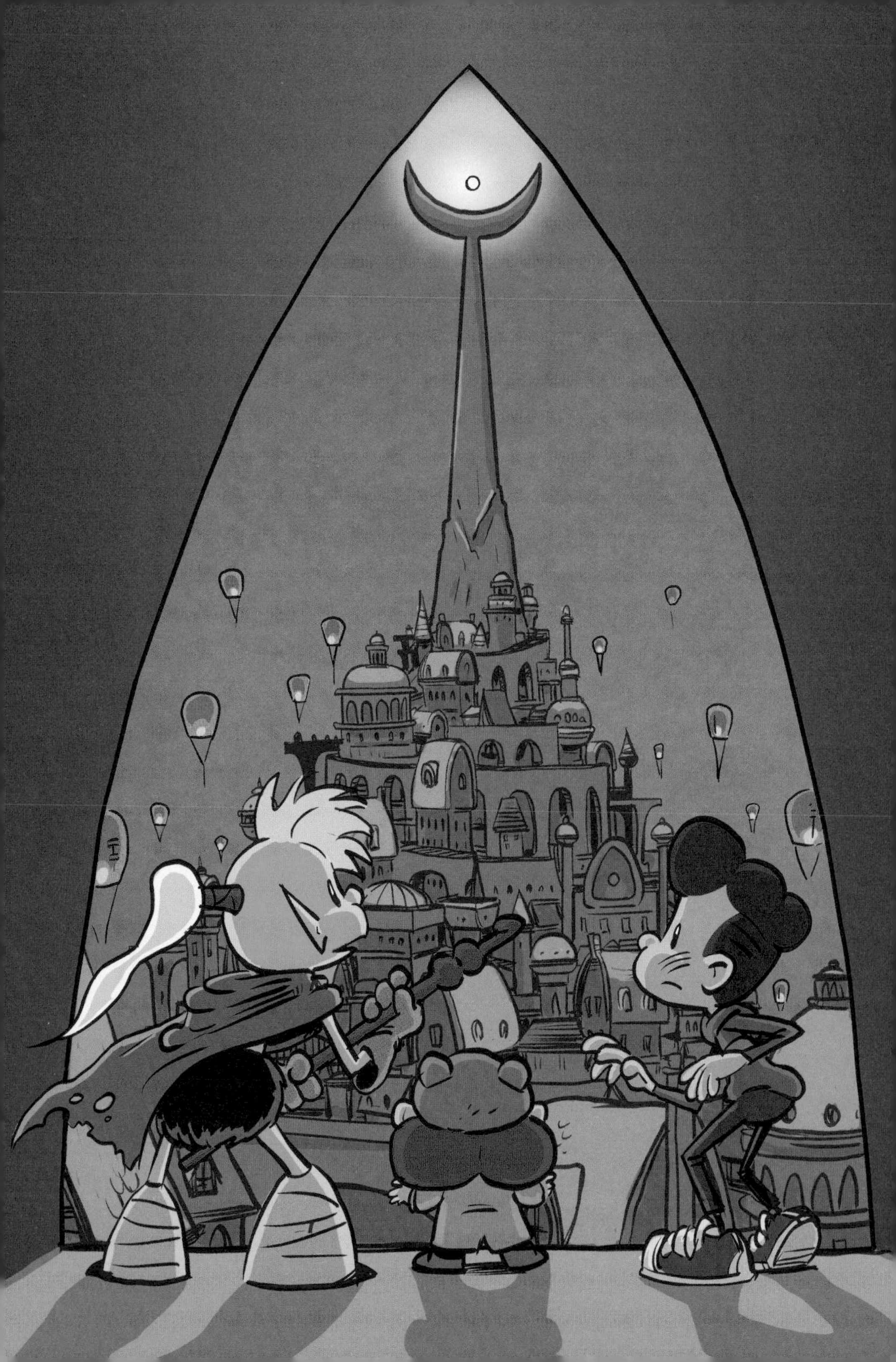

110

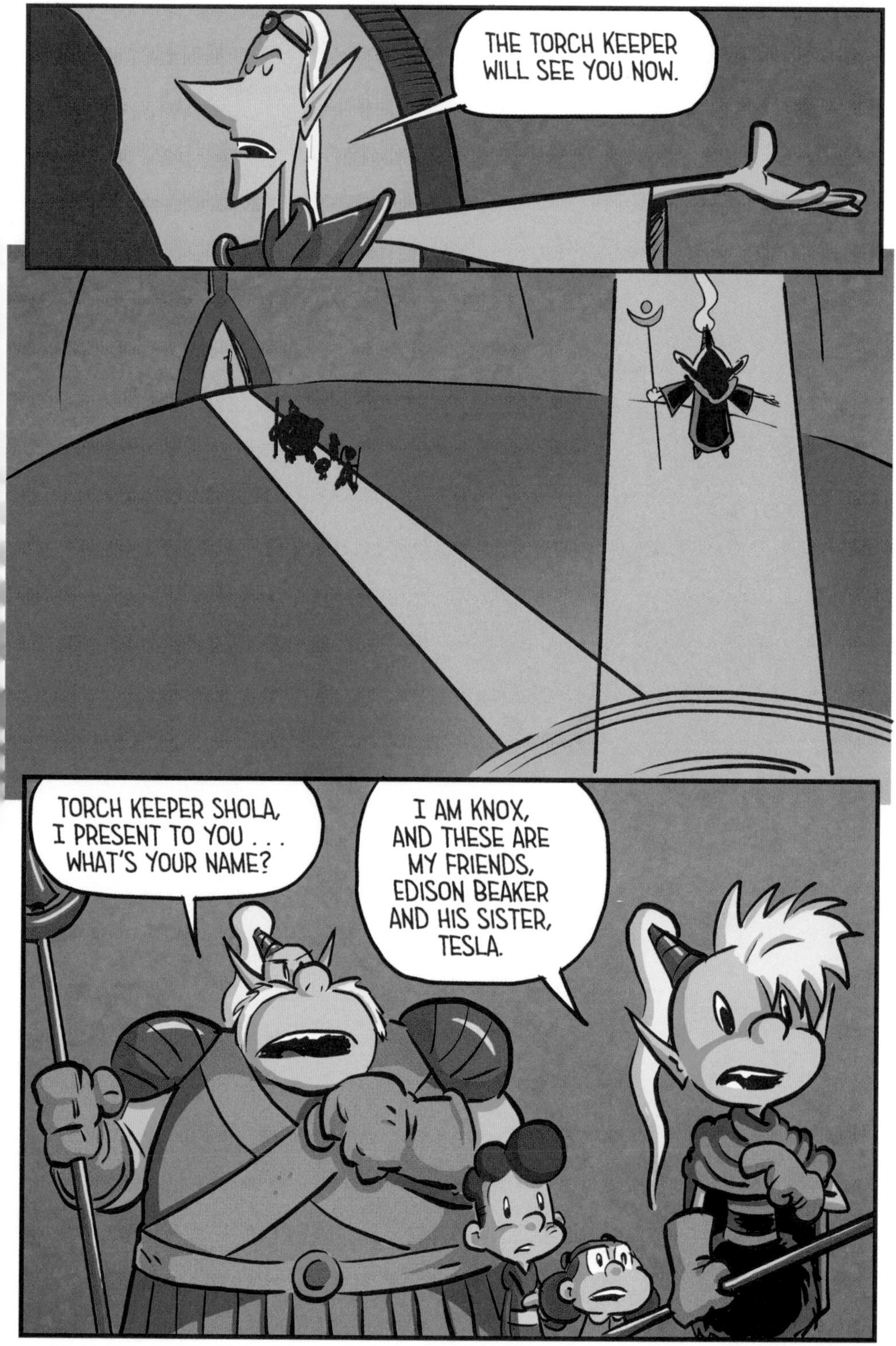
THE TORCH KEEPER WILL SEE YOU NOW.
TORCH KEEPER SHOLA, I PRESENT TO YOU . . . WHAT'S YOUR NAME?
I AM KNOX, AND THESE ARE MY FRIENDS, EDISON BEAKER AND HIS SISTER, TESLA.

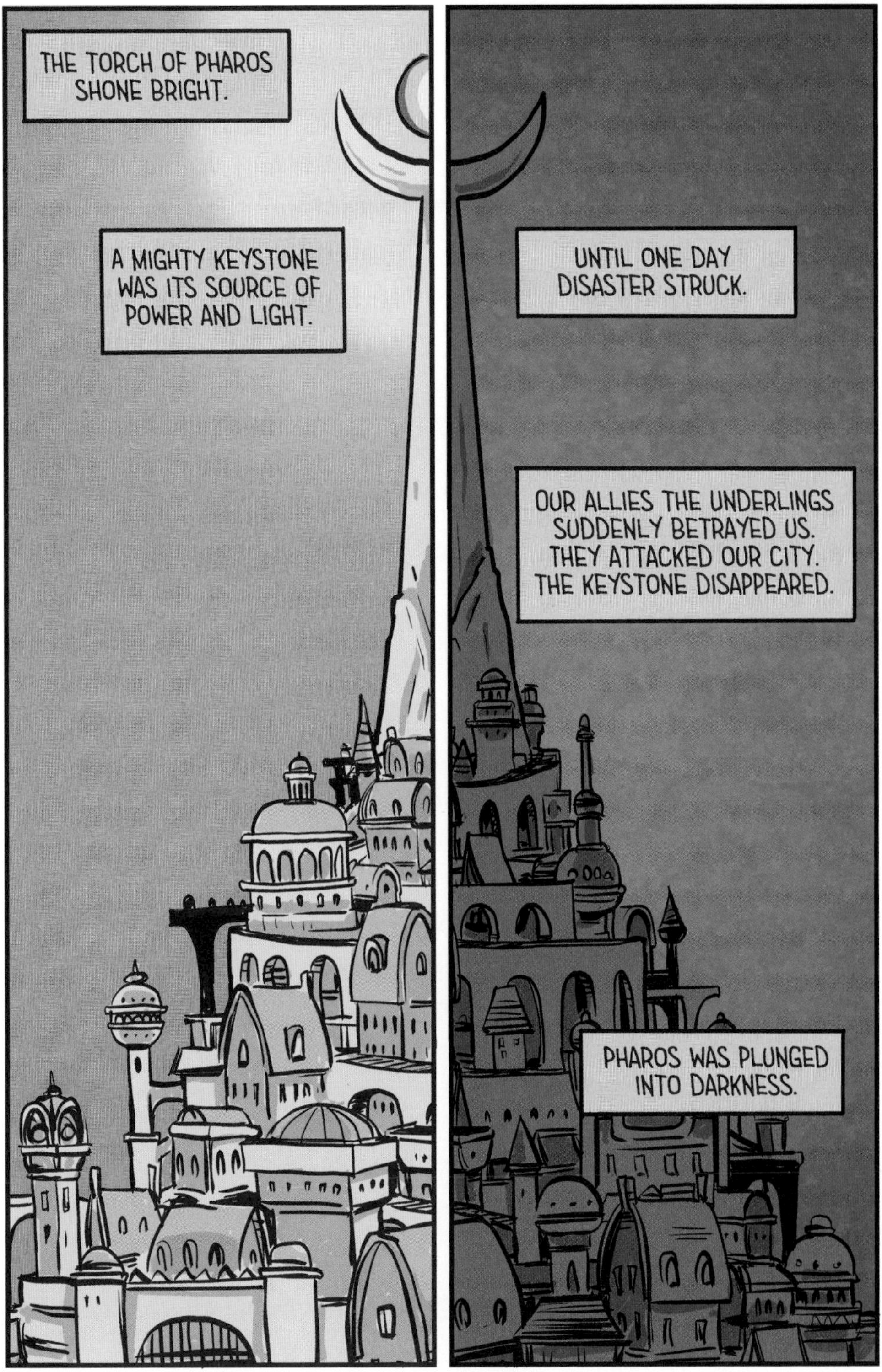
THE TORCH OF PHAROS SHONE BRIGHT.
A MIGHTY KEYSTONE WAS ITS SOURCE OF POWER AND LIGHT.
UNTIL ONE DAY DISASTER STRUCK.
OUR ALLIES THE UNDERLINGS SUDDENLY BETRAYED US. THEY ATTACKED OUR CITY. THE KEYSTONE DISAPPEARED.
PHAROS WAS PLUNGED INTO DARKNESS.

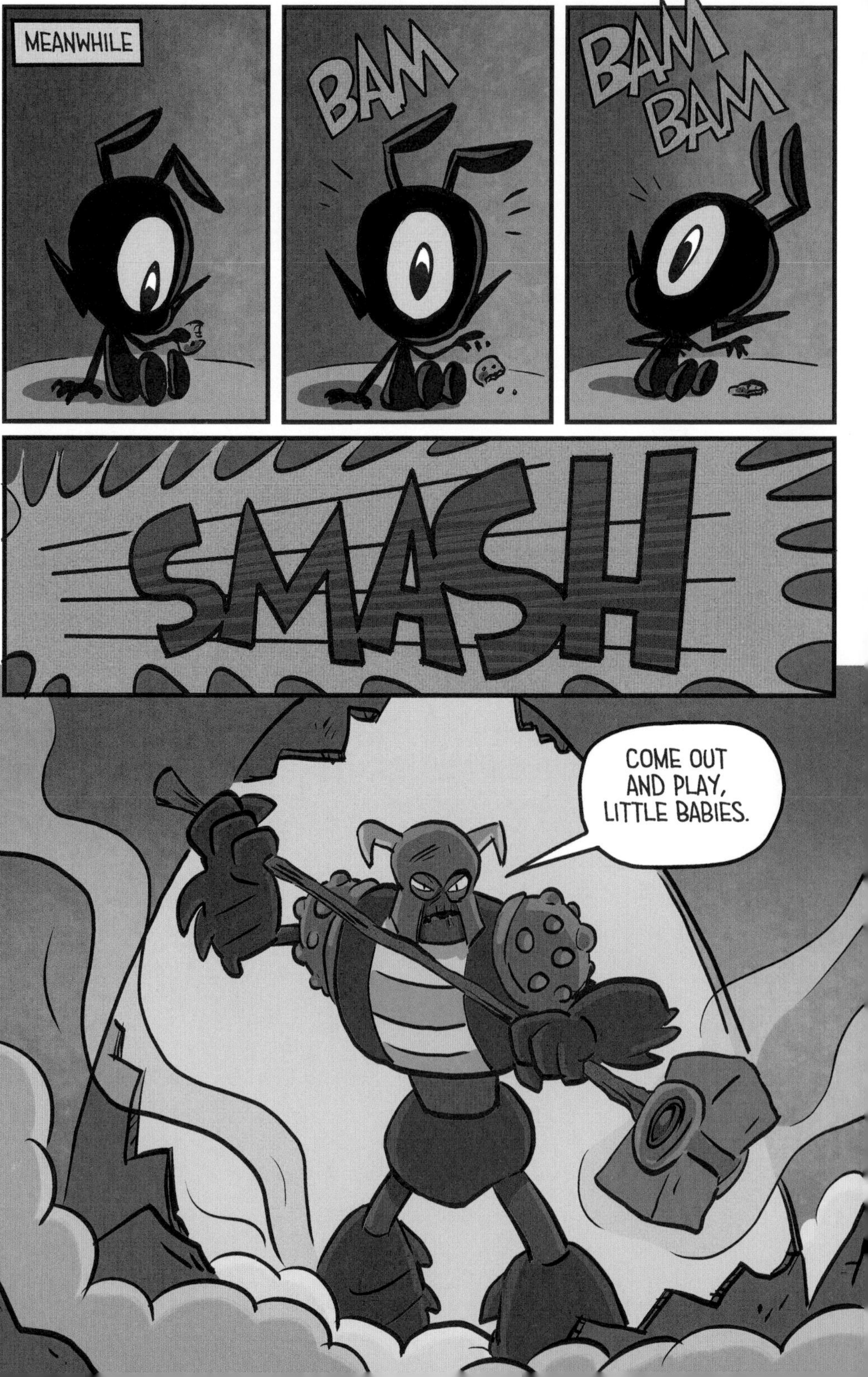
MEANWHILE
BAM
BAM
BAM
SMASH
COME OUT AND PLAY, LITTLE BABIES.

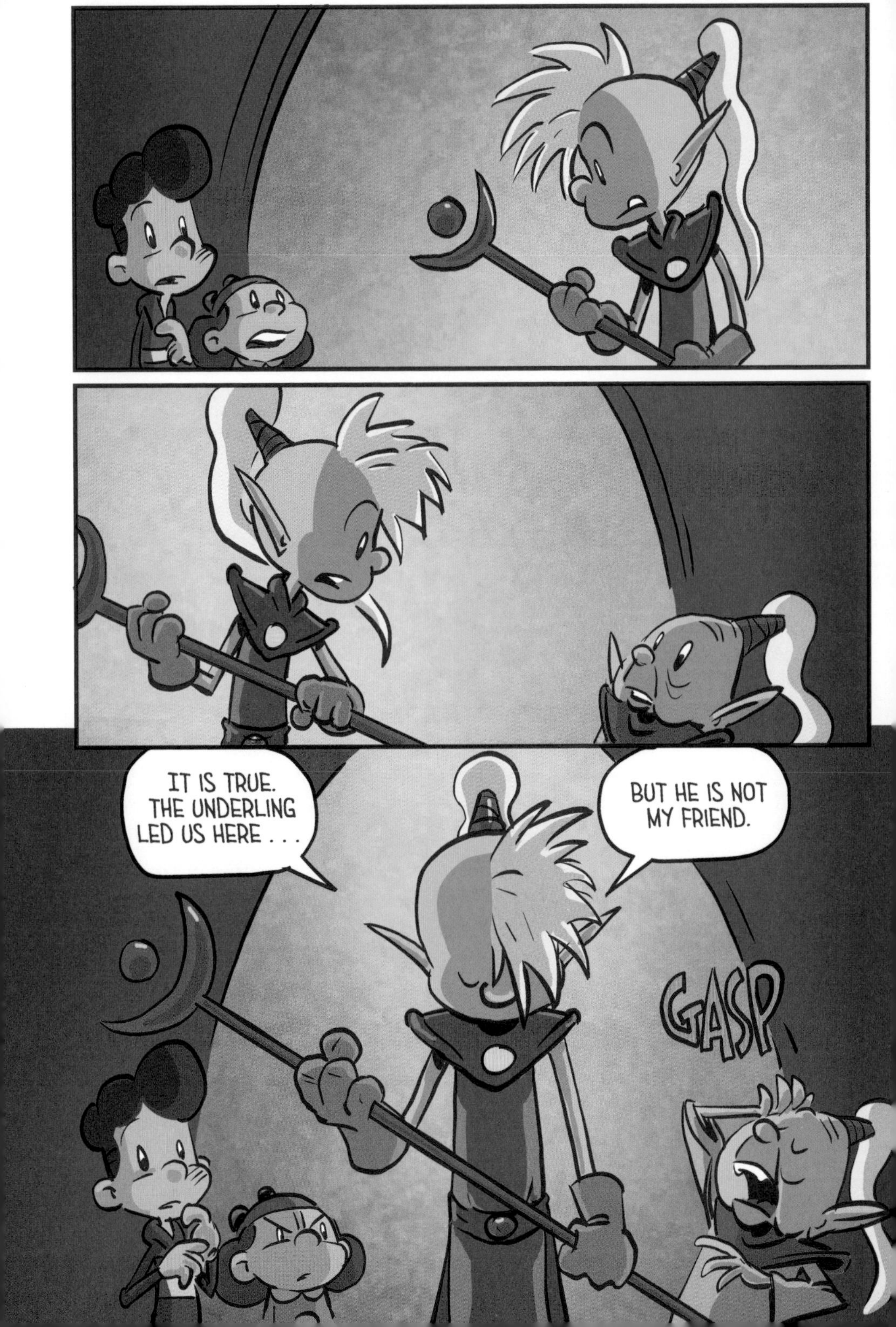
IT IS TRUE. THE UNDERLING LED US HERE . . .
BUT HE IS NOT MY FRIEND.
GASP

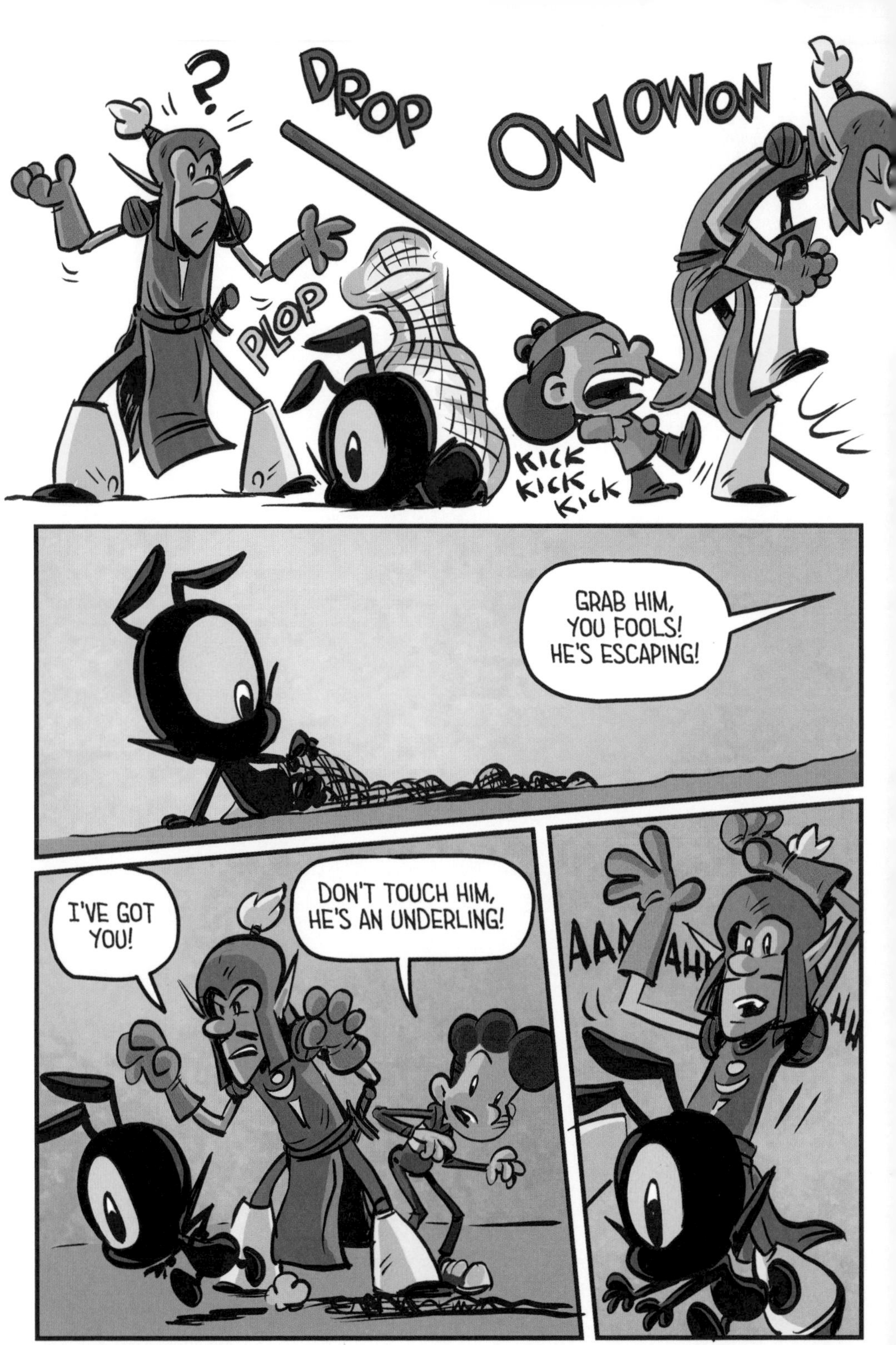
?
DROP
OWOWOW
PLOP
KICK KICK KICK
GRAB HIM, YOU FOOLS! HE'S ESCAPING!
I'VE GOT YOU!
DON'T TOUCH HIM, HE'S AN UNDERLING!

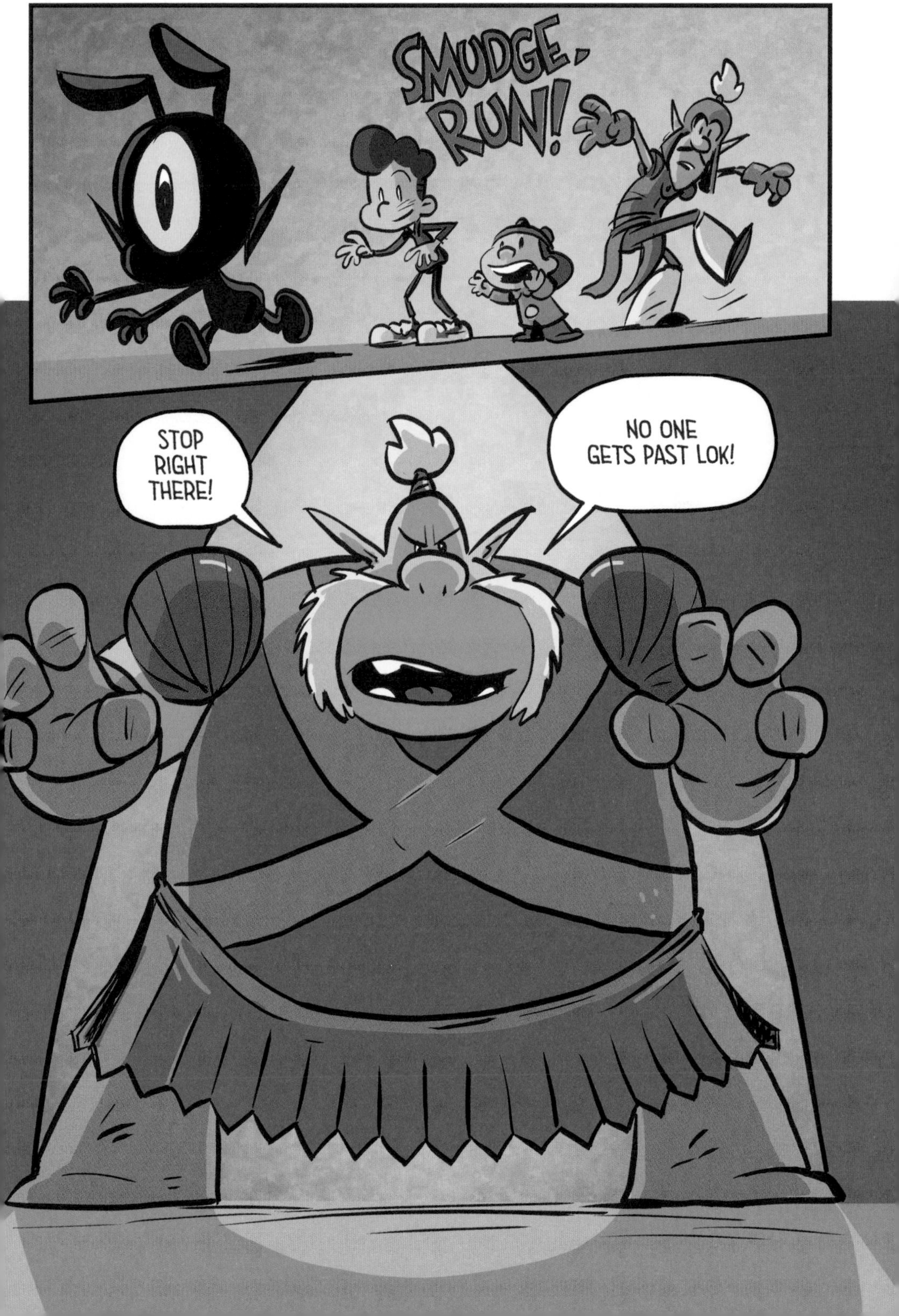
SMUDGE, RUN!
STOP RIGHT THERE!
NO ONE GETS PAST LOK!

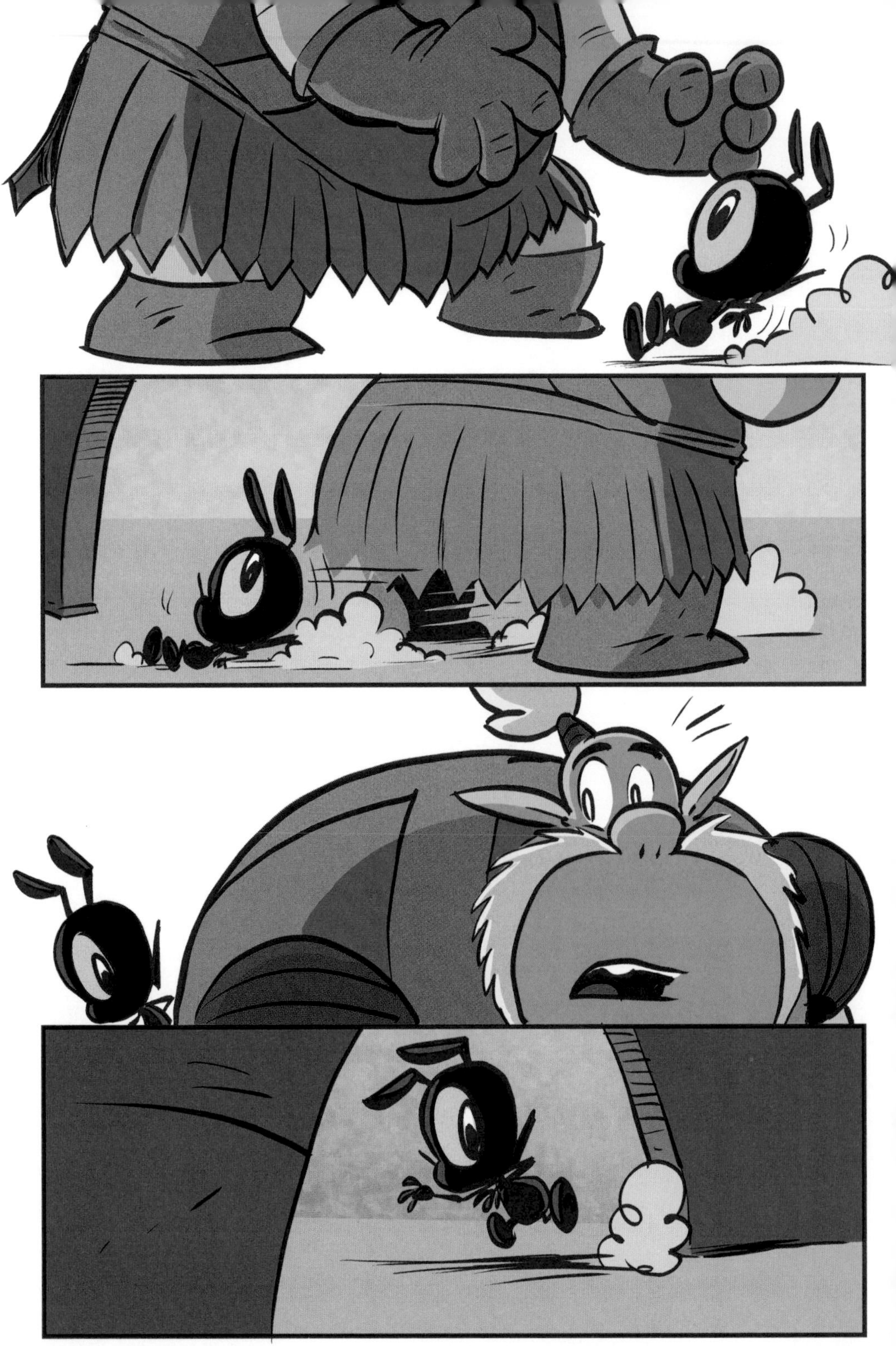

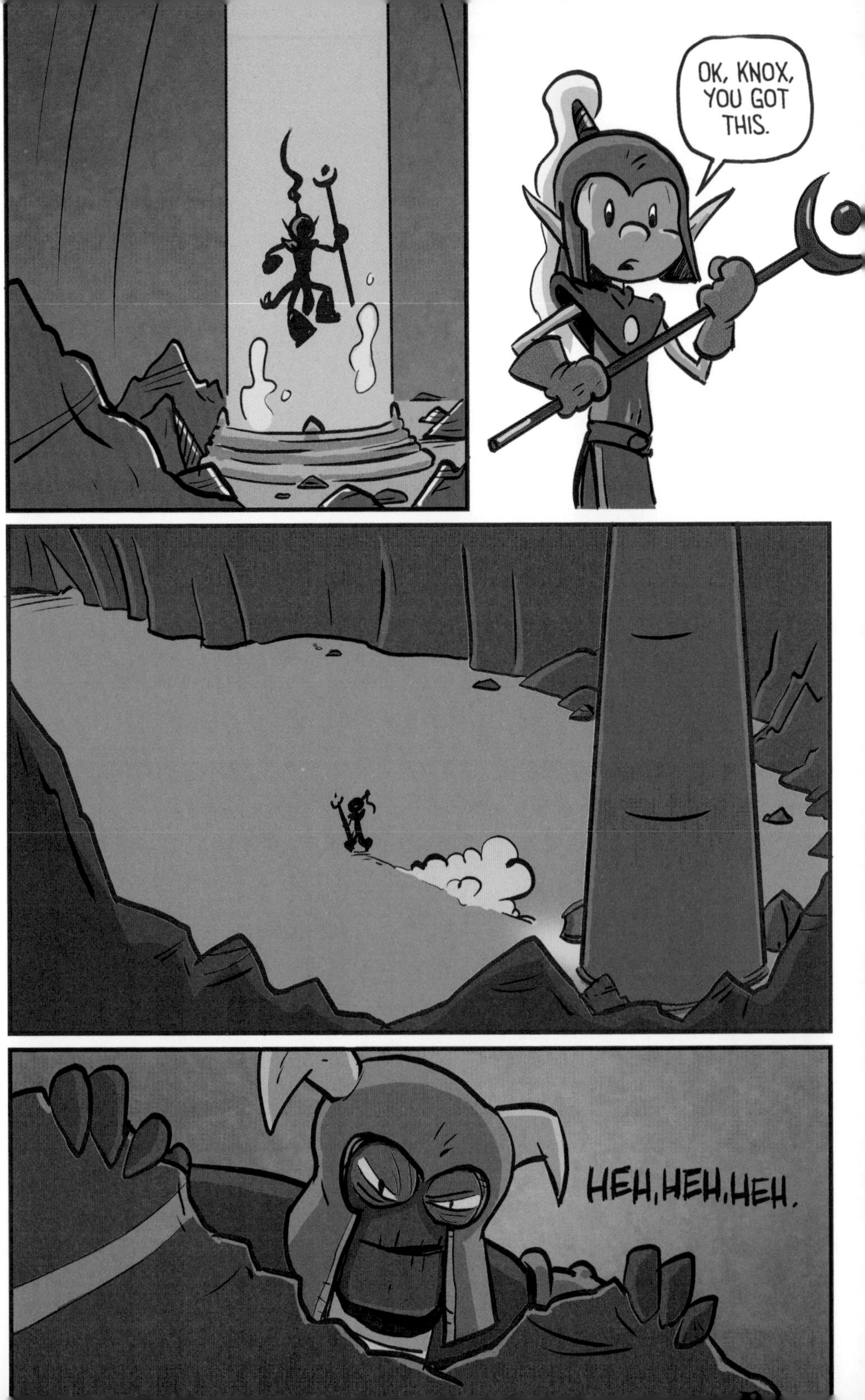
OK, KNOX, YOU GOT THIS.
HEH, HEH, HEH.

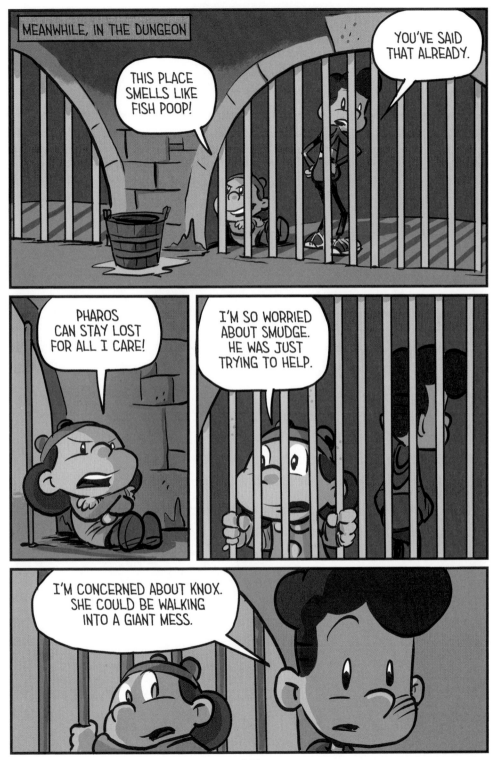

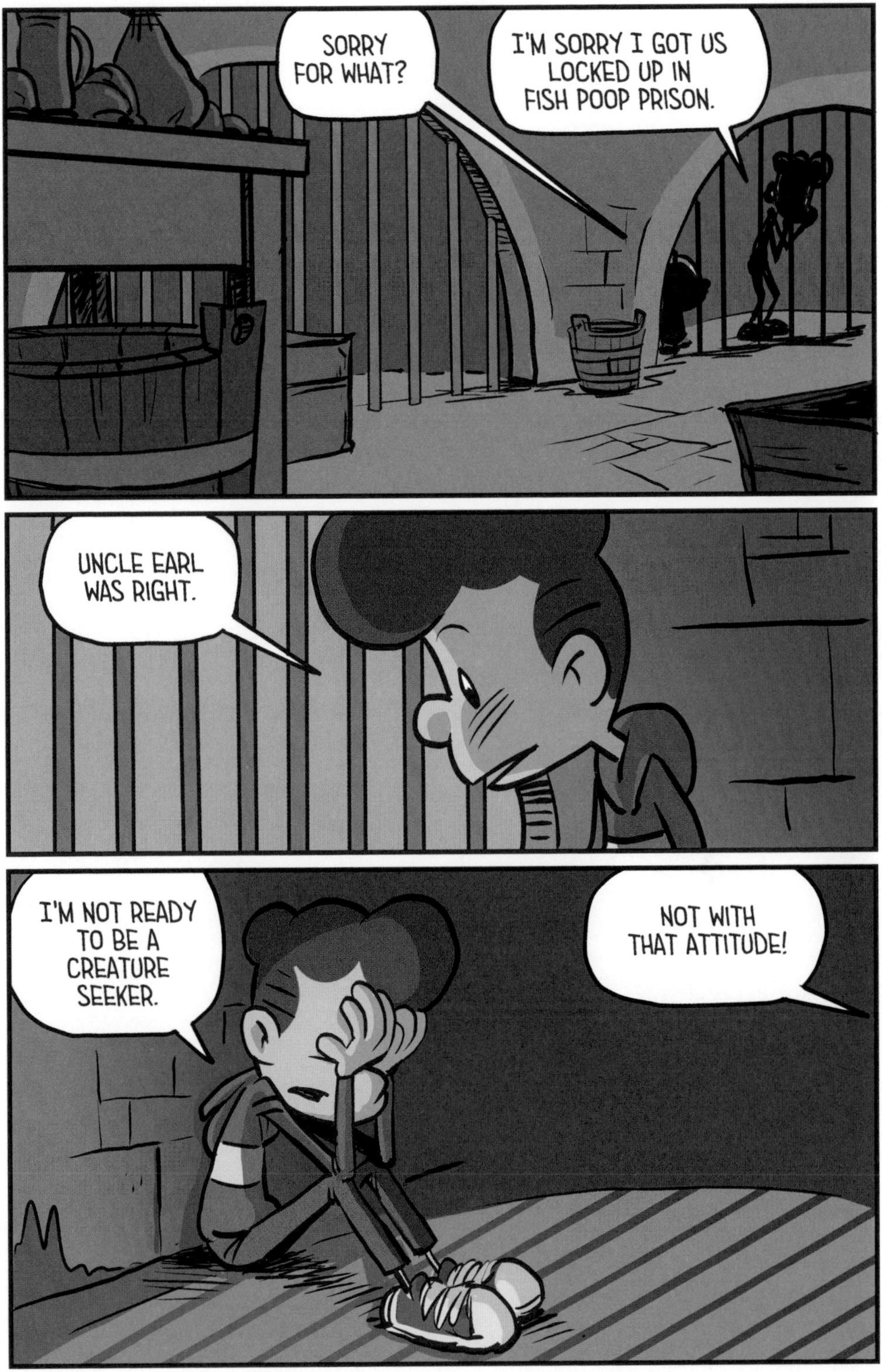
SORRY FOR WHAT?
I'M SORRY I GOT US LOCKED UP IN FISH POOP PRISON.
UNCLE EARL WAS RIGHT.
I'M NOT READY TO BE A CREATURE SEEKER.
NOT WITH THAT ATTITUDE!

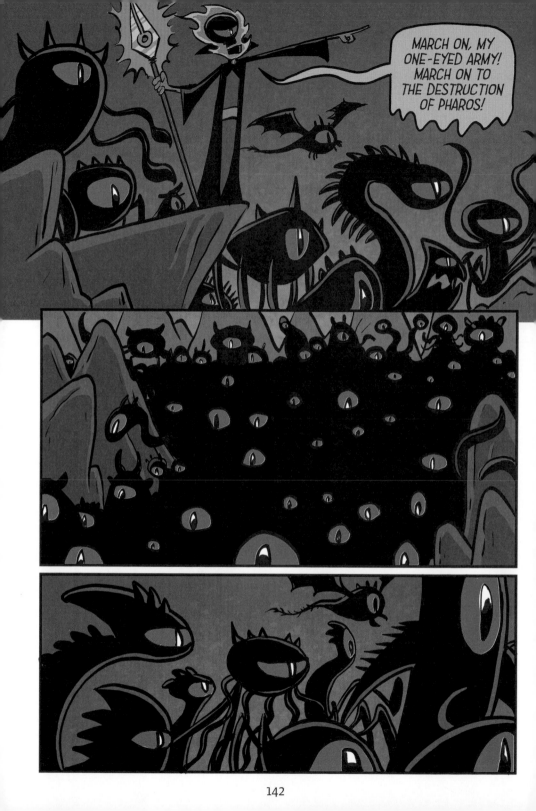

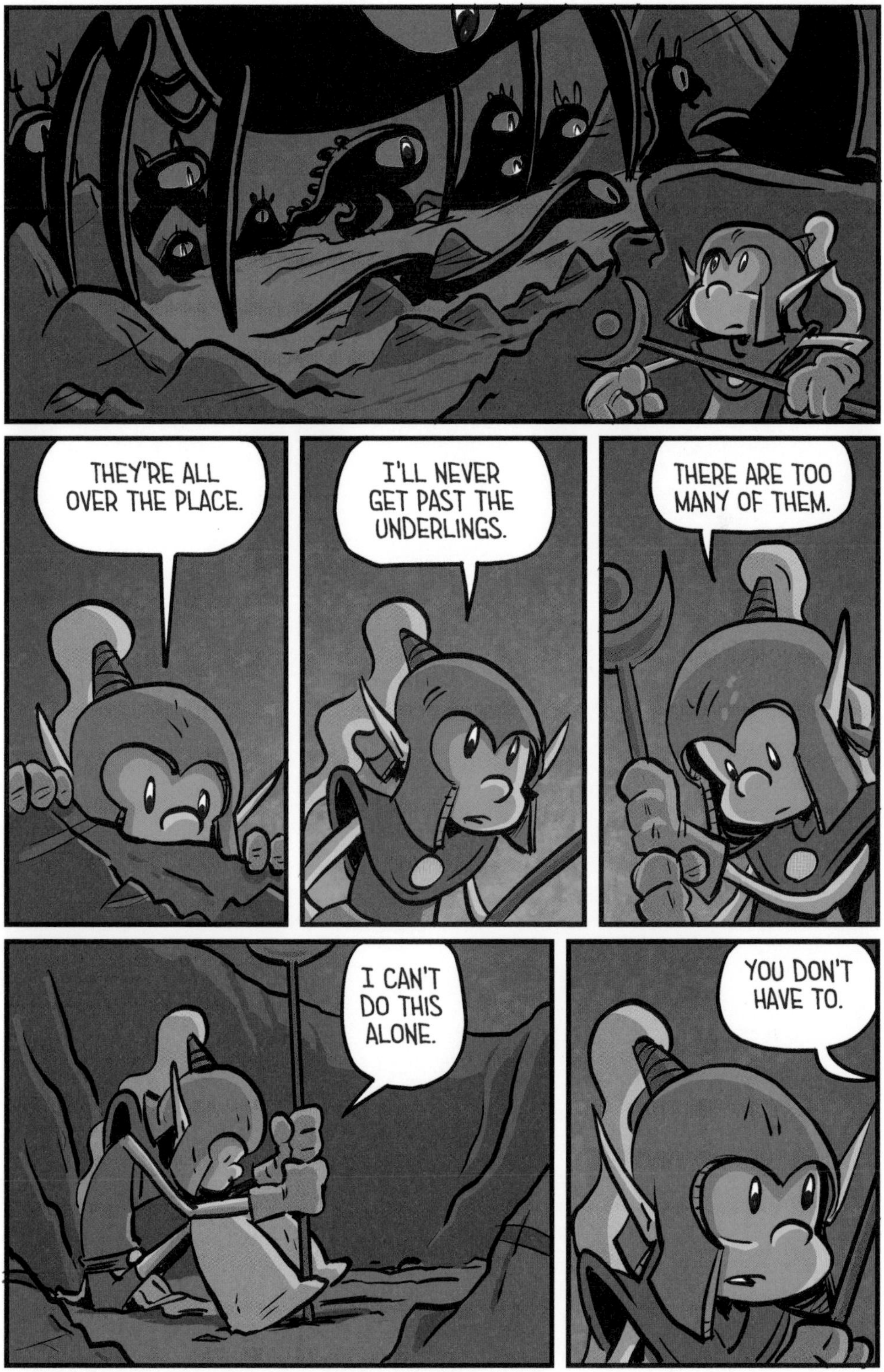
THEY'RE ALL OVER THE PLACE.
I'LL NEVER GET PAST THE UNDERLINGS.
THERE ARE TOO MANY OF THEM.
I CAN'T DO THIS ALONE.
YOU DON'T HAVE TO.

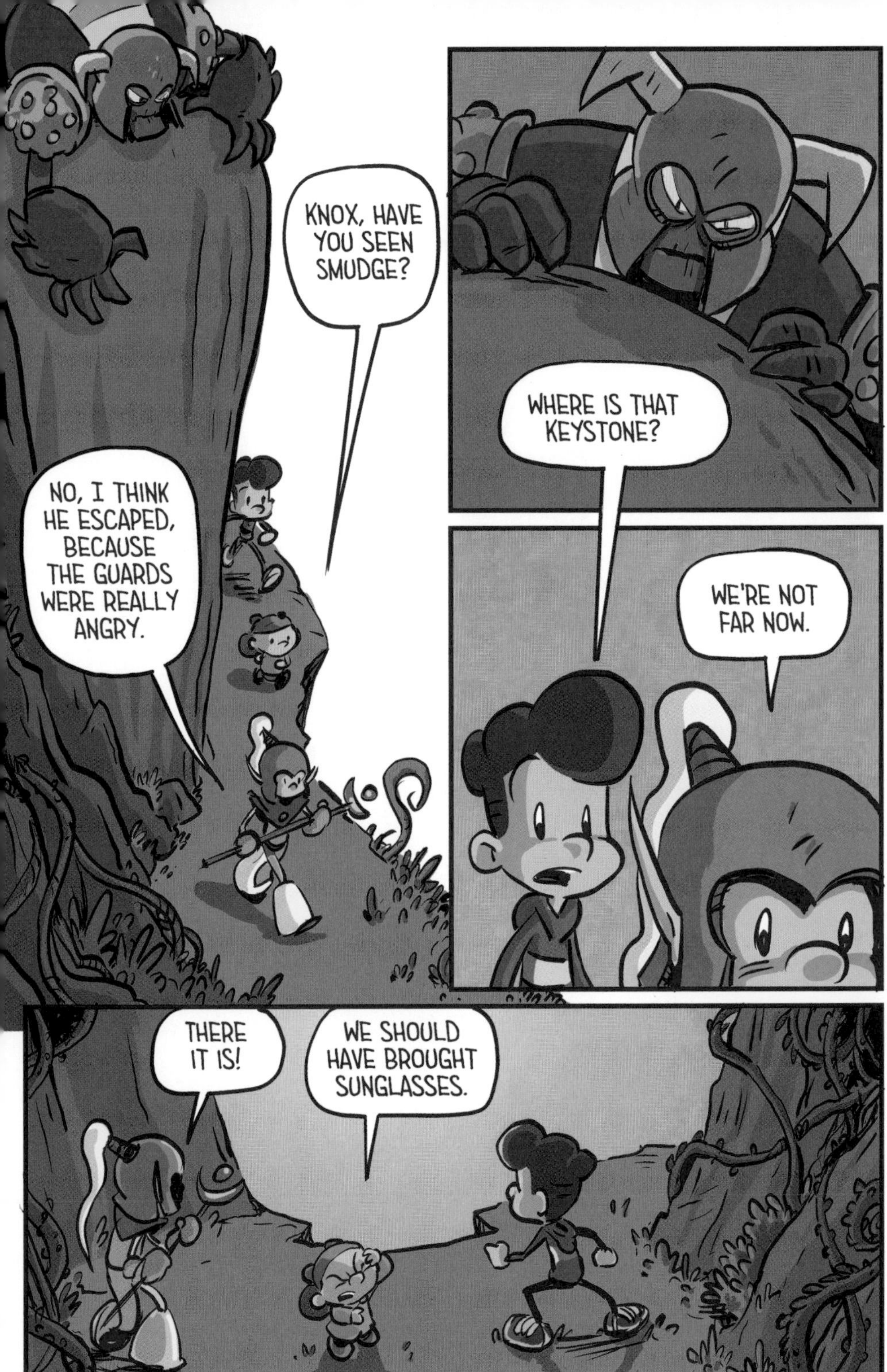
KNOX, HAVE YOU SEEN SMUDGE?
NO, I THINK HE ESCAPED, BECAUSE THE GUARDS WERE REALLY ANGRY.
WHERE IS THAT KEYSTONE?
WE'RE NOT FAR NOW.
THERE IT IS!
WE SHOULD HAVE BROUGHT SUNGLASSES.

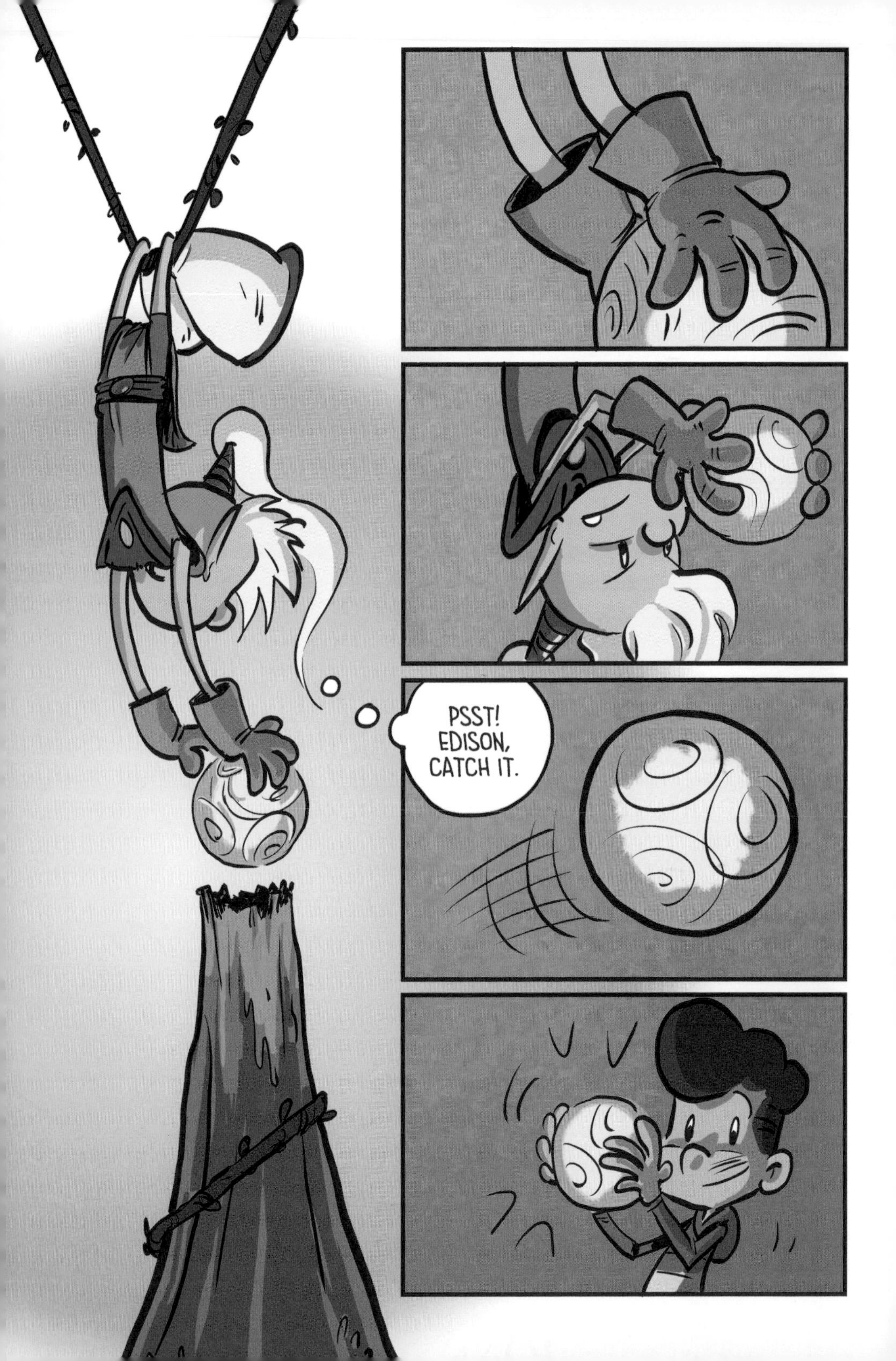
PSST! EDISON, CATCH IT.

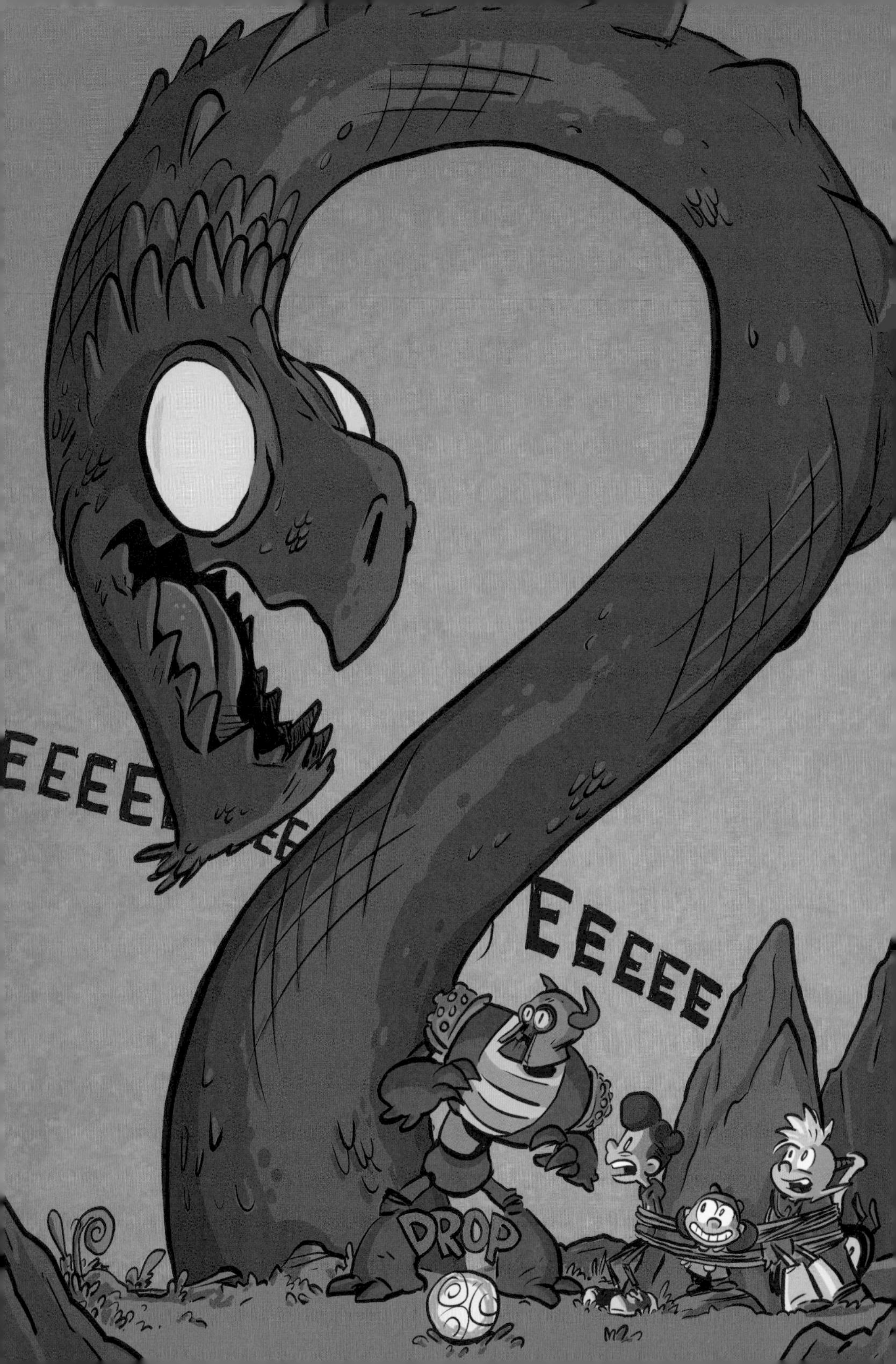
EEEEEEE
EEEEE
DROP

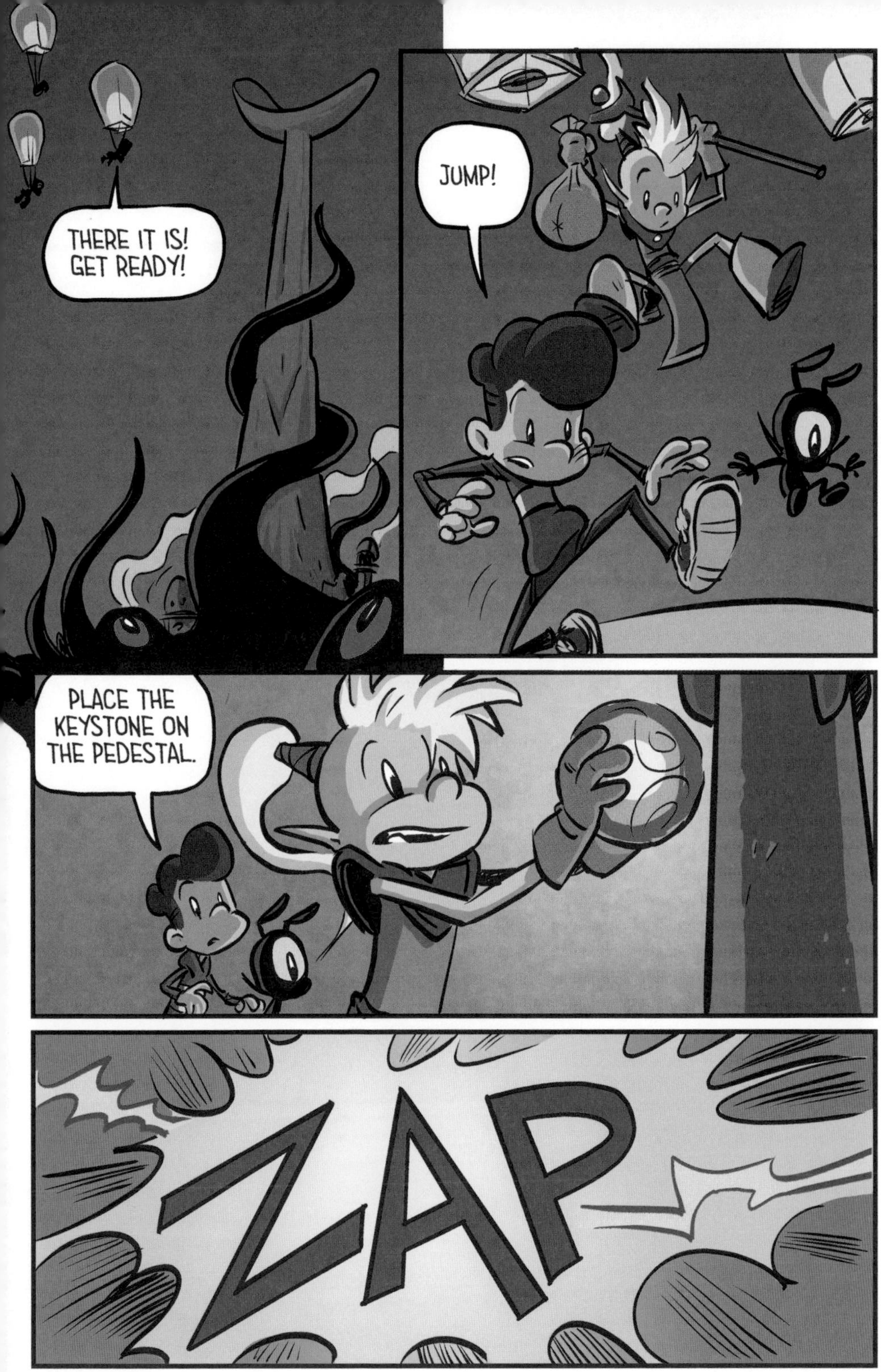
THERE IT IS! GET READY!
JUMP!
PLACE THE KEYSTONE ON THE PEDESTAL.
ZAP

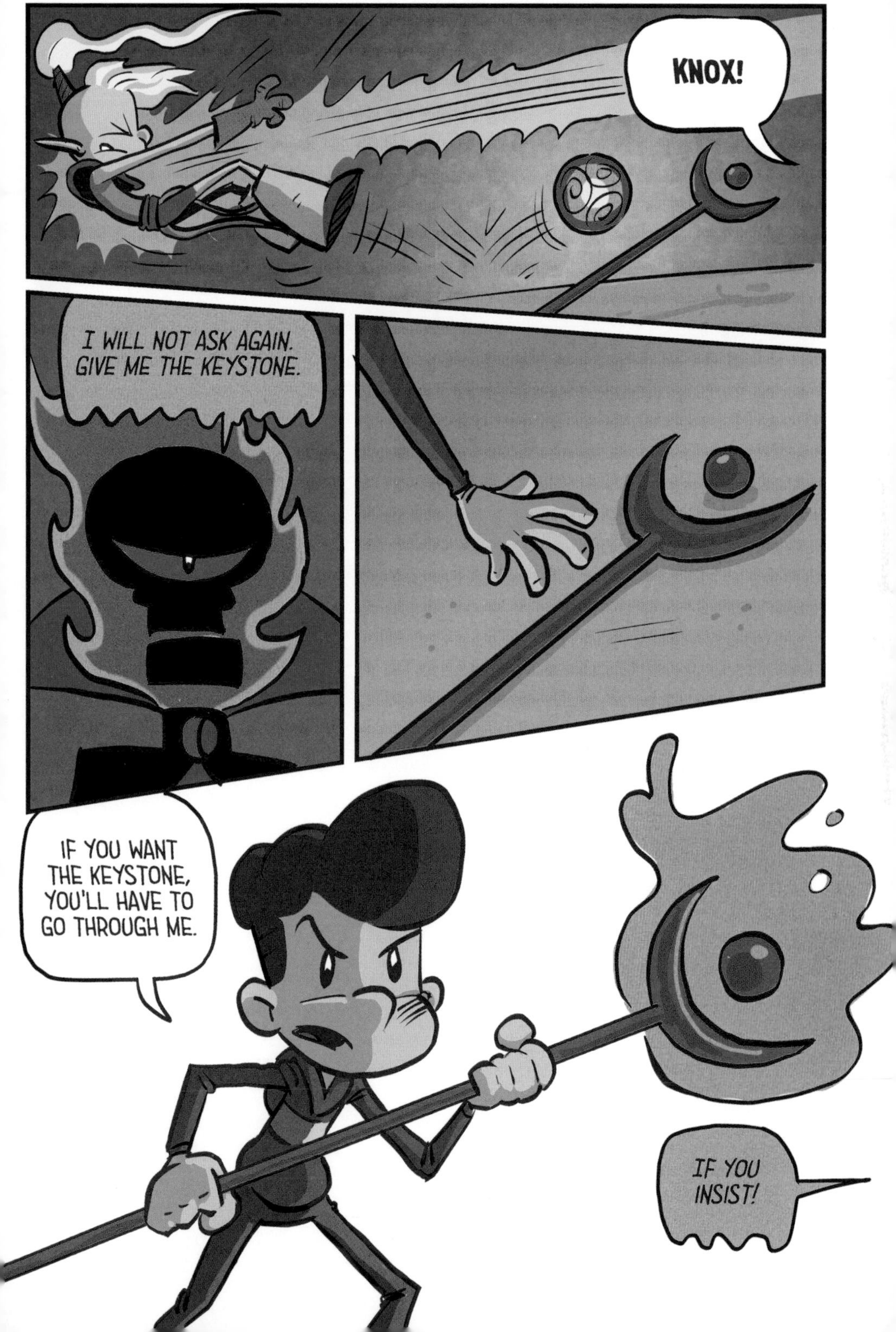
KNOX!
I WILL NOT ASK AGAIN. GIVE ME THE KEYSTONE.
IF YOU WANT THE KEYSTONE, YOU'LL HAVE TO GO THROUGH ME.
IF YOU INSIST!

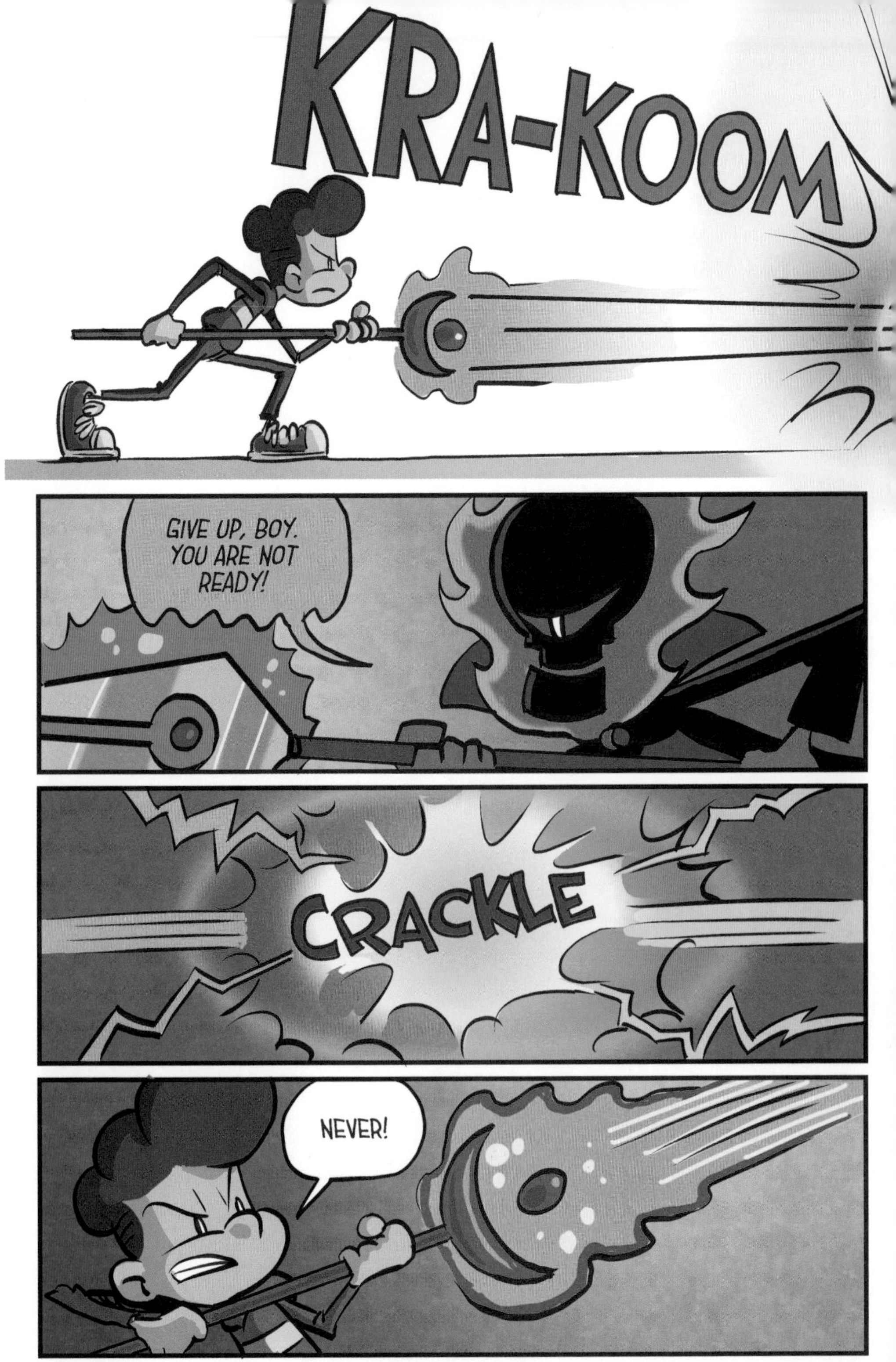
KRA-KOOM
GIVE UP, BOY. YOU ARE NOT READY!
CRACKLE
NEVER!

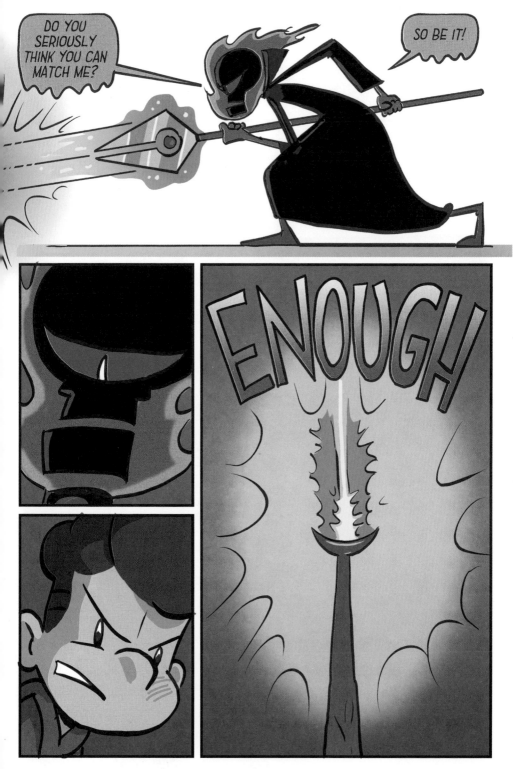

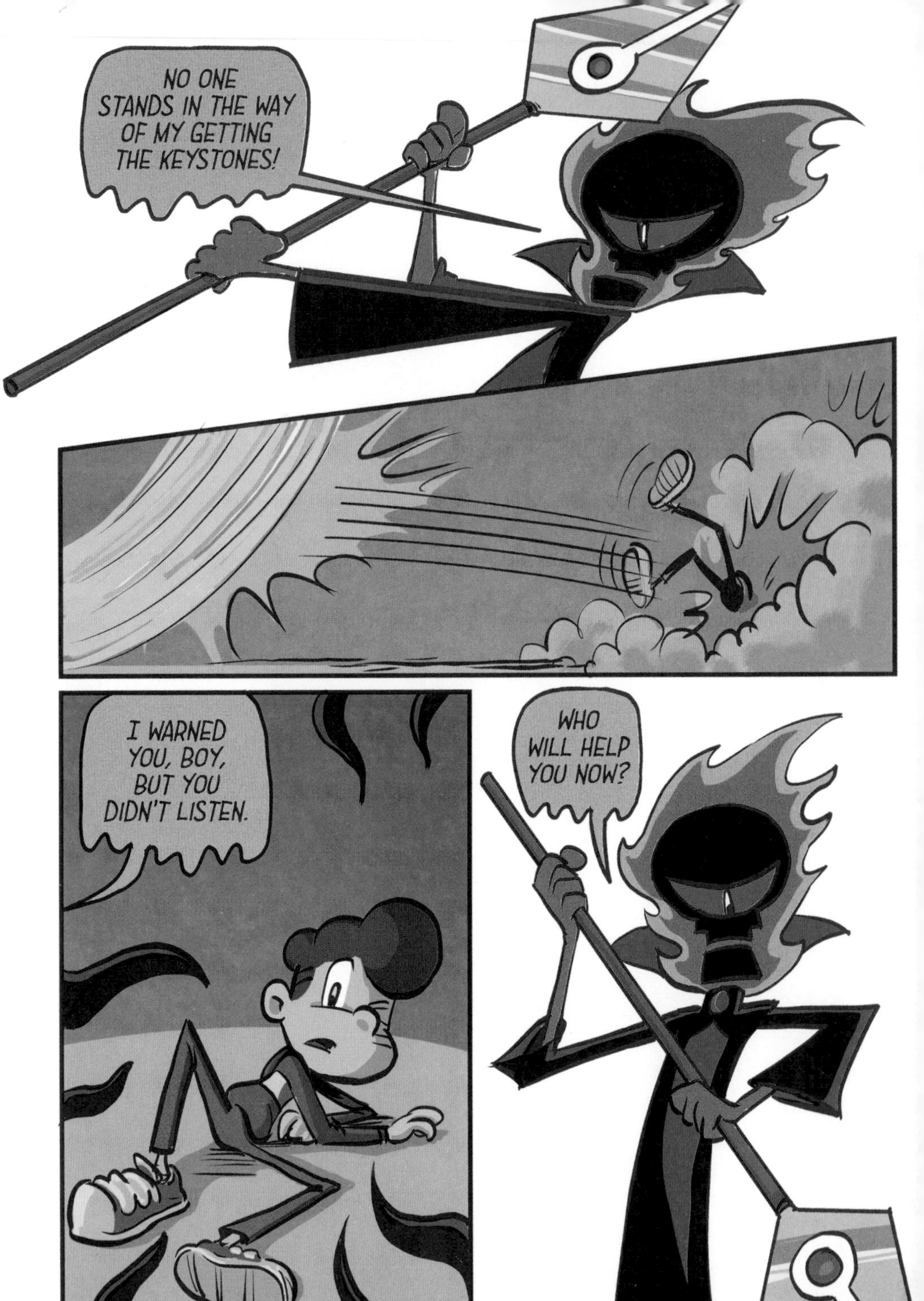
NO ONE STANDS IN THE WAY OF MY GETTING THE KEYSTONES!
I WARNED YOU, BOY, BUT YOU DIDN'T LISTEN.
WHO WILL HELP YOU NOW?

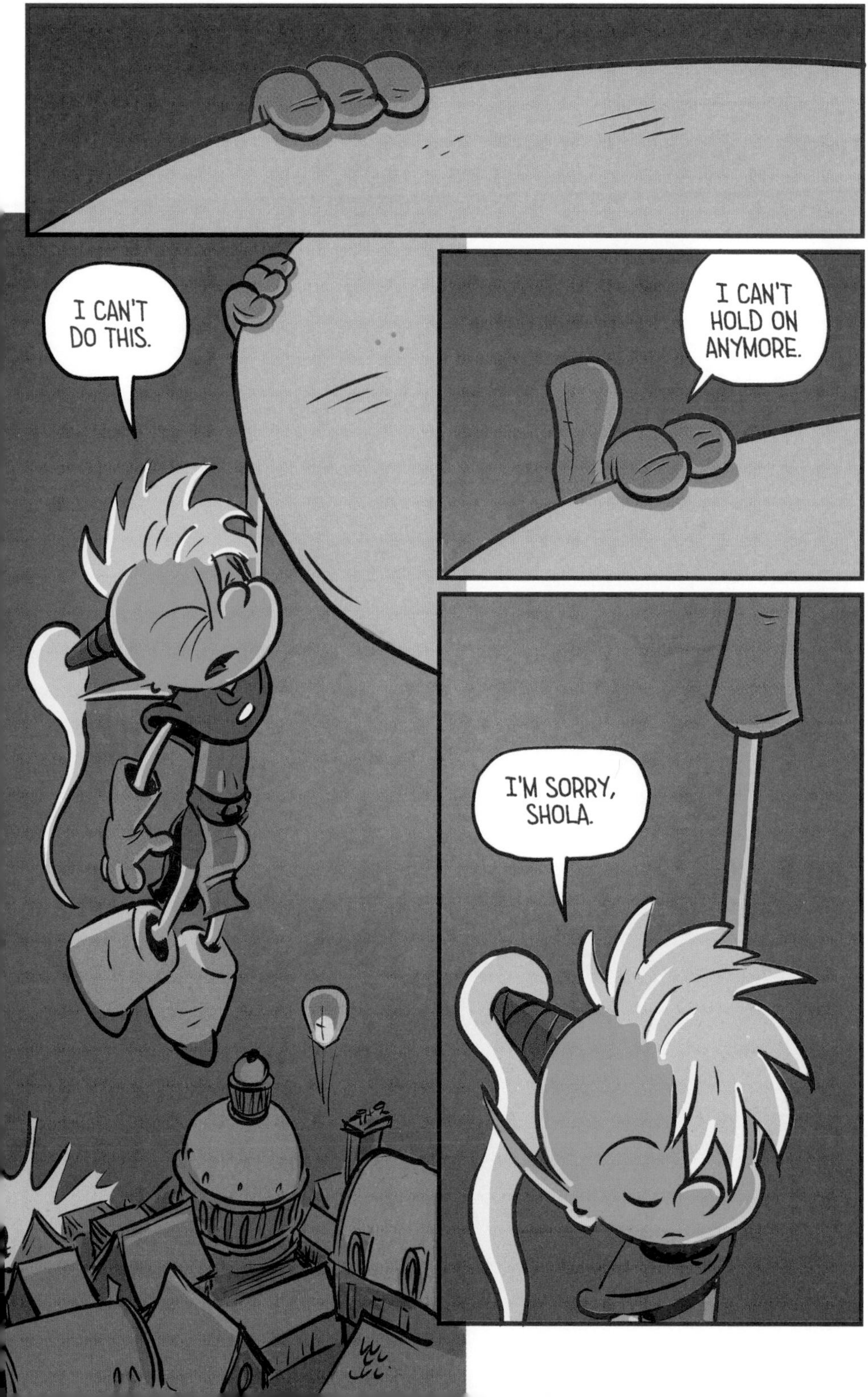
I CAN'T DO THIS.
I CAN'T HOLD ON ANYMORE.
I'M SORRY, SHOLA.

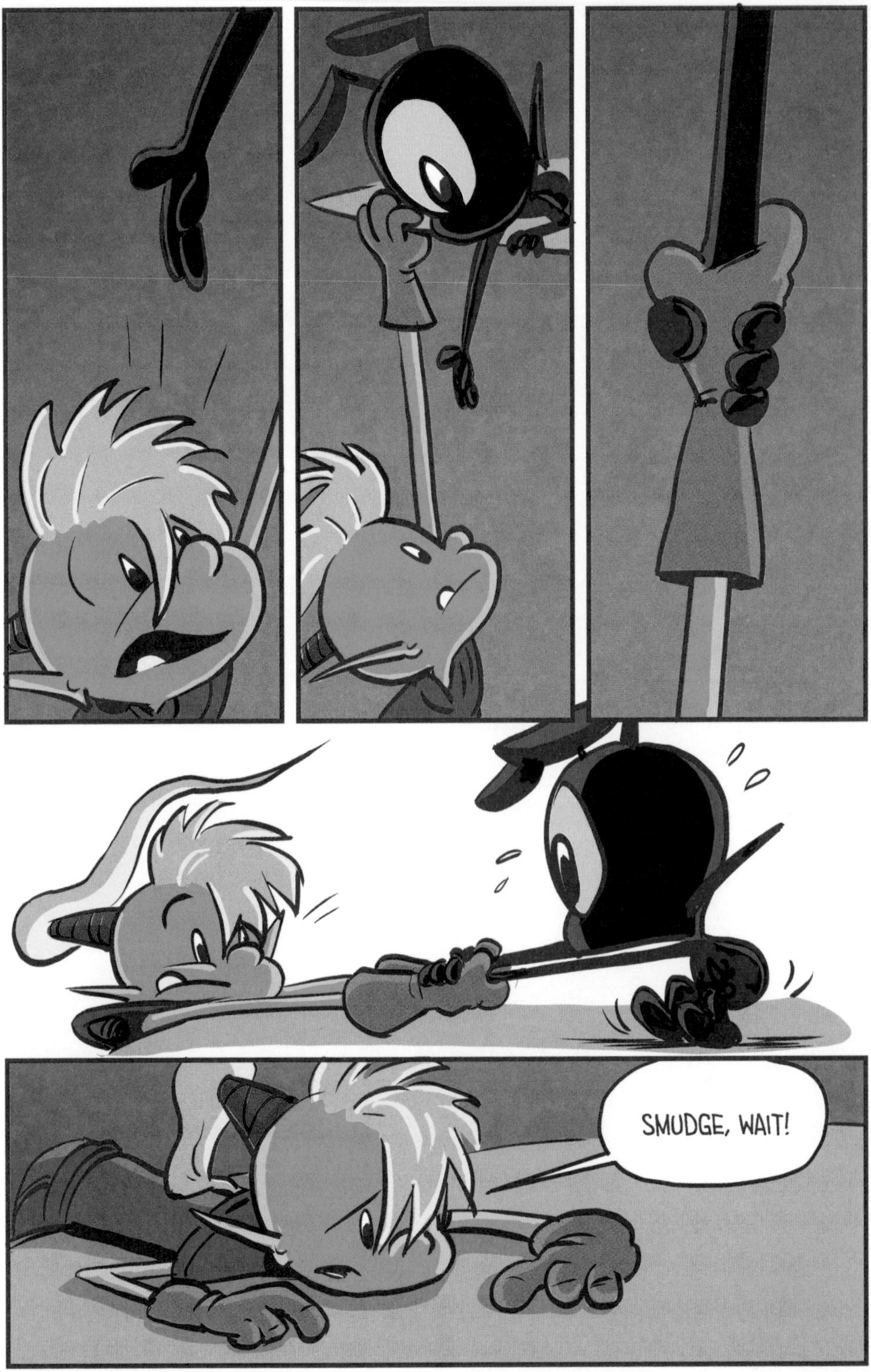
SMUDGE, WAIT!

165

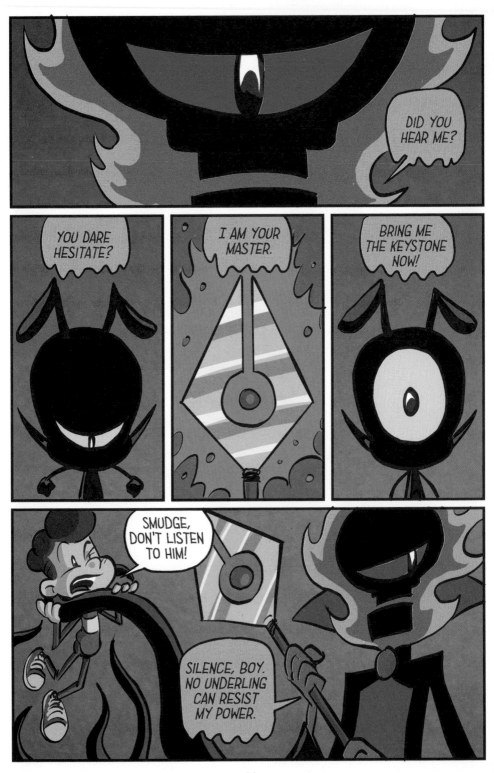

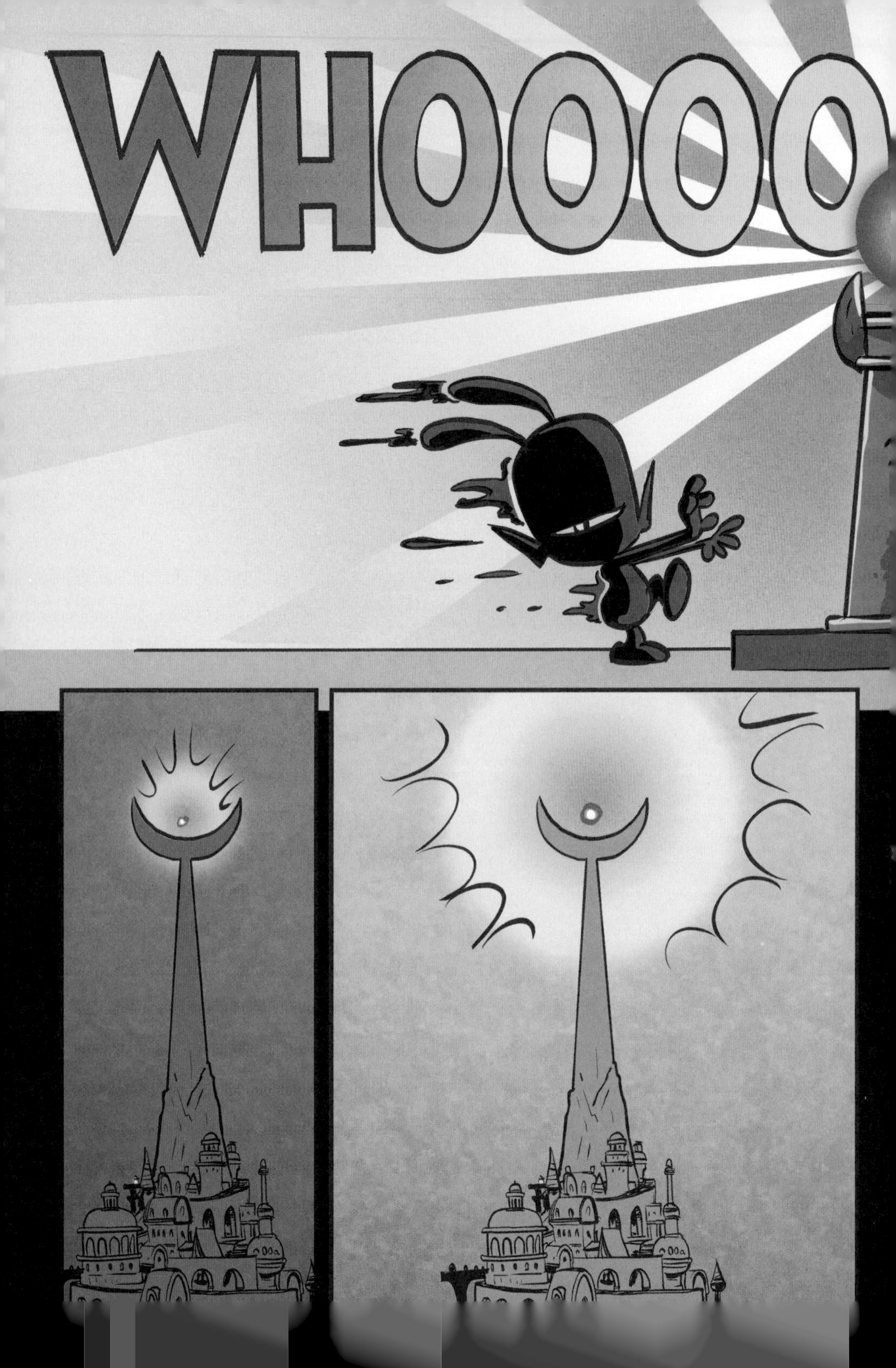
WHOOOO

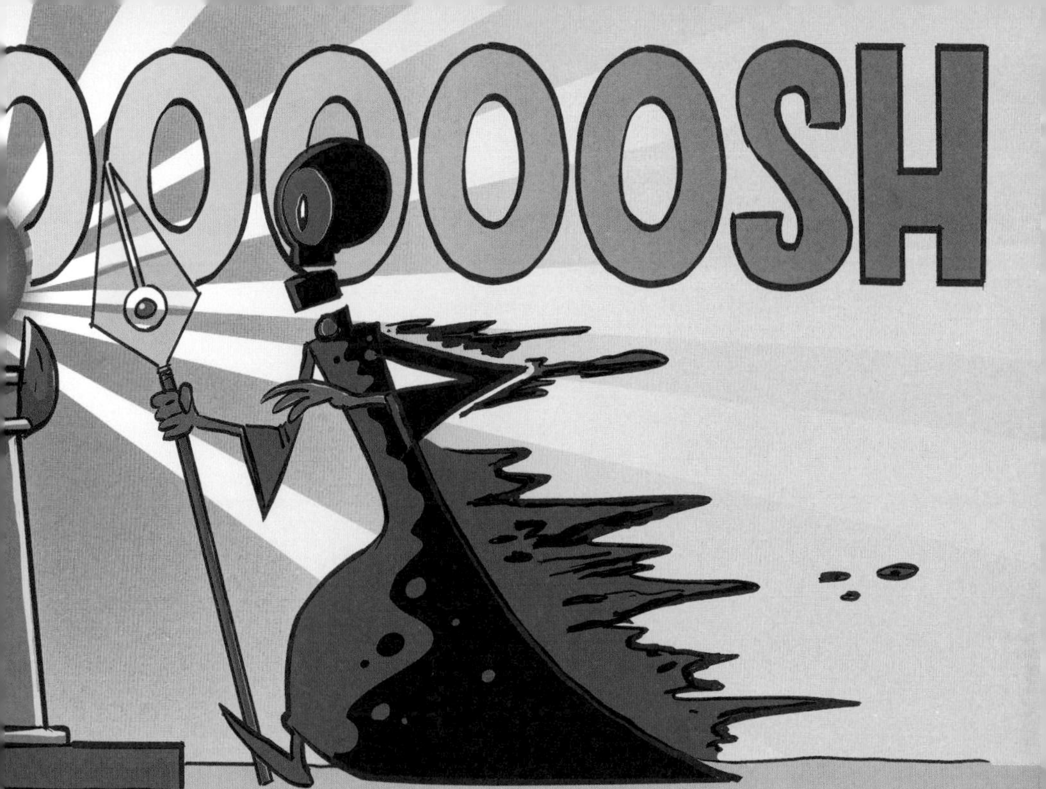
OOOOOOSH
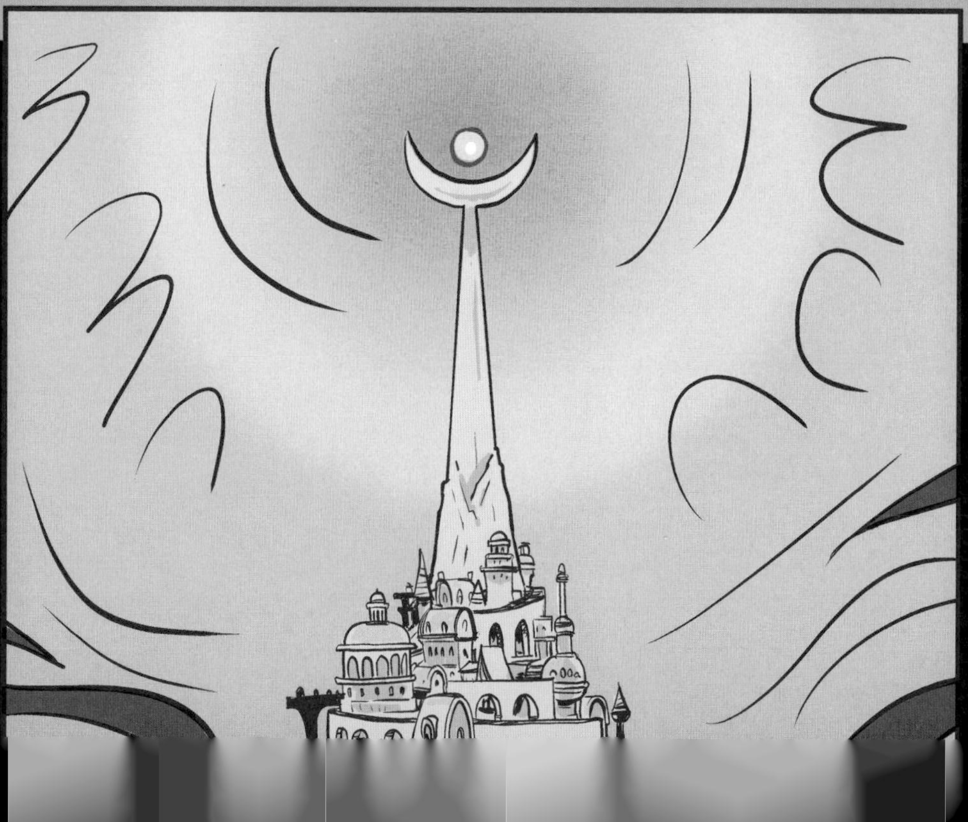

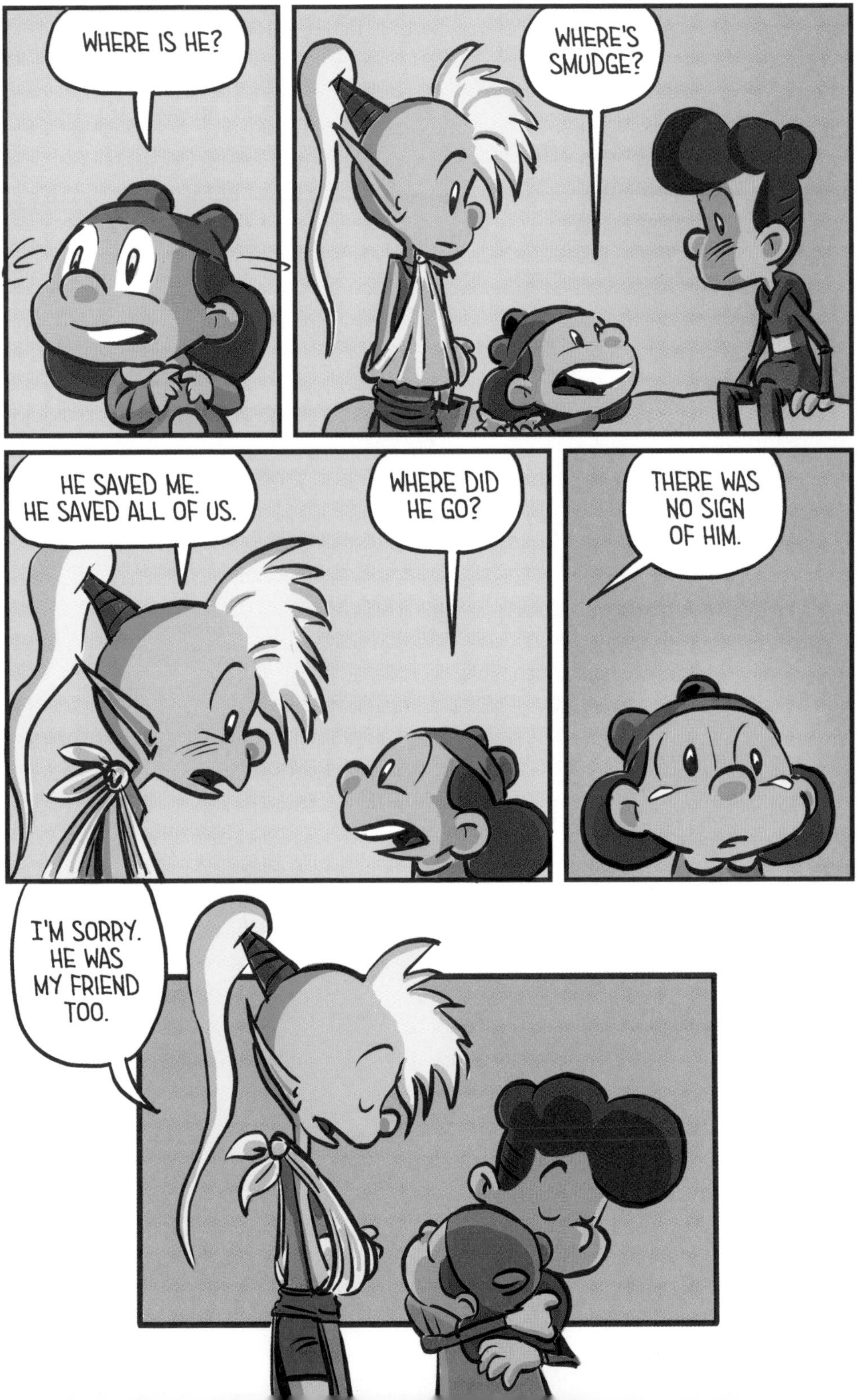
WHERE IS HE?
WHERE'S SMUDGE?
HE SAVED ME. HE SAVED ALL OF US.
WHERE DID HE GO?
THERE WAS NO SIGN OF HIM.
I'M SORRY. HE WAS MY FRIEND TOO.

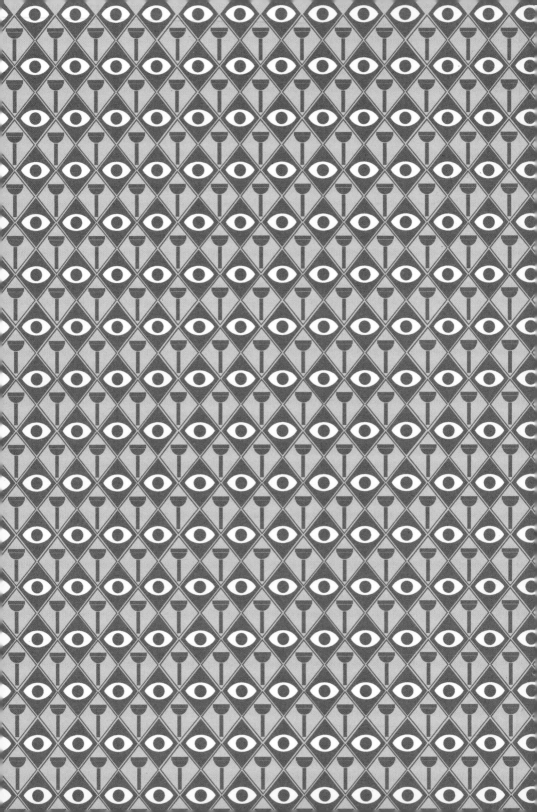